The Frozen Diva

The Amazing Adventures of Rebecca Quinto

Thomas Paul Severino

The Frozen Diva

The Amazing Adventures of Rebecca Quinto

Thomas Paul Severino

Pollywog Pond Communications, Fort Lauderdale

tomseverino.com

tomseverino100@gmail.com

Cover: StockSnap

ISBN: 978-1-7322278-9-7

Also by Thomas Paul Severino

The Kayne Sorenson Mysteries: The Blood Quartet

Seed Blood

Tribal Blood

Stage Blood

Ancient Blood

For Liza

and, of course,

Joanne

Too much sanity may be madness and, the maddest of all, to see life as it is and not as it should be.

– *Miguel de Cervantes*

Fight for the things that you care about, but do it in a way that will lead others to join you.

— Ruth Bader Ginsburg

Prologue: Peter Pan

OBERSALZBERG, THE BAVARIAN ALPS, 1935

The young woman pulled the thick woolen shawl tighter around her shoulders.

The chilly spring air in the Austrian-German border mountains was filled with the awakening calls of larks, barn swallows, and swifts amid the soft rustle of pines – miles and miles of pine trees. Off in the distance, a cowbell sounded as a peasant boy led his herd from barn to hillside. Lights blinked off in the towns across the vista in the promise of a bright morning.

The view from the newly constructed terrace was indeed breathtaking. New greenery shimmered in the valleys below. Rugged mountains, still clothed in snow, towered in the distance along the misty horizon. White and tan houses with soft brown roofs clung to the slopes of the hills and pasture lands. Spiraling roads wound through the panorama. She marveled at how the ivory-colored motor trails, encrusted with low buildings and running wooden fences, climbed the heights and dipped down into the dales as if defying gravity.

From where she stood, she could see the first of the construction workers arriving to continue the renovation of the mountain chalet. They toiled their way upward with tools over their shoulders.

Angela, the housekeeper, and her daughter, Geli, supervised the sweeping of the terrace. Servants entered and retreated into the house, stepping around the scaffolds and setting the tables for breakfast. The Chancellor and his guests would enjoy their morning repast on the broad overlook under the colorful umbrellas despite the chill and the surrounding clamor of the workers. He loved to talk about the construction project and was fond of explaining the design details. The German Leader was passionate about the future, its challenges, and opportunities.

"I trust you slept well, *Fräulein*."

"Yes, thank you, *Frau* Hammitzsch. I was concerned that the cold air here would affect my voice, but the house is warm. Will I have the opportunity to exercise this morning?"

"Of course, the *Reichsminister* had the piano brought up the mountain and installed in the music room last week. The tuner was here yesterday. You will be asked to perform this weekend, no doubt."

"I will do my best."

A dark-haired man in a blue-grey suit stepped from the house and lit a cigarette, blowing smoke in the direction of the mountains.

"Please excuse me, *Fräulein*, I must have Geli get the Doctor's coffee. And I will have her bring your tea. *Ja*?" She hurried away.

"*Guten Morgen*, I trust you are well, *Fräulein*. Have you come to a decision on our Peter Pan Project?"

These Germans, she thought, a minimum of the niceties and straight to the point.

"I am still undecided, to be honest, Herr Doctor."

"That is unfortunate, my dear, as the *Reichsminister* will be sorely disappointed. You see, he was planning this ..." He waved his hand in her direction, taking in her physical form like a magician. "... as a birthday gift for the Chancellor, in April."

The young woman said nothing.

The Doctor took her hand and led her to the low stone wall that served as the parapet for the overlook. They sat and took in the view for a while. Overhead, an eagle swooped, scanning the rocky open spaces between the trees, searching for food.

"Decide judiciously, *Fräulein*. You know that the Minister is in love with you, my dear. He talks as if he was struck by a thunderbolt the night the two of you met at the *Staatsope*r. That Italian piece. Much too frivolous for my tastes."

"*Le Nozze di Figaro*. In Italian, yes, but by your own maestro, Mozart."

The Chancellor's personal physician waved a dismissive hand.

She considered the consequences of her self-exile in Germany. Now, the world's eyes were on the new government leading the country out of the ashes of the Great War. *If I am to reach my potential as an artist, is this the way the fates are leading me? And at what cost?*

She spoke, attempting to change the subject.

"What are they building up there on the tor above the chalet? The surveyors are such early arrivals there on the summit."

"It is to be the site of a government meeting hall commissioned by the Chancellor. He enjoys receiving foreign dignitaries here. His birthplace is not far over those mountains in Austria."

The eagle was joined by its mate, and they soared up the mountainside as the German and the Italian were served their coffee and tea, respectively. The Doctor stood and walked a few steps with his cup but returned to the young woman. He lowered his gaze and sat back down next to her. His tone was insistent.

"You must understand what this will mean to your future, my dear. At Nuremberg, the Chancellor had declared ours to be a thousand-year Reich. There will be much wealth and glory for all of us who give him what he wants and an eternity in which to enjoy it."

The ingénue stared at the older man as if she were succumbing to a spell. The first guests were finding their way onto the terrace from inside the house.

She met his persistent gaze and slowly nodded in resignation. He understood her decision was made, and she would cooperate.

"Capital, my dear. The *Reichsminister* will be delighted."

The Doctor stood, clicked his heels, bowed, and turned to the new arrivals. They exchanged morning greetings as servants circled, showing guests to places at crisp, clean tables and bringing heaping platters and steaming pots of Bavarian breakfast fare. All heads turned as the Chancellor and the Reichsminister stepped through the doorway into the brightening day. They were smiling.

Above them, the eagle rose against the first rays of the sun with its prey dangling from its deadly talons. Its mate seemed to screech in victory, a sound that echoed across the pristine Alpine vales like a scream.

The diva pulled her shawl even closer.

Chapter One: Michele

FRITCHER MUSEUM OF ART, FORT LAUDERDALE, FLORIDA

Mornings were a bitch.

Rebecca Quinto rode the elevator to the executive offices of the Fritcher Museum of Arts in downtown Fort Lauderdale, designer coffee in hand, dressed in chic business couture and a Bao Bao Issey Miyake Tote Bag on her left forearm. *Ya gotta look the part, babies.*

As she stepped onto the sixth floor, she marveled as she did each morning at the panorama of the South Florida urban vista that shimmered beyond the glass wall that curved at the perimeter of the museum building.

By day, Fort Lauderdale was a city of concrete, glass, water, lush greenery, and dazzling sunlight. The Atlantic glimmered on the eastern horizon, and the New River snaked through an assortment of bridges and a mountain range of skyscrapers peppered with the pleasure crafts of the downtown elite. Palm trees, pin oaks, and works of public art enhanced the atmosphere of the tropical paradise awash with the snowbirds. *Who drive like idiots!*

The view never failed to lift her grouchy morning spirits. But this was temporary. Conversations halted among the staff in the outer offices as all eyes were directed at the arrival of the Executive Director and Head Curator of the Museum, moving with the determination of a woman on a mission and with the grace of a fashion superstar.

Exchanges of "good morning" trailed in her wake as she made her way toward her Executive Assistant's suite and her corner office. Micah Vélaz stood up as Rebecca approached. He retrieved the coffee container, which Rebecca drained after a wan smile and a morning greeting. He also took the tote. Three women and a man sat in the executive reception area – her first appointment.

They raised their eyes from coffees, tea, and water to smile and nod her way. She did her best electric smile and said, "Good morning, Darlings. As soon as I get to my desk, we can discuss. I won't keep you waiting any further. I see Micah has offered you our best in 8 AM hospitality.

She glanced at the Kieninger Floor Clock, which stood in the reception area. *Shit, can you really pretend that it is 8 AM when the fuckin' mahogany 'masterpiece of design' says it is 8:45? No more all-nighters, sweetie. Next time, I'll get a jump on these Board reports.*

Micah gently touched her forearm as she turned back and said, "I have the proofs for the catalog for *Tribal Blood*. I will make the corrections before the Board meeting at 10 am. The agenda is on your desk. The documents you sent this morning have been copied and are in the Board's meeting folders."

They moved into her office as he continued, "You have a lunch at 1:30 at Dune on the beach with Mr. Gadarn."

"The wine, the tilapia, and my table? I do not want a booth, M."

"Yes, they ordered the *Pinot Blanc* for you last week. The fish is being caught this morning. You will have your usual table set for two."

The young executive assistant was exceptionally organized, extraordinarily efficient, and a techno Harry Potter. He saved her ass many a time. In her office, Micah was the "Anti-Millenial," showing none of the stereotypic professional flaws of the generational cohort, the 22-37 year-olds. The tall Cuban-American kept the upper levels of the Museum's administration humming along smoothly.

"Micah, please send in my guests."

As the trio of guests entered her office, Rebecca motioned them to the conference table. The young woman sat quietly at the table directly beneath the vent for the air conditioner.

"I apologize for my lateness this morning, folks. I did not mean to keep you waiting this long."

Officer Eshani Shahnawaz pulled her hajib up to the top of her hairline and glanced at her companions. They smiled somewhat conspiratorially as she said, "Rebecca, I need to turn state's evidence on this. When your assistant made the appointment, he told each of us the appointment was for 8:00 but please arrive at 8:30. This guy knows you."

Rebecca smiled and looked through the glass wall at her assistant, who was at the thermostat lowering the temperature in the suite. "That he does, in so many ways. It has always been my habit to surround myself with friends and colleagues who complement my skills and make up for my flaws. Micah is a godsend."

Julia Collins, Social Work Director for Covenant House, got to the matter at hand. "Mikey is looking pretty done in. I was so sorry we had to let her go. Unfortunately, our financial constraints do not allow us to care for so many young adults who age out of the system."

Rebecca said, "Apparently, she has been living on the loading dock of the Museum. One of the staff has been bringing a few supplies and some food for her. This information was brought to me two weeks ago after she had been picked up by the Fort Lauderdale police on suspicion of attempted breaking and entering. How's she doing, Shan?"

"Pretty good, all things considered. My mother's house in the Rio Vista neighborhood is a big old rambler with a garage apartment. We were happy to take her in, but she seemed so frail. I guess she told you about her illness."

Jon Esserman, MD, spoke up. "Mikey has secondary dysautonomia, a result of an injury she has not discussed at this time. Her condition is a type called neuro cardiogenic syncope – she faints a lot."

Rebecca said to the rather shy woman, "Please be aware that while we have no rights to your medical or academic records, you have agreed to allow us to discuss these issues for your benefit." Mikey nodded, glancing at the folks at the table. She sucked back a hefty swig of water.

Rebecca pressed the intercom on the conference table phone. "M, can you step in here a moment?" Returning her attention to her guests, she said, " Please go on, Jon."

Jon Esserman was retired from medical practice but served as a member of City Docs, an urban Doctors Without Borders founded to minister to people without housing in South Florida. At the age of fifty-five, he left a very lucrative practice to seek out and serve those most in need in a city of many homeless, a significant number of them children and young adults.

Micah slipped into a seat at the table.

Dr. Essenmen said, “Mikey’s disease causes her autonomic nervous system to go haywire. Her body is actually at war with itself. In many cases, symptoms are not visible and occur internally. External traits are many and varied, and they come and go. A particular physical activity can trigger more severe symptoms. This may cause people with dysautonomia to avoid overexertion. At other times, she may appear perfectly healthy.”

He looked at the young woman and asked, “Mikey, please tell us what’s been going on.”

“So, lately, I have trouble staying upright– gotta lay down ‘cause of dizziness and vertigo. Yes, I’ve been fainting. Bad stomach, can’t breathe right, eyes fuck up – ahh, sorry. Killer headaches sometimes. Can’t sleep. Flop sweats – always hot. Life on the streets, what can I say?”

“Mikey, your condition is most likely the result of an injury or another health condition. Is there anything you could share with us? Just in case we...”

She cut him off. “Naw, Doc. No other diseases. As for the injury ....” She stared off for a bit. “Rather not say, if you don’t mind.” She looked around at the faces of the group. Her hands checked her hair and smoothed her rather ordinary college-kid outfit.

“I’ll get the jump on this shit. Always do. Don’t worry.”

Rebecca held the conversation at a pause before saying, “Mikey, the Museum has a grant for a paid intern that I will eventually add to the budget line. My boss here...” Rebecca smiled and gestured to Micah.“... needs an assistant, all evidence to the contrary notwithstanding. I tend to be a bit overwhelming.”

“This guy?” The young woman smiled at Micah. “Appears the dude could run Space X with all the organization he has going on, and that’s just the little I've seen." She hoped to lighten the discussion. She pushed a file folder each to Micah and Rebecca.

"Knowing of this chance, I prepared my resumé. Also, some academic stuff – standardized tests, etc.

"I dropped out of Broward College after I got my GED. Profs freaked with all of the faintings shit... ahh, stuff."

"So I need a reason to put your application at the top of the pile. Sell yourself, please."

"Three languages, Ms. Quinto."

"Rebecca."

"Thanks, Rebecca. You get multi-lingual if you are sharp on the streets. I made a lot of 'acquaintances' in my consulting business, so I speak English, Creole, and Spanish. Working on Portuguese– lots of Brazilians here in South Florida. And I know the city, Ma'am, inside and out. I know who gets things done in this town, top to bottom. Made it my avocation to know things as it were. I'm reliable, methodical, and efficient. I come with the highest references, as you know."

Eshani Shahnawaz commented, "Your 'consulting business' as you call it. That's the work you did for police advisors in Wilton Manors and here in Fort Lauderdale. Undercover informant. Any worries there? Recriminations, I mean."

"Naw... um, no, Officer, my little buddy met with the big violence last fall-- wrong place, wrong time. But no one seems interested in me. I keep a very low profile."

Julia Collins said, "Mikey, any idea where Nancy O'Brien ended up. She seems to be off the map."

Again, the young woman got silent before revealing, "The Peeler, as we called her. New Orleans, yeah. Last I heard, she was hooking on Rampart Street." She looked grave and shrugged, saying, "Happens."

Rebecca heard the soft chiming of the antique clock in the outer room. "So, here are the next steps, folks. Micah will send you the contact information for Dr. Lisel Tarek. Her offices are in Las Olas. She is a specialist in autonomic nervous disorders. When she signs off on your health, two things – you start working for Micah and me, and you re-enroll at Broward College in the next semester possible. Here's the job description."

"Yeah, seen it. Piece of cake, as they say." About then, the young woman realized what was happening.

"Holy shit!"

"Here is a cell phone. Use it for work-related ... Well, try to keep the personal stuff to a... Oh, never mind, no one does that anyway. Who am I kidding?"

Everyone smiled and stood to leave. Ms. Mikey Larson thanked one and all.

"Appreciate the trust you folks are putting in me. You won't regret it. See you at home, Shan."

The CEO stood. "You and I will work on our cussing, Darling."

Rebecca nodded to Micah, who handed the woman a stack of business cards. The woman looked surprised and a bit teary as she read the print.

Fritcher Museum of Art
Fort Lauderdale, Florida
Michele H. Larson
Executive Assistant

Chapter Two: Blood

FRITCHER MUSEUM OF ART, FORT LAUDERDALE, FLORIDA

Rebecca was tapping her pen silently, end over end. She knew where this was going. T. Jackson Harkness, Chair of the Museum Board, was giving his report to the Board of Trustees, droning on and on. The mid-morning January sunlight danced behind the rolled-down solar shades of the Board Room. Attendance was excellent; the Museum was famous after the success of the last exhibit.

Lately, having a seat on the Board was a prestigious position in the not-for-profit world of South Florida as well as in the social scene from Orlando to Key West. The Board Committee for the Trustees received member overtures from the well-heeled and success-driven. New blood would be excellent, Rebecca thought, especially among young professionals. Strategic recruitment of a diverse group would invigorate this crew.

She needed an active Board. The days of what she referred to as "Resume Board Members," do-nothings who like to showcase their memberships, were over. With the triumph of *Seed Blood,* even the Development Committee was reporting increased major donor interest and more significant contributions.

Board terms brought about the retirement of many of the "old guard" who lacked the leadership vision for a premier, 21st-century art museum. Most of all, the organization needed to jettison the chair. He had served too long, and she needed a vacancy.

"Jack" Harkness was a South Florida Brahmin. His family came from Glouster, Massachusetts, in the Henry Flager days. His great-grandfather, a relative of Flagler's first wife, Mary Harkness, had worked for Flagler's Standard Oil Company and invested in the Florida East Coast Railway, sparking the creation of the new American Riviera. Oceanfront real estate from Melbourne to Miami Beach brought his family nothing but money and a lot of it.

Once a lightning rod of industrial development and community improvement in the South, now in his dotage, Jack began to exhibit a bit of paranoia when it came to relinquishing power and fading into the shadows as a sage and a philanthropist.

His sons were either presidents of major corporations or politicians. His daughters were pampered, blonde, pony-tailed princesses of Boca Raton and West Palm Beach– blond kids, blond dogs, blond lives. Whenever Carole and "Poppy" came on the scene, Rebecca often thought of the strategic marriage games of the historic European royal families enhancing their bloodlines with the rich and powerful. The extended Harkness family members were frequent guests at Mar-a-Lago. And, the word on the Rialto was that Carole Harkness Inslee's son, Tucker, was in the job market with an MA from Webster University in Fine Arts.

Rebeca was on alert. She listened as the Chair brought his remarks to a chisel point of invective. She thought, *One of us is on the way out, Jack, and it's not going to be me, babe.*

"While the closing production numbers for *Seed Blood* were a landmark in the history of the museum, the violence connected to the gala and the circumstances preceding the opening resulted in quite a scandal. Negative social media went off the charts. My question for the Board is, do we wish to be this notorious of an institution?"

Rebecca casually placed the issue of Time Magazine with the Fritcher's cutting-edge exhibit on the cover in front of her, a move that was not unnoticed by the members of the Board. Her smile was totally a "fuck you, Jack."

"I am concerned that our reputation has been sullied. This institution should be dignified, restrained, and never controversial-- art for art's sake – remaining neutral in the face of politics, social issues, and community controversies.

"Our... forgive me, but it is true, Ms. Quinto... our rather impetuous CEO has taken on the solving of some particularly heinous crimes in Wilton Manors. In addition, she has taken on the plight of the Indians, United States policies on immigration, the international conservative political movement, and most recently, blacks in Australia. Her activism reflects negatively on the Fritcher. Is this what we want to be as a place of public recreation and promotion of beautiful artifacts... as an institution for aesthetic preservation?"

Ruby Ashford, Chair of the Finance Committee, spoke up. "I point out to the Chair with no hesitation that our mission statement underscores the vision of the Fritcher Museum of Art as an educational leader in the local, national, and world community on behalf of the arts. It would seem that you would be taking us back to the days of paintings on walls and statues on shelves, Mr. Harkness."

The young city commissioner continued, "We did all this in the strategic planning process two years ago. The power to inform the minds of the public through embracing the beauty and history of the arts and thereby being a catalyst for action is at the heart of who we are as an institution."

Rebecca appreciated the passion of her friend and colleague. She resisted the rising urge to take on Harkness and was grateful that others on the Board also welcomed the days when T. Jackson Harkness would join the ranks of the Trustees Emeriti. Nevertheless, he did have his supporters and would not go easily. Last year, he had attempted to get approval for an amendment to the by-laws extending the term of the Board Chair. It was defeated by a narrow margin.

"Hey, Jack, for the record, it's Native Americans and Aboriginal and Torre Island Straits People." This from Jorge Diaz, member of the Education Committee and President of Human Rights South Florida."

"I stand corrected."

Jack Harkness did not take correction easily. He pushed on to his critical issue. "The point is Ms. Quinto has given us the roster of planned major exhibits through 2020, *Tribal Blood, Austria-Hungry: Imperial Diversity, Wealth and Power, Ancient Blood.* More contention... You can read all about her escapades on the internet.

He continued, "What I am trying to say is, subject to her continued very controversial direction for the institution, we run the risk of driving away the public and alarming many donors and potential partners."

"Chief, you sound like you are asking for our CEO to step down."

Jack Harkness addressed the speaker while he locked eyes with the molasses-hued stare of his CEO. "I am advocating for some modification in her leadership but if she continues to take on these highly incendiary global issues and refuses to abandon her incendiary international involvement, I am prepared to ask her for her resignation."

Rebecca took a sip of her third coffee of the morning and rose to address the Board of Trustees.

All right, Harkness. Let's do this.

Even Micah, fingers flying furiously over his laptop, stopped to look at the CEO. However, she paused as the oldest Board member stood and signaled that Rebecca should wait and allow the Board to respond to the allegations of the Chair.

Sit back down, girl. Let us do the heavy lifting here, girl.

Arva St. Genevieve was 83 and just as active and feisty as a newborn Florida panther. She waved to the Chair in a gesture that he should keep silent now and listen to the wisdom of folks who know.

"I got something to say, Jack."

She moved one side of her hair extensions off behind her right ear. The soft jangle of her soapstone and bauxite beaded, dangle earrings from Ghana signaled to the listeners that Ms. Arva would do some enlightenment, people, so sit back and pay attention.

"Jack, you are as wrong as you can be, and you know it. So let's start, shall we, folks?"

Arva St. Genevieve had started teaching when she was 17 in a one-room schoolhouse for African American children in rural Broward County. At age 23, she was the principal of a high school for minority students that set records for high graduation rates and academic achievement. Beginning in the '40s, Ms. Arva was a voracious advocate for equality and diversity in the educational system in what was to become the sixth-largest school district in the nation. At age 46, she began the first of her three terms as superintendent of schools. President Kennedy appointed her to the U.S. Department of Education.

"Ms. Arva," as she was known, dearly loved the community of her birth and, in her retirement years, survived cancer twice, served on a host of not-for-profit boards, and accepted honors with humility and legendary grace. When she spoke to an assembly, she was always the educator, instilling the highest caliber of knowledge and experience in her pupils. The woman embodied wisdom.

"Trouble is, folks get forgetful of the most essential ideas and need to be reminded. So, here's your review. Y'all pay attention. There will be a test."

Arva was off and running. "As my good friend, Ms. Asford, said, we discussed the institutional purpose when we created our current 6-year strategic plan. Remember? We started with the nature of art and moved on to the reason for the existence of museums."

Arva moved around the inside of the U-shaped table arrangement. She made eye contact and called on her colleagues. St. Genevieve's Rule: There is no impression without expression.

"Mr. Park, tell me why we have all this art anyway?"

The Vice President for Systems Communications for Kumko International jumped up from his chair like a schoolboy called to recite.

"It is an honor to respond to the distinguished Chair of our Education Committee."

Rebecca smiled at the subtle sense of humor of Nate Park. He was a guy who could make you love his boyish hijinks as he turned the knife.

"Art .. art .. yes, that is what we are about. Ahh, just a moment, please." He drew himself up as if he were a competitor at the International Spelling Bee. Even Ms. Arva suppressed a smile.

He glanced at his laptop as he responded. "The nature of art has been described by philosophers throughout the ages." He scrolled. "I can quote you the theories of Aristotle, Tolstoy, Richard Wollheim, Benedetto Croce, R.G. Collingwood, Kant, Martin Heidegger, blah, blah, blah."

"No blah, blah, young man, and no internet. Tell me what art's purpose is for you and for us. Open up your soul and preach me up, son."

"Ma'am. I agree with the sages who say that art is a means by which a community develops for itself a medium for self-expression and interpretation." The young professional looked off for a moment and then said, "I believe art is characterized in terms of *mimesis*."

Arva said, "My, my, a ten-cent word. You always been so smart?"

Nate smiled. "By that, I mean the ability of art to act as a representation of reality– as a narrative... you know, storytelling and expression– the communication of emotion, or other instinctive or intuitive qualities."

"Excellent. So young and so wise." Park smiled, bowed, and sat down.

Jack Harkness was not amused by Arva St. Genevieve's reduction of his Board to a schoolhouse. He tried to signal one of his supporters to make a motion for continuance.

"What, then, is the purpose of a museum?"

The Education Chair rounded on Julie Davenport, a huge Harkness buddy who was busy with her e-mail. She looked up at the hovering St. Genevieve with the expression of a student who was reading a comic book hidden inside her history textbook.

"Ah, it's where you put the art."

Someone gasped lightly. Another Board member had difficulty stopping a guffaw. Arva looked at Julie with one raised eyebrow. She regarded the woman as if to say, *Seriously? Please remain after class.*

Ms. Arva said, "Anyone else?"

Cambell Lenk raised her hand with the intensity of the proverbial honor student eager to show her smarts.

"A museum as an institution tells the story of humanity throughout our history. It houses the cultural soul of the nation."

Another Member volunteered, "We hold this diverse wealth in trust for all generations. A museum, any museum for that matter, becomes the aesthetic conscience of the nation."

Julie Davenport turned red at the realization that she had been served. All she had to do was pull up the visioning statement for the museum as her colleagues were doing. She looked apologetically at Harkness.

"Arva, I think we all know...."

"Now, Jack Harkness, I've known your family for ages and you since you were in diapers. I have the floor. Show some respect if you please."

Now, Arva turned to the CEO and Head Curator. "Rebecca, what does this mean, the aesthetic conscience of the nation?"

Rebecca stood and started with Jack in her sites. *Ahhh, yesss. Hold on, folks. Wait until you hear this.*

"As it has been pointed out in our previous discussions, the Fritcher is called in the 21st Century to be an agent of change, mirroring the events that shape the human family and becoming an instrument of progress by drawing attention to actions and activities that will encourage us to get better– to be better humans."

She looked up from her laptop notes. "So when we exhibit programs of diversity and unity, we advocate for peace. The Fritcher can promote the ideals of democracy in our outreach to the world community."

"We are not the Smithsonian, Ms. Quinto."

Rebecca stopped the interruption with grace. "Please allow me to finish, Mr. Matheson."

Arva St. Genevieve chuckled at Rebecca's flattening of a Harkness man.

"As has been mentioned, we are a public trust. If we are to remain relevant and continue as positive partners in the development of our communities, the Fritcher must be transformational. We must use our unique resources to become more responsive to the challenges faced by modern society and global change."

Most of the group was a tic away from an ovation.

Rebecca continued, "To further reinforce this, Ms. Arva, please speak to us about the imperatives of our educational mission."

It was almost choreographed. The legendary teacher touched her African necklace and looked up to the ceiling as if channeling inspiration.

"Well, in the final analysis, it is all about education. Isn't it, folks?"

Nodding heads showed approval. The education chair began her expository remarks, rising to the cadence of a southern preacher.

"Education that ignores the cultures of the people is ignorance, plain and simple. We can never abandon our commitment to education. We have the capacity to impart cultural wisdom and knowledge effectively through the artifacts of our collections."

Now she reached the favorite aspect of her thesis, saying, "It is, after all, for the children, Yes? Yes? The children and change. The Fritcher has the ability to educate children and the rest of the public in the understanding and appreciating their history and culture. It is about helping the young folks take pride in the achievements of those who went before us – the forebearers."

The extraordinary octogenarian had reached the vocal tones of what her friends referred to as "The Voice of the Lord."

"Our Education Committee has made great strides in providing instructional resources that can be integrated into the curriculum of our schools. Over the years, we have developed programs for PreK to Twelve and teacher training colleges, technical schools, and universities. Under the leadership of Ms. Quinto, the Fritcher has moved beyond the sedate galleries of previous centuries of curation."

Nate Park jumped in. "You are right, Ms. A! I came here as a school child. It was a silent, pale, and dull place. It even had Musak. Now we have an interactive venue that is open to the world-- bright and integrated – a window, no, a portal on the world."

Arva folded her hands and allowed her students to steer the lesson.

Another Trustee, the Rev. Laurence Bailey, spoke up. "Education is a human issue, and the integration of the wealth and power of museums is transformative. How is it not understood by this group that this museum has to be a big player in the learning that goes on in our schools?"

More from members of the Board weighed in.

"What Ms. Arva says is true."

"We are custodians of heritage."

"The Fritcher is one of the many institutions that serve as keepers and tenders of the soul of the people."

"In these times of conflict and disorder, this means resisting when there is fear and danger in the land."

Arva St. Genevieve sat down.

Ike Matheson tried to get the meeting back where Harkness wanted it to be. He said, "Mr. Chair, I move that the Executive Committee of the Board appoint an *ad hoc* committee to look into the political activities of the CEO and Head Curator."

The room erupted.

Rebecca stood.

"Go for it, Jack. See how far you get both internally and in the public eye. I stand on my three years of extraordinary professional evaluations, my awards, and my accolades for service to both the local and international community.

"Oh, and Ike, start with the FBI. Micah, please send Mr. Matheson the contact information for Special Agent Mary Chaffee of the FBI and Captain Anthony Rota of the US Navy Judge Advocate General's Office in Jacksonville. Yes, and place a call to each of the Sheriff's Offices of Fort Lauderdale and Wilton Manors. Refer to my community activism and ask their advice on the wisdom of firing me."

Now Rebecca was on a roll. "I stand on my scholarship credentials and community involvement. I am on the Board of Florida Southern

University and the Coalition for the Homeless of South Florida. Before you attempt to create a public relations nightmare, a morass of human relations litigation, and a plethora of Board resignations, all resulting in a fundraising disaster for the museum in a thinly disguised maneuver to replace me with…."

The Chair interrupted her. "Ms. Quinto, your mercenary-like engagement with controversial issues has this organization teetering on the edge of disaster. You must settle down as a more sedate leader."

Rebecca took a deep breath and let a bit of silence descend over the room. When she spoke, it was with intense conviction.

"You have an activist as your CEO and Head Curator. I am being honest here." She gestured. "Our Member mentioned that we live in times of great injustice, extraordinary suffering, and the destruction of life in an unconscionable demand for more money for the one percent. We stand at the epicenter of a national controversy that says that the lives of school children, shot and murdered, are the price of our freedom as gun owners. If just for that reason alone, institutional leaders need to be superheroes for justice and peace.

"The arts are evocative. They cause people to think and act. Under my leadership, this Museum will continue to advocate for decisive and deliberative actions on behalf of human rights and for the amelioration of misery across the planet.

"Allow me to be very clear. We are <u>not</u> a tourist attraction. We are an institution for change-- innovative, people-oriented, community-minded, program-oriented, professionally solid with well-trained personnel, and above all, child-friendly.

"Sedate leadership? You got the wrong woman. Never gonna happen. Good morning, folks."

As she gathered up her things and backed out the boardroom door, she heard Ruby Ashford introduce a motion for adjournment. There was a second followed by the vote to end the meeting of the Museum Board of Trustees.

Chapter Three: Dune

HARBOUR ISLES OF FORT LAUDERDALE, FLORIDA

In her opinion, he was by far among the planet's hottest men, and they were a couple. Wavey brown-gold hair, magnificent jaw-line, and features that mixed masculine ruggedness and a bit of classic feminine beauty reigned over by breathtaking turquoise eyes, Mark's physical attraction was instant.

He wore his polo shirt and slacks like a fitness model fresh from the gym, always bringing to her mind the recurring thought, *Dude should be nude.* She was a butt woman, and he had one world-class man-ass.

Mark Gadarn smiled as he spoke to a young server – jock stuff, most likely. The bad-boy journalist for CBN World News attracted admirers just by entering a room. Mark raked his thick mane and gave the young man his card as he looked up and rose to meet his lunch companion and give her a double cheek kiss.

"Hey Beautiful, how 'bout we skip the grub, get a room, and shag like pagans?"

"Jesus, Mark. You have no idea how much I need to be nailed senseless right now."

"Ohhh yeahhh. Sure like the sound 'o that." He was smiling his best shit-eating grin. Their intimacy was as exciting as when they met last year.

The server brought the cocktails Mark had ordered. As they toasted and sipped, Mark nodded to the retreating server. "Aspiring journalist, studying at Barry University. Name's Brandon. Gave him my card."

"Looks like a hot gay boy with daddy issues to me, handsome."

Mark feigned annoyance and finger-combed his hair again. "The grey at the temples is meant to make me look distinguished, not like a daddy."

"You have no grey at the temples, Mark. You are just a hot boy yourself."

At 30, he was two years her junior.

Mark picked up his cell phone as if to voice memo. "Personal note: Convince Ms. Quinto of the difference between a boy and a man. Schedule this demonstration for tonight; allow two to three hours, minimum."

She smiled. "Yes, tonight. Home. Can sure use a romantic evening at home in your arms."

"Cool, today's arms day at the gym." He popped a bicep flex.

Brandon returned, bringing toasted brioche rounds with creme fraiche and caviar. Rebecca thought he would touch the mound of upper arm muscle Mark was rocking. The waiter caught her look, blushed, and hurried away.

"I can see your day has been for shit. How was your Board meeting?"

"Same ole, same ole. Committee reports, finances and fundraising, summaries of 2018 exhibits, bat shit, crazy-ass ideas for the fundraising gala, the Chair called for my resignation, my schema for future major exhibits, two new members approved...."

"Wait, wait, wait. Go back to that middle thing. Harkness wants you gone? What the fuck?"

"The sonofabitch– do you believe that? He called me out for my involvement in social issues. Saying I needed to calm it all down. The jerk wants a cabinet of curiosities on the sunny banks of Fort Lauderdale's New River."

She paused and then said, "No, what he really wants is a job for his grandson-- my job."

"You are so controversial, Beautiful, making trouble on three continents."

She stuck out her tongue and pointed to herself. "This is it, man. I gotta be this– and more."

Mark quoted Victor Hugo, "Wherever men go in ignorance or despair, wherever women sell themselves for bread, wherever children lack a book to learn from or a warm hearth... I am here for you."

"Precisely. As it turned out, it was an excellent exercise for the Board in remembering who we are as an institution. That being said, I am in my "I-hate-the-people' mode."

"Arva was spectacular."

"Ms. Ava *was* spectacular. She is a force of nature and a terrific friend."

"Wanna do something else?"

Rebecca looked at her Marie Laveau and took another sip.

"Honestly? No. The discussion on the vibrancy and power of a museum, and this museum, in particular, was energizing. I think that there are times in life when you raise your head up from all the petty stuff and remember why it is you do what you do. It's like a jump start of your professional passion. Makes you want to run to work every day.

"And fuck it, I am on the lookout for a new caper. Let 'em catch me if they can."

Mark raised his bourbon and soda to toast her conviction. Rebecca reached across to touch his free hand.

I just love that he is in my life. I'd go crazy without him. Intelligent, brave, and hot. But, the kindness of this man surrounds him like a halo- - such a marvel! Times like this, I just want to climb into his back pocket and stay there.

"Those who do not know passion do not know life."

"Hugo again? Have you been re-reading Les Miserables?"

"No, I'm quoting Gadarn. Me. I feel sorry for people who do not live with passion, the struggle, the ecstasy it brings. I think I realized that when I was fifteen and trying out for the wrestling team."

"You must have been something when you were a teen jock. All cocky and ballsy. Showing sexy in that singlet."

"Not so, Beautiful. I was puny, shy, and somewhat of a late bloomer, but I had guts and was lucky enough to have a coach who saw my passion for the sport." He grinned like a movie star.

Rebecca said, "When I was a kid in Puerto Rico, I had a *tia*, an aunt, who believed in me. She was a *prima ballerina assoluta* for *Balleteatro Nacional de Puerto Rico,* the National Ballet Theater of Puerto Rico--Laura Ocasio. Starting in my childhood, she introduced me to the beauty of the arts and the importance of saving them for future generations."

"Very cool. I read about her. Retired but creating theater experiences for the hurricane recovery efforts in Puerto Rico."

"Yes. Laura is staging a series of street performances all over the island entitled *Mi Preciosa Patria.* She put the call out and is attracting some premier artists from across the globe."

She continued, "My aunt has dancers who have come out of retirement and volunteer to either appear or to choreograph. One artist is the dance legend from China, Li Chengwu. He came out of retirement to perform for almost six weeks. They are dancing among the ruins and reconstruction all over the island."

Mark commented, "Talk about risk-taking and visionary leadership... incredible."

Brandon brought the entrees. "The tilapia was caught this morning, Ms. Quinto, just a few hours ago. I hope you find it enjoyable."

"Thank you. Brandon, is it?"

The server placed a top sirloin with Mark and said, "Yes, ma'am. Just want to say, I'm a huge fan. Your police work last year was awesome."

"Have you been to the Museum, Brandon?"

"The Arts Museum downtown? Planning to get there sometime soon. Want to see the blood exhibit.

"Seed Blood. It's breaking all records but soon to close. So, make your plans." She tucked into the Meyer lemon glazed, fresh catch.

Mark had cut into his steak and brought a morsel to his mouth.

Brandon turned to him with the unspoken, *Is it cooked to your satisfaction?*

Mark said, "Mmm, perfect, kiddo. Tell the chef he outdid himself."

"Thank you, sir."

The server uncorked the High Hook Pinot Blanc 2014 from Willamette Valley, Oregon. He poured a small amount into Mark's glass. Mark swirled and examined the legs, nosed the wine, and sipped. He placed the glass to his right, the traditional silent signal to the sommelier that the wine was acceptable.

Brandon was not up on his wine etiquette and asked if the wine was acceptable.

"Good, good, my man."

The wine was poured.

"Sir, If you need anything else, please let me know."

They ate in silence for a few minutes. Rebecca chewed and looked at Mark.

"What?"

"Nothing, Darling. I just have to get used to you being cruised by men as well as women." She pointed with her fork. "He's got it bad. Be gentle when you let him down."

"You're kidding, but I suspect just a little annoyed. Why?"

"Darling, I ordered the wine. He should have made me the primary in the service of it. He is so... the eyes tell all, handsome. He's smitten big time. Are you sure you don't want a glass of red with the beef?"

Mark put his hand over his glass of white wine and made an I'm-good face. He said, "Eating desert dust in Syria and Pakistan has fucked up my taste buds. Ruined me forever as a gourmand."

"The boy would be happy to bring his new man crush whatever."

Mark chuckled. “You are incredible, girl. This continued fantasy of me with some man-on-man action going on-- the stuff of porn and very amusing.” He laughed again.

Rebecca looked down at her meal and raised her eyebrows. “Just sayin’ I can read the heart or, in this case, the sexual appetite.”

“You have an uncanny way of eroticizing the most ordinary situations.”

“Sorry, I guess my libido goes into overdrive when I get frustrated, and the meeting this morning was so irritating. Should I work on the stereotypic, romantic sexuality of the demure and proper damsel? More of the ‘Sir, you disgust me’ and ‘Oh fiddledeedee’ stuff.”

“Never change, Beautiful. I like my bad-girl women. Aggressive yet soft and pliant like an unfolding bloom.”

Rebecca aped a shyer, more delicate flower by twisting a lock of her hair and saying, “Do you ever fantasize me and...?”

“My babe and another woman getting it on? Sweetie, you know I do. When ole Mark boy is getting some of his special solo man-time....” He grinned, made a pumping gesture with one hand, and did a tongue swipe.

“Oh, brother, you men and your toys... It’s you who are too frisky for early afternoon, sexy.”

He did a leering eye-roll worthy of a troll in heat.

Rebecca said, “You know, I’ve changed my mind-- dancing at Hunter’s on the Drive tonight. High NRG. We can kick back the rest of the weekend.”

“Yeah, about that.” It was Mark’s turn to look down at his food as if he were staring into a deep well of ‘here-it-comes.’”

“I got an assignment.” He looked up. “Leaving early Sunday. I was going to tell you, but we have both been so busy.””

“Mark.”

"I land in Djibouti on Monday. It's a base for going into Yemen, across the Gulf to Aden, and then in-country."

"Mark, you're going into the middle of a war."

"Some ground fighting is all. Skirmishes. CBN wants to get the latest on the insurgency war and the horrors of the famine. It's another Syria but has gotten much less international media attention. Many warring factions, and the US is in the middle of it. The civilian death rate is staggering. Disease is rampant, as is the human trafficking that always comes with the horror of armed conflict."

"Will you listen to this guy? You just contradicted yourself."

Rebecca continued, "Holy shit, talk about into the mouth of the beast. Yemen has all your favorites, the Saudis, the Russians, Al Queda, and ISIL. Mark, if any of these groups get their hands on you... Look at what the Saudis did to the Washington Post journalist, Jamal Khashoggi."

"It's gonna be fine, gorgeous. I promise to behave myself."

"Don't give me that. You are totally reckless when it comes to a story. Your reputation as an international media provocateur has gotten you tossed out of... let's count 'em...."

She finger counted. "Syria...."

"CBN pulled me out. My wounds were not all that bad. Beautiful, I saved those Marines... Anybody?" The gutsy reporter looked up and around, raising his hands to the side as if encouraging a non-existent studio audience to agree and applaud.

"Turkey...."

"Yes, I'll admit that was a close one. Erdoğan and his thugs do not like my handsome mug. And I was pretty in your face when I did that interview."

"Vanuatu...."

"Such a cesspool of human rights violations, women, LGBTQ+. Glad to brush the dust of that one off my ass."

"And I do not include that bullet you took last winter."

She doubled back. "How long?"

"Hard to say, love. No exit date. I know you do not want to hear this, but things over there are a bit dicey, hence disorganized."

"Mark, I'm so fearful of something disastrous happening to you. Aren't there less dangerous assignments?"

"Rebecca, I am not a Westminister Dog Show or International Flower Festival kind of journalist. You know that. Been working with my trainers to get into bestial shape to be able to take on trouble if and when it comes...."

"Make sure it doesn't come, tough guy."

Brandon picked up the plates and silently stood by for a dessert order.

Mark said, "Just coffee *pour deux, bachgen*." The lad floated away.

Rebecca shook her head, "Such a tease."

"What? It's French with a touch of Welsh."

"You know what I am talking about. And you are distracting me from my lecturing you on the dangers of your work."

Mark stood, leaned over the table, and kissed his woman.

"Swear on my balls that I will be careful. Three of us going in anyway, nothing's gonna happen."

"Gonna hold you to that, Mark."

"Holding my balls? Naw, gonna need 'em, my gal."

"I'm serious, Mark."

Mark switched to a more sober expression. "All will be well, Rebecca. If I get captured by the insurgents, you can come and save me. Dust off your camos. Anyway, this could be a shot at my dream assignment."

"China."

"Yeah, China."

Rebecca wondered if they should begin sometime soon to talk about living a more sedate life together. There it was again-- that word with its suggestion of a quiet and boring life paralysis. No fucking way. The trade-off for their combined flirtations with danger was staring them in the face, anxiety over the most deadly consequences.

Brandon brought the coffee. They both checked their phones at the same time. Right-hand thumbs skated vertically on the screen.

"Ms. Arva. I'll call her from the office."

"Rebecca, I have a final briefing at the media headquarters, and I have a training session at Crunch Gym. I can meet you at Hunters at 8."

"Sounds good, *chico*. Do me a favor." She placed her credit card in the folder.

"Anything."

"Dress down and goofy. Something that will communicate straightness and unavailability."

"Huh? Oh, wait, I get it, all of this, fresh from the gym... and the men on the make." He grinned and raised his eyebrows.

"No gay boy magnet tonight. I want you all to myself until you leave."

"One tough assignment, but I am up for it."

They both said together, "No pun intended."

Chapter Four: *La Gloriosa*

SOUTH ANDREWS AVENUE, FORT LAUDERDALE, FLORIDA

Arva St. Genevieve wanted a face-to-face, and Ms. Arva always got what she wanted. Rebecca met her at her office, a block from the Museum in the historic Women's Club Building.

"Yeah, that 'Voice of God' thing. That came from my friend Barbara some time ago. My, yes. That woman was a force of nature, swept across this land, did much good, and was gone all too soon. And she was indeed my friend."

Rebecca looked at the signed picture of then-Governor Jimmy Carter, Arva St. Genevieve, and Barbara Charline Jordan, which hung to the left of the Trustee's antique desk.

"Respected by both Democrats and Republicans, she believed in the Constitution of the United States with a courageousness not seen since. Barbara got things done because she knew how to work politics. She was a master at compromise."

Arva sipped her afternoon sweet tea, reached into a desk drawer, pulled out a bourbon bottle, and gave her drink a hefty spike before motioning to Rebecca with the bottle. Rebecca put a hand over her glass, signifying, "No, thank you."

"With all this fighting in Congress, I just hope we get more women of color on the Hill – hell, any color, to be honest, with the charisma of my friend Barbara. Lord, we sure need it."

"Right now, my money's on Kamala Harris, and I do like Hawaii's, Mazie Hirono. The woman got an 'F' rating from the NRA because of her outspoken support for gun control. Excellent."

"Oh, hell yes. We have killed enough school children in this country."

"Ms. Arva, you did not ask me here to discuss liberal politics. How can I help."

The retired teacher and national heroine for civil rights stood and walked around the desk to sit next to her guest. She was a straight shooter and always looked her fellow conversationalist in the eyes.

"OK, my commentary on this morning's meeting: Rebecca, you have taken the Fritcher to the level of national importance as an art museum with relevance and class. We now have an institution playing out on the world stage with a voice for the oppressed and marginalized, which is much needed. Our next major exhibit, the collaboration with Colorado's Phelan Museum of Fine Arts and the Silverman Museum of Native American Arts, will be a voice for justice and reparation."

Rebecca affirmed, "Yes, *Tribal Blood.* We have many Native American communities in on this. Florida's Seminoles and Miccosukee nations will be represented."

"My dear, I want to tell you to keep on going in the direction you are headed. Jack Harkness and his old-school cronies are on their way out. We need new, vibrant leadership on that Board, and you are the one to get it. Such ignorance and foot-dragging. They are so done, my dear. They need to get out of the way."

The Trustee stood and went to her office credenza.

"Ms. Arva, you don't know how good you are for my professional self-esteem and vision for our museum. That meeting just put me off. Sonofabitch!" She reached for the whiskey.

Waving away the praise, St. Genevieve placed a framed picture in the hands of her guest. "Seems like all I have these days are old pictures. Rebecca, I want you to meet another friend of mine. This is *La Gloriosa,* Victoria Ricci."

The framed photograph was a vintage shot, circa the 1930s, of Floria Tosca from Giacomo Puccini's eponymous opera set during Napoleon's invasion of Rome in 1796. In the photo, the tragic heroine is standing over and placing a crucifix on the body of Baron Scarpia, the corrupt chief of police she has murdered.

The inscription was in Italian. *Alla mia amica Arva, vivi per l'arte, vivi per amore, Vickie.*

Arva translated, "To my dear friend... Live for art, live for love. The inscription is based on the first line of the signature aria from *Tosca,* 'Vissi d'arte.' It was taken in 1942 at the Staatsoper in Berlin. Italian operas were rarely staged during the Nazi regime. This production was a rare exception."

"She is gorgeous. Was she a big star?"

"She was the diva of divas. The best of her age, or of any age for that matter, an Italian coloratura mezzo-soprano, opera singer, and recitalist. It was the end of that age of creative genius between the wars, and she was a goddess superstar. She opened opera houses across the world. She gave recitals staged amid the ruins of classical civilization. *La Gloriosa in the Jungle* – she even appeared at that fabled opera house built in the Amazon."

"Wow, *O Teatro de Amazonas*, amazing."

"Victoria had a considerable repertoire. Her interpretation of the renowned soprano and mezzo roles has yet to be surpassed. She was a model and mentor for many of the post-World War II great ones, Callas, Albanese, and Tibaldi. She was known for her versatility in prominent female roles. Critics lauded the force of her electrifying acting and her youthful, bright vocal expressions.

"I met her at a recital in Dresden in 1945, ten months after the massive bombing by the Allies, which totally destroyed the city."

With a dreamy look on her face, Ms. Arva tapped the picture's inscription. "This was one of her arias. Her performance was for a Red Cross benefit for the children of Dresden. She was 35 years old and in the prime of her art."

She returned to her desk and cued up a YouTube. The room was filled with a lustrous yet plaintive voice of a woman entreating her father to allow her to marry the boy she loves, "O Mio Babbino Caro" from Puccini's *Gianni Schicchi.*

Rebecca felt a stab to the emotions and the tears that come in the throes of a mystical experience. The intensity of the character's heartrending torment over the tension between the devotion to her father and the passion for her lover seemed to be a tangible entity that pulled with evocation at the human heart.

They sat briefly in silence. Rebecca tissued tears on her cheeks. "You have me a few seconds from a huge snot cry, Ms. Arva. What a voice!"

"We sure did it up right in those days, girl. The world just can't seem to keep up with the caliber of the artists of that great generation. Something about being formed and fired in the cauldron of two world wars."

"So, how did she die?"

Arva St. Genevieve poured a bit more spirits into her sweet tea. She walked to the window that looked out on the lush gardens of the Broward County Public Library. She said solemnly.

"Sister ain't dead."

"Get out. She'd be about a hundred and ten – a super-centenarian. That's incredible. No one writing about her and doing PBS documentaries?"

The wise older woman shrugged. "No, they're not, and they won't."

"Arva, you are as mysterious as hell."

The slightly eccentric educator and sage turned to her guest and continued her fantastic story.

"Rebecca, when a person who has achieved greatness gets old, you lose friends and loved ones. The bastards who lived each day just to bring you down are all gone, too. As a woman, you are no longer desirable to men, and so your power diminishes."

Rebecca nodded and said, "It's just the opposite as men grow old. Their power increases. Look at the good old boy's club in Washington."

"As she ages, a woman eventually comes to the time when she can afford to become radicalized and kick ass with a special kinda I-don't-give-a-fuck attitude. Now she can say exactly what she thinks and believes in her heart, raisin' the hell that needs to be raised."

Arva continued, "As a woman grows even older, stories arise, legends. It's the flip side of notoriety. Sometimes the stuff people believe and say about you is true, sometimes not, and sometimes the bullshit is just plain unbelievable."

Rebecca smiled as she asked, "Ms. Arva, are you really descended from Thomas Jefferson and his mistress, Sally Hemings?"

"That one is pure hogwash and infuriates the hell outta me."

With her right hand, she wagged a resolute index finger. Her other hand was on her hip, completing the pose of a no-nonsense instructor who meant business – *no time for ignorance, child.*

"For starters, Sally Hemings was not Jefferson's mistress. She was his property. Mr. All-Men-Are-Created-Equal owned more than six hundred men, women, and children at Monticello. When he died, Jefferson granted freedom to only seven people, and that slave woman who bore him six children was not one of them. Anyway, how that revision of history came to land on my front porch is beyond me."

"But you were lovers with Thurgood Marshall. That one's true, right?"

"Ut ahh. Mr. Billy Dee Williams. Ohhh, that man was fine, girl. Made love like he invented it."

They both stopped and looked at each other, watching to see who would crack first. After a beat, Rebecca and Ms. Arva exploded in simultaneous laughter at the joke.

"You are so bad."

Arva responded, "Oh, my yes. There's still some fire in the furnace, girl."

They laughed again.

"Getting back to Victoria-- at the end of the war, there were many stories about the woman. The fact is she was a paramour of some very important Nazis. In the past, she has refused ever to speak in-depth about that time of her life."

"Hold on, Ms. Arva. The great soprano Victoria Ricci was a consort of the Nazi High Command. Yet in 1945, by the end of the war, she was giving recitals for the support of the Allies. Why wasn't she condemned for her Nazi sympathies?"

St. Genevieve said slyly, "Umm humm. Churchill stepped in and saved her ass. No legend there. Fact."

The conversation stopped for a few seconds. Rebecca's quizzical face changed to an expression of sudden realization.

"Jesus, she was a British spy."

"MI5. Snuggling up to the balls of the enemy. That she was. She was decorated to huge acclaim and had a tremendous international operatic and concert career up until 1975."

"Sick and hospitalized?"

Arva feigned annoyance. "No. Now, are you going to let me tell my story or what?"

She walked to the credenza and tossed some ice in a glass-- a tall bourbon and soda. She handed it to Rebecca in two moves, a gesture that said, "Here, take this," and another motion (when a refusing hand went up) that said, "Do as you're told. Gonna need it."

"On December 11, 1975, She performed again in Dresden on the 30th anniversary of her *Children of War Concert.* Following the performance, she walked out of the theater by a stage door and was never seen or heard of since."

"She pulled a Greta Garbo."

"You got that right."

"Ms. Arva, that was almost forty-five years ago. She is most likely gone."

"Wait. There's more. *La Gloriosa* was a woman of intense passion. Art was one of them, children another, and one rather strange interest, spiritualism. During her last public years, she never went anywhere without her psychic, a notorious voodoo queen who goes by the name of Madame Ondine Rillieux."

Arva made the sign of the cross.

"Three weeks ago, I received this, sent by mail. The postmark was New Orleans, Louisana." She handed Rebecca what appeared to be a playing card.

Ms. Arva explained, *"L'Impératrice,* the Empress. The deck is New Orleans Voodoo Tarot. She represents the productivity of the subconscious, growing ideas. She is the embodiment of the growth of the natural world, fertility, and what one knows or believes in one's heart. She is the personification of Art."

Rebecca slowly turned the card in her hand. She looked up and said, "Ms. Arva, help me out here. What does this have to do with La Ricci still being alive?"

"Open the back of the photograph's frame."

What Rebecca found caused her to take a long swig of her bourbon. Attached to the back of the photograph was a tarot card...

The Empress.

Chapter Five: Strip

HUNTER'S NIGHT CLUB, WILTON MANORS, FLORIDA

The entrance to the nightclub was guarded by two bouncers. The exit was about 25 feet down the glass-sided building and had another two guards supervising the outflow near the back dance floor bar. The gays usually obey the rules, lining up in an orderly queue that snaked down the parking lot on Friday and Sunday nights. An outdoor bar helped to make the wait more congenial.

Rebecca excused herself and stepped up to the muscular, head-shaved bouncer, reminding herself, *This baby does not wait in line.*

"Jimmy, I did it again, left my purse in the Ladies." She did a half-turn to make sure she was heard by patrons waiting close to her. She lightly touched the bouncer's chest. "Do you think I could just run in and...?"

"Ms. Q, you gotta stop doing this, rab jab." He winked, signifying that she was only fooling the customers at the head of the line who were watching the beautiful drag queen jump the queue.

The other bouncer was about to object, but Jimmy waved him off. He continued the charade, saying, "It's OK, Dan. She'll be right out." As he stepped aside, he whispered to Rebecca, pointing to her gold-chained shoulder bag. "Girl, your purse is right fuckin' there."

They both laughed. She was in.

Gay men everywhere, all makes and models, ages, and body types. Eight-thirty PM-- the silver daddies would be gone in an hour, and the muscle boys, twinks, and disco queens would fill the place. The energy and camaraderie of the crowd were in high gear, the music palpable.

Rebecca thought, *God, I just love my gays.* She acknowledged that this was their club, and she appreciated that most of the clientele acted as if there was "room for us all." The front bar was three deep, and the cocktail tables along the opposite wall were full. She could see a large crowd around the pool table at the rear of the room.

No Mark.

No return text to her "Meet you at N's drink station."

Rebecca eased into Natalia's service area. The Russian beauty smiled and leaned across for a triple-cheek kiss. She had already begun squeezing the lemons for Rebecca's cucumber lemon drop on the rocks. As Natalia reached for the Effen Cucumber Vodka, Rebecca put her credit card on the bar alongside her purse.

"Keep it open?"

"Oh hell yes, Darling. Gonna stay a while and dance my ass off."

Natalia locked the Coach shoulder bag in a cabinet under the register. Rebecca said, "Mark?"

Natalia smiled knowingly and pointed to the crowd around the pool table. The men erupted in a prolonged and lusty cheer. Everything at Hunters had a strong sexual vibe.

She squirmed her way over to the pool table. Mark was pulling his t-shirt over his head. He was grinning and accepting encouraging slaps on his bare back as he let the "T" hang from a side belt loop. He retrieved his Michelob Ultra from his muscled-up, shirtless opponent. The guy wore a ball cap with "Studly" emblazoned on it.

"Rack 'em, pretty boy. This next one's for your jeans. Hope you're not goin' commando."

The man's buddy jumped in with, "Hope you are, dude!" Audience approval erupted.

Mark sucked his beer between his shit-eating grins. He slipped the top button of his jeans to better show the waistband of his Calvin Kleins, ending speculation.

The sexy journalist arranged the billiards, flipped up the frame, picked up his cue, and signaled to "Studly Man" that it was his break.

Rebecca touched his shoulder. He turned.

"Hey, Beautiful, where have you been?" He smooched her.

Rebecca responded by pulling him in for a deep boy-girl kiss-up, backing up his butt to the edge of the pool table.

Totally getting it, the spectators reacted with a conjoined "Ewwww!'

"Told ya he's straight."

"Damn. They're fuckin' everywhere."

Rebecca stepped back with a smug look on her face, and the two shirtless men resumed the third game. Tight jeans-clad butts bent over the green felt while equally fit upper bodies stretched and reached to take the perfect shot with agility and precision. The Strip 8 Ball match progressed evenly between Mark's solids and studly Jerad's stripes. The spectators were slightly drunk and very frisky. The Welsh-American jock with the porn star physique was the evening's favorite bar hottie, admired by many, ignored by none.

Mark soon commanded the table, but his opponent kept pace. Solids disappeared, and stripes followed along, sinking into pockets, all but two. Jared scratched, and the cue ball rebounded from a side cushion to sit in direct line with the 8 Ball and the far corner pocket.

"Wanna unbuckle right now and save us the wait, big guy?"

Jerad smirked, "Bring it, sexy boy. Make the shot. Oh, yeah, and I am going commando." He did a half-turn and exposed the top part of his left butt cheek before pulling back up. "Any interest in upping the stakes?"

The crowd loved it, roaring and making salacious remarks. Rebecca moved a bit to get an unobstructed view of the half-naked man ass. *God, I love this place.*

Mark widened his stance and bent, overreaching with his pool stick for the cue ball. The pool table lights played across his muscular back, misted with a light layer of sweat. The pressure was on, and he relished it like a drug. He rocked the stick back and forth, teasing the cue ball but never touching it. The tip finally kissed the white surface, and the ball mated with the 8 Ball with a determined click before stopping dead.

The black ball rolled straight to the open mouth of the hungry corner pocket. The momentum would just about carry it over the lip when a hand reached out and caught the winning shot. Pandemonium erupted.

Mark exploded. Jared was open-mouthed. The crowd yelled their frustration.

"Fuck you, Cam, what the hell? I gave you the twenty-bucks."

"Take 'er easy, hot stuff. We said one hour, and that was up thirty minutes ago. Mark, you know I can't keep the table open on a Friday night. This place is balls to the wall with a mile-long waiting line. I need the space."

Cameron Stone, Hunters' manager, gestured to a nearby barback to cover the table. Jared stepped up, took the still bewildered Mark's cue, and placed it, along with his, on the wall rack. He returned and did an alpha-to-alpha handshake-shoulder bump with his opponent. "Another time, bro."

"Count on it."

The crowd would not be placated.

"Strip! Strip! Strip!"

Mark looked at Rebecca with a mischievous grin.

Rebecca knew not only could he not resist, but she wasn't about to stop him. She shrugged and smiled.

Mark raised his arms up over his head, commanding attention, and then dropped his hands to his jeans. The fly went down, and he pulled his pants to his ankles, bending over in his tighty whities as he did. He came back up, arms stretched wide in an is-this-what-you-wanted-to-see gesture.

The fans went wild.

Chapter Six: Bayou Shadows

SAILBOAT BEND, FORT LAUDERDALE, FLORIDA

In the dark shadows of the night, soft, haunting vocals of Billie Holiday floated out between the trees. They wafted over the glistening waters of the slow-moving river. A solitary fishing boat, nets held high from the mast like lacy shrouds, slid quietly upriver to its home berth. Late-night river ducks went rear-end up in the marshy shoals, catching a bedtime meal, ever watchful for feral cats on the poorly defined shoreline in search of their duckling broods.

In a cottage close by the sluggish waterway, an elderly woman sang in the shadows and night lamps, along with Lady Day and a moaning saxophone, "How can I go on without you...?"

Arva St. Genevieve lived in a salt-box style antique of a home at the western reaches of the New River not far from downtown. Many over a hundred years old, the pre-war houses were tucked into small streets lined with overhanging pine oaks dripping with green-grey Spanish moss. A forest of monstrous ficus stands, leather-leafed rubber trees, twisted sea grapes, and exotic Indian banyans created a mysterious urban jungle. Branches, trunks, and ariel roots were home to iguanas, peacocks, snowy whooping cranes, and their cousins, the sandhill cranes. The banks of the drowned river bed were peppered with other tin-roofed, pastel-colored human abodes. Opossums and raccoons were the night roamers, scavenging and playing in the trees and open spaces.

The winter night was quiet and cool, lit by a full moon dressed in the shadows of a slowly moving total lunar eclipse. Arva looked up from her back porch. It seemed that the moon goddess, Selene, was donning some dark red and black, sexy lingerie in a slow, suggestive dance with the earth and sun against a curtain of stars. Screened windows and doors allowed the fragrances of the night and the sound of the river and its wildlife to move through the house like a restless spirit.

Arva filled the bird feeder that hung from the porch rafters, left sliced oranges for the rodent and coon population, and brought her calico cat, Rosie, inside. The lights in the house were scattered pools of amber emanating from lamps on tables and bookcases. This was Arva's favorite time of day, evening, the "lamp lighting time." She moved to the bedroom to switch on a bedside lamp before returning to the kitchen to pick up her bowl of Cajun jambalaya and take it to the dining room.

On the way, she popped out *The Best of Billie Holliday* CD. She replaced it with *The Concert in the Forbidden City: Victoria Ricci in Bejing,* one of the diva's last public appearances. The soprano intoned the luscious aria *"Tu che di gel sei cinta*" from Puccini's *Turandot*. Breathtaking strains of operatic perfection filled the cottage and spilled out into the night.

Arva sat amid the books and papers on her dining room table, serving as her home desk. She had done an excellent job on the jambalaya. She paused a moment to savor the dish's delicate and robust spicy balance. The house seemed to snuggle into the aromas of her cooking, reluctant to part with the delight and warmth of the rustic odors. She poured a glass of a French Syrah and nosed the fruity interiors of the dark wine.

The aged teacher listened to her friend, *La Gloriosa*, sing of love and death as she finished her meal. She reached for a deck of tarot cards with one hand and made space in front of her with the other. Nearby was another gift from her diva, a shopworn book on the meaning of the tarot. The wine brought new sensations to the night as she sipped.

She opened the ornate ormolu card box, which she had previously placed in the moonlight on the porch, and held the cards in her hand. Her thoughts drifted to the years she spent with Victoria Ricci during the rebuilding of Europe. Such misery, but it was also an exciting time of hope for the future.

She separated out the twenty-two cards of the Major Arcana, setting the others aside. The smaller pile of picture cards would focus on the material world, the creative mind, and the realm of change.

As her friend taught her, Arva knocked the pile in her hand, spreading her energy into the deck. She shuffled for a few minutes and cut the cards into three groups before gathering them into one.

Arva dealt the cards in the pentagram spread, the star layout. The star pattern was six cards dealt face down. At the top was the Spirit Card. The Winds of Intuition Card and then the Water Card were to the upper left and right. Beneath them were the Earth and Fire to the left and to the right.

First, she turned over the center card, the Significator. This would be the representation of her-- The Hermit. Arva flipped the pages of The Meaning of the Tarot for an explanation.

She read aloud, “Standing upon a mountain top, the Hermit beholds the rest of the world. He raises the lantern of truth to guide all seekers.” It seemed to Arva that the Tarot was referring to her lifetime of teaching and lecturing.

“Humph.” The sound was sharp and soFort *Yes, that’s me, all right, and I am here to say after 83 years, it has not gotten smooth and easy. Lord, no.*

She turned the card on her lower left, the Earth Card. This brought stability and security. Here would be revealed any restraining forces that would prevent completing the pursuit. Now, the image of the Lovers stared up at her, signifying a temptation of the heart. A stable relationship hung in the balance. The card was “reversed,” upside down, foretelling conflict, disharmony, and threat. She scanned the book and stopped.

Outside, the trees were rustling, but she felt no breeze through the open windows or the screen doors. In the grate, the fire logs blazed unexpectedly before damping back down. She looked at the Lovers and seemed to hear a voice whisper in the movement of the branches and leaves as well as the crackling of the fire.

One in danger. One will save.

Next, she turned the card on the upper left, the Air card. This was the place on the spread that showed the Winds of Influence, important forces that would come into play. The flipped card revealed the High Priestess, enthroned in blue robes, wearing an Egyptian-style crown. The figure stood with one foot on the moon. Arva read aloud, “She reigns between the columns of the Temple of Solomon. Behind her, the

Veil of the Temple embroidered with pomegranates hides the mysteries she guards."

Rebecca.

Arva said, "Definitely her. Girl is as unconventional as they get. Rarely does anything by the rules. I need to draw her further into my confidence on this."

She lifted her wine glass and drank to her friend. Rosie jumped to the table, checking things out with her large green eyes. Her purr motor was running in high gear as she settled into a lounging position just beyond the cards.

"Welcome, Your Majesty."

The cat batted at the card in the Fire position on the lower right of the spread, the Ultimate Destroyer. Its message would carry a warning of significant harm, destruction, and peril. Rosie looked as Arva flipped the card in that position and timed the reveal with a part meow and a part growl.

The Devil

"First, I hear voices, and now up jumps the devil himself. This is scaring me a bit, Your Highness. And I am here to tell you, Ms. Arva's not afraid of a whole hell of a lot."

She stroked the cat and read for guidance.

"OK, so what we got with His Satanic Majesty here is an individual seduced by the material world and physical pleasures. It says that there is much fear around him, domination and bondage, being caged by an overabundance of luxury. Humph." She tapped the card with a slightly shaky hand.

"We best be careful of this one."

One of the neighborhood peacocks, Doctor John, began to screech on the back porch. A burning log in the large fireplace shifted, sending a few sparks against the screen and puffs of smoke into the room. The opera music grew louder.

The Tides of Intuition, the Water Card, was flipped next on the upper right. It showed where Arva would find the twistings and turnings of her journey. In the pentagram, it was the Hanged Man, *la pittura infamante*, who occupied this position and looked up at her. He was a traitor being hanged upside-down by one ankle.

Judas is among us. Who will he turn out to be?

What she saw before her were the characters charged with a perilous quest, a dangerous journey to conquer the forces of evil, destruction, and death. There would be grave obstacles and, along the way, the need to gather faithful companions for the expedition.

But whose quest was she seeing? Her's, the Evil One's, Rebecca's, the turncoat, the man or woman in peril? "Rosie, I am one confused woman right now."

Arva shook her head, thinking that this was most troubling. She drank from the glass and gently stroked the cards. Flipping back and forth between the pages of the guidebook, puzzling over the meaning of the cards' messages, a feeling of foreboding caused her to shiver.

The old teacher poured more wine as she said aloud, "Feels like someone is walking 'cross my grave, Rosie." The cat looked at her with bright, green eyes. She let out a mouth-stretching feline yawn but seemed to focus on a movement just beyond the engrossed Arva. There was something there by the window. In a flash, the agitated familiar transformed into a hissing arch, tail straight up, and fangs bared. The cat flew off the table.

Arva looked up and then back to her Tarot reading. She dismissed the growing sense of dread. *Shit, I don't believe in this crap anyway.*

She was about to scramble the deck but stopped, seeing the one lone card she had yet to turn over in the spread. Arva reached for it at the top point of the star, above her image. The ignored card was the Significator. This was the Tarot's representation of the Spirit, the entire self. It would depict the divine companion that would guide the resolution of the journey.

She never got to it.

The dead flowers scent of patchouli filled the dining room. A small, naked arm reached over from behind her. Tattoos covered the thin, dark appendage. A slightly deformed hand extended a bony finger to flip over the Spirit Card.

The Empress.

Chapter Seven: Strike a Pose

HUNTER'S NIGHT CLUB, WILTON MANORS, FLORIDA

"I'm pretty sure you two are drinking for free tonight. Your balls are so spectacular, Mark." Natalia placed Rebecca's martini and Mark's beer on the bar mat between them. Rebecca hissed at her like a cat ready to fight. Natalia played along with a feline swipe of her right hand and a precious meow. She was a dark-eyed beauty who, in Rebecca's estimation, "... makes the best cocktails, Darling."

Mark's left arm wound its way around his lady love's waist as they accepted the drinks. Otto, a muscle-boy barback, took Natalia's place as she moved to make other orders. He swiftly pushed glasses into a soapy sink, rinsed them in another, and set them up to dry. He said to Mark. "Seriously? Johnson's the strip club just down the Drive. Bud, most of the dick dancers are straight anyway. With that body, you will crush. That is if you can dance, Papi."

"He's got a job, cutie. A damn good one. And he dances like a male hustler in a wet dream." Rebecca said. Turning to Mark, she added. "Speaking of, let's hit the dance floor. Seems like we both could use some release. 'All I ever needed was the music and the mirrors and the dance....' Let's go." They made their way through the crowd to the mobbed dance floor.

"Cassie in *A Chorus Line* – perfect mime, Beautiful." Mark looked at her disco wear as they endeavored to get to some space near the center of the dance floor. Rebecca sported a teal sequined mini dress, t-strap pumps, also teal, with silver accents, and a peacock blue fan from the Wilton Manors Pride Festival 2018 with the *message #expressyourpride – Absolut.* She wore her long, dark-brown hair up, held in place by a rhinestone hairpin modeled as a mardi gras mask, purple, green, and gold. *Girl was styling.*

Dianna Ross was singing to the beat about how right, so right she was and that she could turn emotion on and off. The Boss drew posers and conversationalists onto the dance floor to crank it, and lip-sync. Some joined the group on the narrow stage and disco boy boxes. Lights and smoke swirled like a portal into another dimension, one of total inhibition, abandonment, and complete body sensuality.

Ms. Ross performed Ashford and Simpson's luscious lyrics on flat screens throughout the club in a white, sleeveless pantsuit, sending it up in 1979 with a full orchestra and dancers on roller skates. The club took its patrons back to the 70s, 80s, and 90s. Tonight, Hunters was the rockin'est place on the planet.

Mark pulled Rebecca in close, pointed to the monitor, and said, "On Diana's resumé – Queen of Disco."

"No, my man. That's Donna Summer. Do not blaspheme her, especially here."

They busted some ballroom moves in the tight space. Rebecca snapped her cha-cha fan at the crowd as she turned and rocked out. Total precision and extraordinary body heat, sultry, inviting, and graceful, they were caught in the net of watchful eyes, sensual desires, and genuine admiration.

The DJ was "hottern hell." As the songs piled up, couples intruded in a friendly, dance-moves appreciation of Rebecca's and Mark's smooth and supple gyrations. Those who had imbibed heartily thought the smiles and the pagan atmosphere assumed an invitation to touch. Rebecca's fan use as a dancing accent was a well-executed skill.

Mark was gracious to any freak dancers that came his way but managed to wiggle closer to his beautiful partner, avoiding a few salacious activities. He wiped the sweat from his torso with his t-shirt and was intercepted by a man in jeans who huffed it and handed it back to the very amused Mark.

He said, "Go for it, man."

Next, the DJ heated it up with the great disco anthems: "I Will Survive," "I Am What I Am," "It's Raining Men," "You Make Me Feel," "Don't Leave Me This Way, "Got to be Real," anything Cher and everything ABBA. Dead and retired disco stars, their bands, and their backup dancers swirled across the giant video screens above the dance floor and below the flashing ceiling lights ricocheting off chandeliers.

And then... there was "Vogue."

Yasss, Queen! *Vogue!* Madonna's performance at the 1990 MTV Awards-- Louis XIV drag, signature attitude moves, and surreal backup dancers. Hunter's on-stage boys aped the choreography like the denizens of the New York City 80s Drag Balls. Gliding, pouting, and "rocking dat ass." Even club patrons on the stairways and balconies of the upper bar-- "You're a superstar..." and they knew it. Chair-dancers on bar stools were not immune to the invitation to "Let your body move to the music."

Rebecca was on fire. Like Rita Hayward, she "gave good face." Arms up, out, and around her head, moves rapid, sharp, and crisp. *Snap that fan, gurl!*

Mark was doing a twerking thing in front and around her, then spinning from a boxing crouch into a balletic move, which he tried successfully to copy from the video. The man danced on air, and his Ginger Rogers also dazzled. Couples and singles moved close, sharing the energy of a lost era of sexual freedom recovered in the music, the lights, and the hot bodies every Friday and Sunday night on Hunter's dance floor.

A scorchingly hot woman began to dance with Rebecca, turning and spinning in synchrony. Mark exploded from a floor crouch to a cross-legged sitting position on the edge of the disco dancer's box. He aped a hand-to-chin mug that was straight out of Timberlake.

He spun to the floor and then executed a kip-up, pushing into the air with his arms to land up on his feet, creating a small smattering of applause. Shirtless men, some in leather harnesses, circled him, going mad to the music.

Rebecca noticed that Mark suddenly had a partner. Brandon from Dune was gyrating with her gorgeous straight man. The star-struck server was in Disco Boy Heaven. How cool to have found his afternoon crush, wet and wild, with the top button of his jeans open in a fabulous gay bar. Mark did not discourage. Brandon moved so that he was in front of Mark, who embraced the young man so that they rocked together to the ecstatic music.

Olivia Newton-John told them to "Get Physical," so they did. Bodies touching in pairs, in threes and fours, they explored each other and invited further intimacy in a haze of riotous light, pumping music, and sweat-soaked movement. As the cut switched, Rebecca's female partner kissed her solidly on the lips, a thank you, and spiraled off through the crowd.

Mark smiled at Rebecca's pleasure and excitement. To The Boss' *I'm Coming Out*, he turned to his young dance partner and said something to him. As Rebecca exploded with laughter as Mark took the young man into a "Hollywood Kiss," leaning him back, almost to the floor, Mark extended the other arm up and above him and his lip-locked dance partner.

Rebecca thought that this was the definitive goof– Mark was such a showboater and the ultimate tease.

Mark dropped Brandon on his butt but quickly pulled him back up. They both shared a laugh, a chest pat, and a hug up before Mark grabbed his lady love and squirmed them both through the crowd.

"Got one of those for me?"

The kissing hunk turned and gave her the most romantic, tender lips/tongue/face smooch-up that seemed to go on forever.

"Always, Beautiful. You're my one and only. 'Cause I really, really, really like girls."

Rebecca did a combination eye-roll and a smirk, aspirated by a heavy sigh.

They came up to Natalia's station and reached for the Mick Ultra and the Cucumber Lemon Drop on the rocks she had ready for them.

"But Darling, I can see little Brandon's diary entry for this evening: 'The Night Mark Gadarn Kissed Me.' So, bromantic."

Chapter Eight: The Wolf Moon

HUNTER'S NIGHT CLUB, WILTON MANORS, FLORIDA

"It's like I told the police, Rebecca. I usually check on Ms. St. Genevieve before going to bed. She just lives across the *cul-de-sac*." Micah Vélaz leaned on the front porch railing and gently touched a flowering vine covering one side of the cottage. He spoke to Rebecca and Mark in the semi-darkness. Rebecca could see he was visibly shaken. In an exotic chiaroscuro, soft light and silken shadows played over the front of the house and the adjacent garden. The moon was in total eclipse, a spooky disc reflecting an eerie red glow as they spoke.

"Micah, tell me what you saw and heard."

"I could tell something was wrong from my house. Ms. Arva's fireplace never smoked as much as what I could see through her windows. I thought she had forgotten to open the flue, but there was smoke in the chimney.

"I came across, and when I got in the house-- she never locks-- two fireplace logs were smoking in the space before the hearth as if they had fallen out of the andirons and grate. The fire screen had been folded up and set to the side. I smothered the small blaze with a scatter rug and turned to find her. She was at the dining room table."

"How did you know she was dead, kiddo?"

"Well, Mr. Gadarn, I could tell she was not breathing, and she did not respond when I called her. Also, no pulse."

Rebecca asked, "How did you happen to be home on a Friday night?"

"Bad date. The dude could not stop talking about his ex. Like, I need that, right? I made an excuse– a 'bad stomach' and Ubered home."

"You touch anything besides the rug and Arva's wrist."

"No, ma'am. I remembered your advice on crime scenes."

"Mark, let's go inside. I want to see this up close."

County law enforcement had placed the body on the floor and covered it with a sheet. The police were bagging evidence, the Tarot cards, and other items from the table. Nina Simone crooned "*Ne Me Quitte Pas*" as the playlist continued softly.

Detectives, medical examiners, and beat cops carefully combed the interior of the house. Small, numbered traffic cones marked important spaces, like the now quenched logs, for investigation.

A police officer nodded to Rebecca and Mark, and another important-looking policewoman looked up from the corpse. Rebecca asked. "OK to intrude, Dian?"

Sheriff Dian Crawford said, "Hello, Rebecca, Mark. Yes. To be honest, I'm not sure what we got here. Appears to be natural causes; the woman was almost eighty-four, I understand. No wounds; the wine and food will be run through toxicology ASAP. I'll see that you are briefed on the report."

Mark asked, "Playing solitaire, listening to the blues, and had the big one?"

"Appears so, but we need to do a full investigation. Very odd."

"How so, Sheriff?"

"Well, the logs, for one thing. Couldn't have fallen to where they were, as indicated by the burn marks. Thanks to this young man, the house was saved." Micah did not respond. He looked a bit like a sleepwalker just coming out of a bad night.

They moved carefully through the quaint house filled with the memorabilia of a woman who had lived an exciting life. Framed photos chronicled Arva's accomplishments, travels, and accolades. From Eleanor Roosevelt to Tony Bennett and Lady Gaga, Arva St. Genevieve made her mark throughout history advocating for quality education for all and arts education.

They moved to the back porch and its midnight river view presided over by the January Wolf Moon. Mark said, "Rebecca, remind me again why you get such a cordial entrée from the police."

"Simple. FBI Citizens Academy. I also know that our little caper with INTERPOL last summer got some local attention. Then there was that serial killer thing. The higher-ups love me."

They were interrupted by the soft closing of the back screen door.

Micah stepped out to join them. "Such an awful thing and so very strange. I am going to take the divine feline here home with me. Right, Rosie?" He cuddled the cat under his chin. She loved being caressed and carried around.

Mark said, "You sure you're OK, bud? Hope you have some spirits to mellow you out tonight."

"Yeah, thanks. Lock my doors and have a stiff cocktail."

A high-pitched screech pierced the night air, mocking the humans inside and outside the house. Micah said, "Our neighborhood watchdog, Doctor John, the peacock. He knows something's wrong."

From inside the house, Nina scatted softly to "I Put A Spell on You." Micah put the cat on the railing and pulled out his phone. "I thought you would want to see this."

Micah had taken a few photos of the expired Arva before the police arrived. Rebecca scrolled. Arva was seated rather than slumped over the table. Her head was thrown back, and her mouth and eyes open as if she had seen a horror. Heart attack or stroke, the body would have fallen face-first on the table, most likely. This was something different.

"Holy shit! Send me that one, Micah."

The picture was of the arrangement of the cards on the table, all turned face up. Not solitaire-- Arva was doing a reading.

"Something else, folks. As I came from my house, I saw the shadow of a creature. I would say a monkey, but the primates we have around here are small spider monkeys. This was bigger, but the arms were all wrong. Not as long as a baboon or orangutan. Anyway, it jumped up from the front porch into the branches of that big banyan." He pointed to the enormous tree that overhung the entire west side of the house.

Mark was waving his cell phone flashlight over that side of the porch.

"Fuck! Check it out. I thought I saw something odd in the dark."

On the floor, near the banister, adjacent to the corner post of the porch, was a white and brown curved object about three inches long. It had a hole in one end and was covered with arcane markings. The carving on the reverse was of one of the Major Arcana images, Death.

Chapter Nine: The Octopus Trap

FORT LAUDERDALE, FLORIDA

"It will pass. Please do not be concerned. I am going back to the serving area in the rear of the plane, Rebecca. I will come back here just before landing."

Michele took her water bottle and headed to the rear of the airplane. She had spoken to the flight attendant and was reassured that stretching out on the floor would provide no safety issues or spatial inconvenience. It was a relatively short flight, just over two hours, and serving had been completed.

As Michele took off, Rebecca reflected on her last moments with Mark before leaving on their respective adventures, New Orleans and the Horn of Africa.

***

They had discussed the death of Arva St. Genevieve well into the night. Because of her status as a leader in the community and the mysterious circumstances surrounding her death, Arva's autopsy would be performed immediately. Rebecca was on the phone with Special Agent Mary Chafee, getting intel on the forensics part of the investigation. When they left the dead woman's house, media vans were pulling into the cul-de-sac. Arva St. Genevieve, so well respected, a person who spoke and the world paid heed, had died while eating her jambalaya. It would be a front-page sensation.

And it was.

Fresh lox and bagels (courtesy of Uber Eats), orange juice, and strong coffee were laid out on Rebecca's granite kitchen island. The media covered the story as if there were no other news on the planet this Saturday morning. Mark scanned the Sun Sentinal, the Miami Herald, and the New York Times for coverage. Rebecca flipped through online news services.

She mused, "Murder most foul – there it is. The media is implying it out the ass. Who would want to kill Arva?"

She had chosen one of Mark's white Oxford dress shirts for her morning ensemble. He originally had selected his birthday suit– *a stunning male without the hindrance of clothes.*

She thought, *I am so in lust*.

Their lovemaking in the wee small hours of this morning was a pornographic epic in his mind and a fulfilling romp of desire and romance that reached into her body, heart, and soul.

To accept the food order, Mark threw on a red, black, and ivory plaid bathrobe, a Christmas gift in his family's Welsh tartan, which now hung suggestively open as he criticized the journalism.

"Fuckin' tabloidism at its worst. Listen to these assholes. Conspiracy theory and not a shred of evidence. The woman was totally noncontroversial unless calling for equality in educational opportunities for women and girls on the world stage is incendiary."

"You, of all people, should know that it is, Mark. You have seen the disparity of human rights in so many of these backward countries that exploit women and girls. I remember when Arva introduced us to Malala Yousafzai at the gala last season."

"Yes. I realized how ludicrous my remarks were as soon as I said it. I guess you got me a bit distracted this morning, beautiful, in that white shirt."

He reached across to undo one more button while saying, "I will admit it is a deadly horror when you eliminate the hopes and dreams of 50 percent of your country's population. But Arva was someone who raised the cry and dreamed of equality. My concern is that these commentators and reporters are inciting sensationalism into a story before checking out the facts. Fuck, the woman was in her mid-eighties – hello? Heart attack."

"But she was in perfect health. Wait, it's Mary. I need to take this."

Rebecca made a gesture as she listened to her FBI friend. Living with, traveling with, and loving the delightful Ms. Quinto for almost a year, Mark recognized her silent gestures with familiarity. As she listened to the Special Agent, he handed her a pad and pen.

Rebecca took on that appearance of entirely being present to the caller but looking at the person to whom she was physically present. Her eyes looked Mark up and down as he sat across from her at the kitchen island. They were filled with an interior gaze as she listened to the facts of the autopsy.

After a short time. "Octopus what… unbelievable… yes, I guess I will think of a thousand questions, but nothing is coming to me right now. A bit of a shock... yes. If I think of any, I will text or call. Right… he sends his best also. Thanks again, Mary. Bye."

She looked dazed. "She died of fright."

"Holy shit. Seriously?"

"Apparently, the autopsy showed a sudden malformation of the heart and its total calcification. The examiner said this occurs when large amounts of adrenaline flood the circulatory system. The result is a sudden weakening of the heart and instant death."

Mark's fingers scrolled and typed on his cell phone.

"Amazing. Found it. It's called 'takotsubo cardiomyopathy.' It's a condition where the heart muscle becomes suddenly weakened. Caused by sudden and extreme stress."

Rebecca consulted her scribblings.

"The heart immediately loses its ability to pump enough blood to the rest of the body."

Mark added, "*Takotsubo* is Japanese for 'octopus pot.' Says here the heart changes shape with a narrow neck and rounded bottom."

Rebecca said, "That's how the autopsy report described it."

"What could have frightened Ms. Arva so much? She was having a late dinner, listening to music, and playing cards."

"Not just any cards, Mark. The Tarot. I suspect she saw something terrifying in the reading or…."

Mark snapped his fingers and pointed at Rebecca in an *Eureka* moment. "Shit! The medallion. Someone else was in the room."

***

NEW ORLEANS, LOUISANA

“The captain has turned on the fasten seatbelts sign as we prepare for our landing at Louis Armstrong New Orleans International Airport. We ask that all passengers....”

“How are you feeling?”

“All good. I get a kick out of passengers' reaction when they see me stretched out on the floor at the back of the plane. The attendants couldn't have been more accommodating.”

Michele took her seat and flipped open her laptop. “If you’ve no more changes to the draft of the Board meeting minutes, I will forward them to Micah for sending to the Board Secretary, Dr. Kenner, as soon as we get WiFi. Also, the car is ordered and waiting at the Gold Club .”

“Talk about hitting the ground running. Nice work for just a few hours in your new position.”

“I sure appreciate your trust in my abilities. This short trip to New Orleans is a welcome holiday before I start my classes.”

“Glad to have you along. You will love NOLA. Our main objective, aside from meeting with the folks from the Art Museum, is to find her.”

Rebecca showed Michele a picture on her phone. A grey-haired beauty with an other-worldly stare looking out at them. She was dressed in bright colors and exotic Caribbean patterns. Elaborate gold earrings hung to her collarbone. Rows of beads, colored stones, and shells wound around her neck and across her chest. The whole image imparted a sense of the wondrous and strange.

“This is Madame Ondine Rillieux”

Chapter Ten: Remy

NEW ORLEANS, LOUISANA

"You'll soon have dis place all to yourself, *cherè*. I have been called up to New York tomorrow. They are moving forward with a plan to exhibit my paintings. Ahhh, but you, my beautiful one. You will pose for Remy, no?"

Their host took Michele by the hand examined her profile, and then stepped back to take her in a full view. Michele smiled but was not as entranced as most were when first encountering the swarthy and tantalizingly rugged Cajun artist.

"Dis, gal here ver' fine, *cherè*. Keep an eye on dis one, hear? Quarter *mecs* gonna be all over her. But is guaranteed y'all will pass a good time in N'awlins."

Remy Brasseaux and Rebecca had spent some time in a very torrid and intense interlude in former days. She referred to it as "my starving artist period"– love, sex, and divine decadence in the elegant squalor of a 300-year-old city. Their passion was steeped in high drama, romance, intrigue, tragedy, and sensual inspiration – incendiary, but when it was over, they were both the wiser for it.

Remy's three-bedroom flat was on Rue St. Ann, on the second floor of one of the two landmark Pontalba Buildings facing Jackson Square. The matching red-brick block buildings, 4 stories tall, were completed in the 1840s. Beyond the floor-to-ceiling French doors, one could step out on the balcony to take in a panorama that included the Cathedral of St. Louis, the Presbytére, the Cabildo, and, through the trees, the Embankment on the Mississippi. It was a unique section of the *Vieux Carré* where one could take in the sights, sounds, and smells of the Quarter's rich and unique cultural and architectural heritage.

Some starving artist. Remy was ensconced in luxury. The flat and his studio in the nearby Marigny district had been set up by an older, wealthy woman with a passion for art and roguish Cajun men.

Remy was devilishly handsome and engaging. He had a rich history of intense *liaisons dangereuses* with both sexes. Michele thought he looked like a hero from an 18th-century novel-- D'Artagnan in the French Quarter, with his long black hair, tight, wiry build, and Hollywood good looks. The man turned heads. That was a fact, but he was yet to be discovered as an artist.

"I put your t'ings in the spare bedrooms. Come with Remy, we go for brunch, yes?"

Rebecca sparkled. "You are a love, Darling. On the entire flight to get here, I dreamt of some premium roast with chicory and beignets."

"Right, *cherè*. Forget dat dere Café Du Monde. Too late now and be packed with the tourists. We head on over to Revolution on Bienville, 'bout six blocks, and do da brunch. Dey know Remy dere, and da Creole is authentic. *Ça c'est bon*!" He looked like temptation itself as he smiled at Michele, saying, "Mmm ummm, 'lil *cherè*, get ready to taste the sweet ass of dis here town."

He made a call. They had a table.

As they walked, they switched back and forth from Remy's description of the Quarter for Michele to a conversation that allowed Rebecca and him to catch up.

"How's ya man, girl? He doin' fine?"

"Mark is amazing, Remy. On assignment. He left yesterday. I miss him already."

Remy winked and slipped an arm around Rebecca's waist.

"So you gonna let Remy fill in for dat hot man while you here, *cherè*?" She cuffed him, laughing at his audacity. "Does it ever go down, Darling? And what would your Baroness think?"

"Naw, no problem dere. Ms. Angela, she know her Remy go *rougarouin'* quite a bit. No harm."

"Michele, allow me to be your translator as we continue to converse with the devastatingly frisky Mr. Brasseaux, Cajun male extraordinaire. '*Rougarouin*' means to go about causing trouble—partying but a tad rougher."

The young woman was entranced by the architecture along the Rue Royal as they headed toward Canal Street with their gregarious guide.

"Mark, so fine and sexy. I 'member when we went to dat *fais do-do* over der in da Marigny. Dancin' to the fiddle and da zydeco-- too bad he only has eyes for you, *cherè*. Remy can t'ink of…."

"That's it, bub." Rebecca did a friendly push-off, saying. "Watch what you say. Michele works for me, after all. Do not scandalize her."

"Pshaw, *ma cherè*. Remy just being Remy."

This was a man you forgave for many things, a total enchanter.

***

"Who dat?"

"She is Mambo Ondine Rillieux. And I need to find her." Rebecca put down her phone and continued, "Can you help?"

"Ooo – eee, *cherè*, you gonna mess wit dat occult shit-- dat voodoo?" He looked at his erstwhile lover. "Damn, you serious, gal."

They had shared beer-battered crab stuffed beignets complete with delicious remoulades. The coffee was robust, savory, and exquisitely bitter– a jolt to the taste buds and the nervous system. They moved to the bar and sipped decadent cocktails.

Rebecca said, "This voodoo priestess is the key to a mystery surrounding the murder of a friend."

Michele asked, "Remy, do you have any contacts familiar with voodoo culture here in New Orleans? They may know of the Mambo."

Remy picked up the phone and examined the picture. "She old, 'lil *cherè*. Most likely died. Not many of da old ones around anymore." He spread his fingers on the screen to enlarge the image and moved it around. "You search?"

Michele said, "She's on the web, yeah. Her website has been archived, however. Nothing about her after 2010."

The music in the bar was soft jazz, suitable for a crisp winter's afternoon. The crowd had dwindled so they could speak confidentially. As if suspecting their desire to have a private conversation, the bartender moved to the opposite end of the bar and wiped glasses. However, she could not take her eyes off the dashing Remy Brasseaux and his animated face and gestures.

"OK, you two listen to your Remy. Deese t'ings, dey best be spoken about in the darkness. Yes, Remy has a contact, 'lil *cherè*. I gonna arrange to get him tonight wid you at Lafitte. I t'ink he gonna help you find what you lookin' for."

Rebecca said, "Thanks, handsome. I knew we came to the right guy on this one."

"How 'bout you listen to a piece of advice from ole Remy, huh *cherè*?

Rebecca and Michele both looked at him. His serious tone indicated an entire switch in his light and breezy persona.

He tapped the phone. "You forget dis here, see. Do not do dis. Leave it for da po po. We can stop by a precinct on da way back and give dem a heads-up. No way, this shit gonna come to no good."

The Cajun prince shook his head, "A ver' bad business."

Chapter Eleven: Oz

BOURBON STREET, NEW ORLEANS, LOUISANA

"Where y'at?"

Remy stepped outside Oz to take the call. "Right, boy. Be der inside an hour." He headed back in to find his guests.

Rebecca was handing Michele cash to stuff in the boots of the strippers. Oz dick dancers went all the way down to a hand towel or a plastic drink cup held over their business. The place was mobbed for a Monday night – make that Tuesday morning. The Bourbon Street tourists had left the late-night hours to the regulars and the visiting stalwarts.

Patrons sat at the bar or wandered the lower floor and the interior balconies of the bar. Some watched the strollers on the street from the upper-story galleries behind wrought iron balustrades. A few caught the spell of the music and the lights and danced. Patrons quaffed drinks, held hands, embraced, or moved with the intention of stealing another's man or woman. Possessed by total enchantment and much alcohol, the adventures of the night seemed endless.

Michele toasted with her club soda and lime as another dancer mounted a recently vacated platform to a few cheers. "OK, so no one is that big. It's gotta be fake, right?"

"We should see pretty soon. Here, give him this five."

Remy was looking up and talking to one of the strippers, a muscled-up jock type. He handed the kid a few bills in exchange for the dancer's light blue thong. The beauty set down his "privacy cup" and went down on one knee to sign the article of erotic wear. Remy stuffed his purchase into the back pocket of his jeans. His t-shirt hung from the other hip.

Moving away, Remy pulled into a small group of dancers and accepted admiring hands and a few kisses as he gyrated seductively.

Rebecca said, "I love this city. So lost in depravity and passion. Looks like your guy is the real deal, Michele."

"I am so speechless, Boss."

Remy came up from behind and nuzzled each of them in turn. "Ahh, *mes belles femmes*, you miss your Remy, no? Dis here song is a fav, so we dance. Come, come. Dose *mecs*, dey not going anywhere, you two tip *très grand*."

He took each by hand and led them to the dance floor to rock to the music. Michele did not last and called over the din that she was stepping outside for air. The DJ switched up the mood with "Hello Josephine" by Queen Ida and Her Zydeco Band. Rebecca pulled her sweating partner into a classic two-step. The set continued with "Your Man Is Home Tonight" by the master, Buckwheat Zydeco. Remy held his partner close.

"You, me and *ce bel homme*, Mark. We gonna go Cajun crazy sometime soon, *cherè*. 'Les you want to start somt'in wid out him." He moved in for a lip lock.

Rebecca turned her face and spoke into his ear. "Easy tiger. This baby being true to my man, as enticing as your offer may be." She pushed back and said, "Don't we have a man to see tonight about my missing queen."

"For sure, *ma belle*. He right down the street at Lafitte in Exile. Yes, we go now. Where is 'lil *cherè*?"

"She stepped outside. Let's pick her up on the way out."

As they passed, Remy's naked dancing jock bent down to provide a sexy kiss to his departing admirer and the single hand gesture that translated "call me." On Bourbon Street, Rebecca looked for her companion. Turning to look up, she caught Michele's eye as the young woman leaned against the railing, seemingly caught by something disappearing up the cross street, Rue St. Ann. She soon joined her friends on the ground as they headed to the next bar.

"What's going on, kiddo?"

"Not sure. You two were the main attraction on the dance floor when two badass-looking dudes came in and parked themselves near the inside of the doors. They were checking you both out and not in an admiring way. I could tell.

"At first, I got pretty close, but then I went upstairs to keep a bit of distance. From up above, just before you came out, I made the jerks as two gangsters. They headed up the other way."

Rebecca felt a chill and looked over her shoulder as they moved up Bourbon. Michele said, "Let's move out of here quickly, folks. They will be back and soon."

"And why you say dat, *ma cherè*?"

"They are going to find out soon that I lifted this."

Michele took Remy's and Rebecca's hands and, reaching behind, placed them against the small of her back. The trio had the appearance of three friends staggering up the street after a long night of *rougarouin'.*

Beneath her overhanging jacket, tucked into her belt, they felt the outline of a gun.

Chapter Twelve: In Exile

BOURBON STREET, NEW ORLEANS, LOUISANA

Café Lafitte in Exile, one block down the street, initially opened in 1933 in a famous building that had been the infamous pirate Jean Lafitte's blacksmith business in the 18th century. In the 1950s, the owner moved the notorious "gin mill" to its present location, a few doors down. The establishment claims to be the oldest continuously operating gay bar in the country.

Frequented by the notable and the notorious, Lafitte's has numbered among its rogue's gallery John Steinbeck, Truman Capote, and Tennessee Williams, to name a few. Throughout its two floors, dark corners, and balconies, legends abounded. Bar patrons claim to have occasionally seen the ghosts of Café Lafitte's departed luminaries inside the bar.

Rebecca and Remy wound their way through the remains of the night's revelers to the stairway to the second floor. Remy explained that, earlier in the evening, the bar had celebrated an anniversary with a costume party called "Diaspora," an annual event where patrons and employees dressed as famous exiles. In the early Tuesday morning hours, Dante and Napoleon joined Julian Assange, the Dali Lama, and Idi Amin at the first-floor bar.

Heading upstairs, Rebecca and Remy were stopped by a bare-breasted woman in an 18th-century style peasant's dress and a red Phrygian cap. A knot of ribbons, the tricolor cockade, was pinned to her hat. She was sitting on the stairs, quite intoxicated. Before they could get by, a tall man descended the stairs. He was dressed in a French army officer's uniform circa 1940.

He twitched his mustache and said to the woman, "Come, my dear, we do not want to disgrace the memory of the Provisional Government of the French République. Get yourself together, bitch."

Marianne, the allegoric figure of the French Republic, stood with the help of General Charles de Gaulle. As Remy and Rebecca passed, the leader of Free France in Exile tossed out a saucy remark saying,

"Winners, couples division." The besotted drag queen and her soldier joined the denizens of the lower bar. They pandered to the cheering customers with the opening lines of the *La Marseillaise*.

At the top of the stairs, Salman Rushdie, Eva Peron, and Imelda Marcos fought jokingly for the attention of the shirtless bartender who sported Trotsky's iconic beard and wire-rimmed glasses.

Rebecca said to the fierce-looking Evita, "Darling, I understand that you died before being sent into exile with your husband."

"Which is why I lost to this Filipino cow." The ersatz Mother of Argentina hiked a thumb at the deposed First Lady of the Philippines. "I hate people who read."

Tucked in a back corner was a lone pinball player who had chosen 3:45 am to break his house record on a machine dedicated to Elvis with colorful, electronic highlights of the career of The King.

The young man danced with the flippers and stroked each shot with loving but urgent caresses. He used his hips and lower body to manipulate the blinking game in glass, metal, and glimmer. The machine responded with flashing and ringing orgasms of light and sound as no ball was wasted until it had given up all its penetrating movement, exploding with a surge of high scores.

The gamer greeted Remy– hands, arms, chest bump, and affectionate kiss. He was dark and animated with hooded eyes and a lean frame.

They spoke a few sentences in French before Remy reached into his back pocket and presented his friend with his Oz purchase.

"Ouch, man. You seriously giving me this?" He read the autograph. "Samson? He's my longtime crush. You fuckin' rascal. I owe you big time, bro." He slipped the thong into his pocket as Remy introduced Rebecca.

"Dis here my good friend Rebecca Quinto. Meet my man, Benoît Duplessis. He go by Benny."

Rebecca smiled and said, "Nice to meet you. Not in costume?"

The man waved a hand in dismissal and cued up one last ball. As he spoke, he stroked and bopped the machine, sending the silver ball through the flashing obstacle course.

"These queens-- sad, really. Don't have to be so elaborate. Most of us were thrown out by family anyway. Gays in exile. Met a street kid who was twelve the other day. Family disowned him 'cause he a little queer boy. "

Remy said, "Covenant House. Yeah, 'dis one got him there before he could start selling his *derrière* for food and housing. Sad."

Benny slapped electronic Elvis, and the round ended with flashing lights and ringing bells. He turned his full attention to his visitors.

"So what can I do for you, Ms. Quinto? I hear tell you're looking for some *gris-gris*."

Rebecca showed Benny her picture of Madame Ondine.

"Ohhh." The slick gamer paused and looked around suspiciously. "Let's take this outside, fellas and gals."

Out on the second-floor balcony, they rounded the corner that faced the Rue Dumaine side of the building and sat at a table under a green umbrella. The fire escape to the street below was at their backs. Across Bourbon Street, they were in sight of the early morning patrons of the Clover Grill. The smell of burgers wafted in the pre-dawn air. A waiter dressed as Benazir Bhutto took their drink order.

Benny opened, "Be very careful with this one. Some bad things have been going on, and Madame Ondine's name seems to be coming up more and more. Time was when she was a very popular mambo, especially with the international elite. Then she just kind of disappeared, but she is still around. You want to meet her, I imagine."

"Yes, can you arrange that?"

"Let's talk first. What do you know about voodoo?"

"Not much, I am afraid."

“OK, so, can you see that apartment window across the street? There on the second floor. Tell me what you see.”

“Looks like burning candles.”

“And there’s another one you can see up that way in the Uneeda Biscuit Building. They are voodoo altars. People put them in their windows, candles, fetishes, incense sticks, and pictures of the saints. It has all kinds of *gris-gris* to ward off evil and bring the house and family protection and blessings. The voodoo is like an ancient specter that hangs over this city, especially in the Quarter. It is quiet but very powerful and, in some cases, can bring harm.

”Voodoo comes from West Africa– Benin, with the slave trade. It’s mostly harmless-- healing practices, ancestor worship, and elder veneration all rolled up in traditional Catholicism– assimilation out the ass.”

Rebecca was distracted for a moment. Considering they had bad guys tailing them earlier, Michele acted as a lookout on Bourbon Street near the Clover Grill. She did not accompany them inside the bar because of the gun.

Rebecca thought, *Best to hurry this along.*

“Voodoo religion in the 19th-century thrived among *the gens de couleur libres,* the free people of color including the *voodooienne* superstar, Marie Laveau, who lived and practiced not far from here.”

Benny continued, “While the traditions, ceremonies, charms, and kitschy wares – curios, potions, and whatnot have become heavily ‘tourist-afied,’ Marie Laveau once hexed a rival and drove her insane. There is death and terror in this thing. Make no mistake.”

Rebecca said, “Benny, Madame Ondine. Can we see her? I need to ask her about the sudden death of a friend who should not have died.”

The young man paused. He looked from Remy to Rebecca. He felt an eerie dread creeping over the situation-- secrets revealed and evil unleashed. He checked his watch.

“Yes, I know exactly where she is right now.”

Remy said, “How come you know dis’ bro?”

As the sky over the French Quarter turned from the raven hues of the evening to the pre-dawn-streaked canvas of greys, Benny Duplessis raised his eyes to stare at the flickering candles that had seen the family across the street through the darkness of another night. He looked back at his friends.

"Madame Ondine is my Aunt."

Chapter Thirteen: The Ritual

BOURBON STREET AND CONGO SQUARE, NEW ORLEANS, LOUISANA

The corner of Bourbon and Dumaine erupted behind them with the lights and sounds of police cruisers careening into a driveway behind the Clover Grill. Shouts and pointing indicated a dark fleeing figure hurrying up the side street beneath the balcony of the Exile, where Remy, Rebecca, and Benny sat in the final hours of the night.

Michele.

Remy stood and stretched for a look, saying, "Dat's a lot of po po. Sometin' bad goin' down back o' da Clover." Benny looked around and said, "Quick, we go this way."

Remy and Rebecca followed him down the fire escape to the street below. As they passed bystanders, Rebecca heard a young man explaining the pre-dawn melee to his friends.

"Yeah, I saw the whole thing in the alley. Two guys. It happened so quickly. The smaller guy jumped up on the bigger dude with a legs scissors stranglehold around the neck. Classic! The big guy goes down, and the other one headed up that way, running hell-bent for leather."

The street in the direction he pointed was empty.

***

"*Bonjour, ma tante*. How was mass?"

The older woman moved through the trees at the perimeter of the square. She did not return the greeting but eyed the two strangers accompanying her nephew. Leaning on a carved wooden cane, she overcame the crippling effects of osteoporosis which bent her over but did not slow her down.

"This is Rebecca and Remy, my friends, *Tata*."

Her eyes sparkled with unspoken secrets. Her gnarled hands were covered with rings, and jangling bracelets covered both wrists. A colorful turban held back her hair and blazed like a crown on her regal head. The voodoo queen pointed to Rebecca.

She inspected the beautiful woman with an acute gaze. "You seek answers to some serious questions, but there is danger near you. Come, you speak with Ondine."

She next addressed Benny. "I pray for you, my Benoit, at the mass, took the Holy Communion and ask that you may turn back to Lord Jésus. Too many nights with the rough menfolk. You must change your ways. Make your confession." The older woman was eyeing Remy as she chastened her nephew.

"No, Auntie. This here is my good friend Remy. He's a good man, a very talented artist. No…."

Benney made a rubbing gesture with the index fingers of both hands. His aunt sneered at his response like a mother who knew her son all too well.

Madame Ondine took the handsome Cajun's hands and gazed into his eyes. "You, eh? You are a lady killer. All a dat…" The old mambo woman waved a hand at the virile man and continued. "Humph. It is no surprise. Cajun male beauty brings so much trouble. Philandering and charmin' up folks." Her look went from Remy to Rebecca and back again.

She continued to assess the man whose hands she held. "The dark eyes of a devil, but wait, Ondine can see into the soul. Yes. You are blessed with inner visions. Your art, no?" She straightened up a bit and turned her grip into a loving pat of Remy's hands before letting go. "Are you good to your family, my son?"

"Ahh, yes, *ma tante*. And good to 'dis one here." He squeezed Benny's trapezius. "Keeping away the bad spirits from him, *les mauvais esprits*." He winked at his bud, who made sure the dick dancer's thong was buried deep in his pocket and out of his Aunt's view.

She pointed across the square to a small shop on Rampart Street. "You buy me a cup of tea, and I talk to this one here." She leaned on Rebecca's arm as they walked.

The four early morning strollers made their way across Congo Square in the mists of a city rising from a night of ghosts, debauchery, and mischief.

Rebecca checked to see if Michele responded to her text. There were only two words, "All good."

In the spaces between the trees of Louis Armstrong Park, drums began African rhythms despite the early hour. The smells of freshly brewed, strong coffee and sizzling bacon caught on the breeze. The Tremé neighborhood was waking up.

The grizzled mambo spoke as they crossed the square, "Way back, the enslaved people of New Orleans were allowed one day off, Sundays. Many worshipped at St. Peter's, where I go. White folks restricted their gatherings to spaces at 'the back of town.' One such place was here – *Place du Congo.* The enslaved people would set up a market, sing, dance, and play music. At the time, the slaves could purchase their freedom and could freely buy and sell goods in the square to raise money to escape their slavery."

She continued as they walked, "Ahh, ma Tremé – the African dancing and music, the rhythm of the beat of the bamboulas and wail of the banzas. You know much survived throughout the years despite suppression.

"You hear? The rhythms played at Congo Square can still be heard today in our jazz funerals, second lines, and Mardi Gras parades. That famous Nawlins jazz festival each year is right here."

Madame Ondine pointed to the square they had crossed. She leaned a bit more heavily on Rebecca's arm as they walked. Passing her tote bag to her companion and lowering her voice, she added, "Besides the music and dancing, Congo Square also provided the blacks with a place in which they could express themselves spiritually. The voodoo rituals performed in this plaza were a form of entertainment and a celebration of African culture.

"True voodoo rituals were much more exotic and secretive. They focused on the religious and spiritual lives of the folks. The great mambo queen, Marie Laveau, led voodoo dances here in Congo Square.

Still, her darker, secret rituals were hidden along the banks of Lake Pontchartrain and St. John's Bayou. Powerful spirits with that gal. Oh, yes, powerful *gris-gris."*

***

The Amnesia Tea Room faced the square across Rampart Street. Madame Ondine took a seat across from Rebecca at a secluded table in the rear of the shop. At the counter, Remy and Benny ordered breakfast and took it outside. Rebecca breathed a bit easier as she saw Michele stroll up the street and join them. The young woman came into the Café to order and gave her boss the "thumbs up." Rebecca turned her attention back to the old voodoo priestess.

Madame Ondine reached into her tote bag and withdrew a Tarot deck. "This one has been with me for many years. You cut the cards three times, child. Make piles."

Rebecca did as she was told. The spiritualist recombined the stacks and held the reshuffled deck in her hands. She looked at Rebecca and said, "Now, you tell me why you have come here."

"Two women. One dead and one lost."

"Stop."

She turned five cards face up and spread them out, all picture cards of the Tarot's Major Arcana. Her lips moved as she prayed silently and made the sign of the cross. Ondine placed an amulet in Rebecca's hand and then took it back. Something unseen tapped once on the table. Rebecca felt the soft breath of an invisible kiss on her cheek.

The mambo pointed to the first card – the High Priestess.

"This is you, my dear. This card says you must rely on your inner sight, but child, things are not what they appear to be. Much information has been held from you. It will take strength and insight to conquer the mysterious evil that I see surrounding you over…."

Madame Ondine moved three cards into a row and pushed one out of the lineup, sliding it next to the High Priestess. "… the death of this one."

The Hermit.

Ondine asked as she tapped the card and looked into the eyes of her supplicant, "One who was withdrawn and is searching. But this one reaches for you from the spirit realm. I sense she is distraught and has left something unfinished in this world."

Again, one loud knock sounded on the table.

The *voodooienne* asked, "Who was she, and what happened?"

Rebecca related the events of Friday night in the lonely Fort Lauderdale bayou home.

"Ms. Arva. Yes, I have heard of her. So tragic. Make no mistake. Her death resulted from encountering an unspeakable evil connected to the one who is lost. The evil spirits reach out for the hidden one."

Rebecca showed the older woman the picture on her cell phone of the talisman found on the house's back porch.

Madame Ondine drew in a soft breath and said, "This is a powerful fetish, Rébecca-- an amulet with much power for protection. It is usually tied to animals who provide for the family's welfare. Some people wear them also. It is made of bone, and the carvings here and here invoke the saints and other good spirits...."

"But this one. Look. It is different. It calls forth the darkness and the malice of the evil one. See? It brings death."

Rebecca said, "It is unlikely that it belonged to Ms. Arva. She was not really a believer."

"No, she was not." Ondine's face filled with an enigmatic expression as she continued, "It is the murderer's, then. The one who descends from the trees to kill with fear." She tapped the picture. "But the demons on this medal guide the wearer's evil deeds. They make him do the bidding of another man. Both are damned, and you must be aware that he will kill again."

Madame Ondine Rillieux looked carefully and long at the remaining cards in the setup. She pushed forward a third card – the Empress.

"Tell me, Rebecca. You know this one." Ondine tapped the card with a withered index finger.

"Yes, the Opera Diva, Victoria Ricci. Arva told me to find her."

Ondine's eyes glistened over as she gently picked up the card and lightly stroked it. "*La Gloriosa*, the Immortal Diva. *Ma chère* Victoria. So beloved and so tragic, like the many operatic heroines she portrayed.

"Please tell me of her, Madame."

"She was a member of dat one—dat Hitler... his inner circle. Well, as much as a courtesan could have been at the time. She was exceptionally fashionable, artistic, and forever young and beautiful. I met her in Paris in 1940. I was only four years old, but she would remain close to my family and me. My mother and I were trapped in the city the year it fell to the Nazis. *Maman* was her spiritual advisor, and when she died, Victoria turned to me for advice."

"It must have been a very fearsome time."

"Certainement, ma chère. One never knew from day to day. Hitler was very interested in the sacred arts, especially the esoteric Tarot. The same thing like Napoleon-- powerful men who trusted in the divine powers to gain insight into the past, the present, and to affirm their plans for the future."

Madame Ondine held up the card of the Empress as she spoke. "Interesting. Dat Hitler and his generals claimed to be irreligious, so they left it to friends, especially the women, to access the powers of the occult for them."

She placed the Empress card next to the Hermit. "Arva and Victoria, they were good friends from the war. That diva had many secrets. She needed to go into hiding. Many seek her even now and would do her harm."

"You were her seer and friend. Where is she, Madame? Please tell me."

Ondine touched the Victoria/Empress card and made a series of arcane signs. She tapped the image on Rebecca's head and once on each shoulder. The mambo's eyes grew wide and sightless. She sat back in her chair and began to tremble. Her breathing quickened, and the tone of her voice deepened. She entered into a trance as she communicated with her spirits.

"Ohhh, *Les dieux au sein de Dieu me montrent le chemin. Montrez-moi la vérité. Écoutez ma prière pour l'illumination, ma mère."*

Rebecca felt the air around them go cold as the Mambo rocked in her chair. The spiritualist repeated her entreaty to her guiding spirits and her deceased mother to open her visions.

When she spoke again, there was a dry huskiness in her throat.

"I can see the Frozen Diva. She is embedded in the ice of solitude. She has been hiding in the steel cage... the swords and daggers of kings protect her... saints of the Three Faiths look down on her and guard her... *La Gloriosa* is deathless ... never to be found. No one can wrest her secrets from her... she is the one never to be conquered. Not even by death itself."

Ondine snapped upright in her chair and shrieked, "Many are suffering. Yes, yes, and many will die. Only the ice princess can save the lost. She can touch great divine power. That which is sought by the demons and their minions, she alone guards."

Outside, abruptly appearing clouds seemed to squelch the early morning light. An unusually strong wind swept up the street and through the open doors of the tea shop, battering the shutters as it entered. Dust and darkness gathered above and around the card players as servers backed away into the recesses of the dining room, pulling aprons over their mouths and noses. More than one made the sign against the evil eye.

Rebecca stared in wonder at the shaking and groaning old *voodooienne*. The Mambo's hand reached out and pushed the fourth of the five cards forward, the Star. Her hands continued to hover over the Tarot, making secret signs and arranging the five into a cross with The Star at the intersection.

Her voice got slightly louder. "The Star is a man. Evil? I cannot tell... wait... No, no. He will... be a guide... come suddenly out of the danger surrounding you... not evil... no, no. I see him flying in the air far above the land and water. He is a strong and brave friend for you."

She slowly came out of her trance and blinked at the open-mouthed Rebecca. Around them, the din of the air's disturbance abated as quickly as it had appeared. Clear morning light filled the tea room and the street outside.

Ondine's hand moved to an untouched card in the formation. At the same time, she took Rebecca's hand and slid it next to the High Priestess, pointing to the naked man on the Lover's Card.

"My dear, *you* must find the Frozen Diva for the sake of this man."

The Mambo tapped the male figure on the card.

Mark.

Chapter Fourteen: Jackson Square

ST. ANN STREET AND CHARTRES STREET, NEW ORLEANS, LOUISANA

Remy never stopped talking since they returned to the flat. He seemed to want to replay every detail of an exhilarating evening among the denizens of the night city.

"What was dat, *cherè*? Me and Benny and 'lil *cherè* eating our grillades and grits, and da wind whip up outta nowhere like the breath of the devil hisself. Remy said you was messin' with t'ings best left alone. You listen to Remy sometime, eh? Do you whorl a good, *cherè*?"

He spoke through the open door of his bedroom to Rebecca and Michele, who had crashed on the divan in the front room.

"I should not leave you two here. Benny and I both agree that you are stirring up much trouble wid this here shit. Gonna bite you on your beautiful *derrière, ma chère*."

He stepped through the door in only a towel soaked from his shower. A valise was spread open on his bed, half packed. "But, dis here is a once-lifetime chance for Remy, as dey say. Dis New York exhibit--no way can I pass on dis one. Remy's Miss Angela go to great expense for da Remy. Gotta show some appreciation. *Me comprenez-vous?*"

He did a crotch grab punctuated by a lascivious wink.

"Yeah, yeah, studly. I get it."

Michele did an eye roll as Rebecca continued, "Go, Darling, go. We got this. Nothing to worry about. Things that go bump in the night... That's all."

He stood with his fists on his hips and looked at Michele. "There are killers out der, lil *cherè*. You stirred dem up tonight. You must be careful. You both are mere women with no man to protect you in dis town." He smiled wickedly as he spread his arms wide and, accidentally on purpose, allowed the towel to slip to the floor.

Rebecca reached for a throw pillow to fire at him but was too exhausted to take the bait. She sank back into the couch.

Michele said, "Mr. Brasseaux, if I can take out a thug in an alley, I assure you, using his pistol, I can turn you from a baritone to a soprano for your insulting remarks and flashing that... Just saying, I'm that good of a shot."

She smiled and added, "You will miss your plane, and you should dress for the occasion."

Remy glanced at the wall clock. "*Baise-moi*!" He reached over the coffee table, snagged, and opened his cell phone. He tossed it to Michele. "You Uber Remy, *s'il vous plaît*. Southwest terminal at Louis Armstrong." He dashed bare-assed back into the bedroom to dress and finish packing.

He threw a final remark over his shoulder, "You keep dat pistol close 'til you leave Nawlins, you hear?"

***

"I feel like I've slept for days, girl. How you doing?"

As the early evening settled over Jackson Square, Michele stood in the window watching the folks below. She rubbed her neck and said, "Bit of a headache, Boss, I'm afraid. It will pass in a few hours."

"You know, that Dennis-Quaid-Cajun-Rascal thing of Remy's is all an act, don't you."

"No kidding?"

Rebecca smirked. "He speaks English like an Oxford Don, actually. He does the roguish, sexy male animal as a self-promotion thing. It gets him art patrons and generous lovers. He's all about the fantasy of the rugged male from the Louisiana bayou with the killer bod and the revved libido. Trouble is... he knows it, and he shows it."

Michele laughed at the circumstances of their present situation. A soft evening breeze stirred the sheers of the open French doors. Somewhere on the square below, a lone sax player added to the decadent atmosphere of the city, crooning out a moaning piece of New Orleans jazz. Folks within earshot around the square would dreamingly recall lost loves as the blue notes stoked long-forgotten memories of fiery passions that had burned down to smoldering embers.

Rebecca gestured to the Baretta on the coffee table and said, "Tell me about that guy."

Michele said, "While you and Remy were talking to Benny, one of the guys who was stalking you at Oz came back along Bourbon and caught sight of you guys on the upper level of the Exile. He slinked back and decided to hang out in the shadows, where he could keep an eye on the situation. So, I am doing my best secret agent shit when he spots me and remembers the bump-up at the stripper bar.

"Asshole wants his gun, but all he got was a throw down, and he lost. I booked and kept very out of sight, and the police – da po po, as Remy calls them, lost interest in finding me. So, I end up at Amnesia with you guys."

Rebecca slipped the gun into her Hermes bag.

"How did it go with Madame Ondine, Boss?"

"She was like a character in a novel, royalty of the voodoo culture with no apologies whatsoever. Absolutely timeless. I hate to think about what that woman has seen throughout her long life. She has influenced a lot of important people with her spiritual guidance."

"And Ms. Arva and the Diva?"

"Cryptic – not that I expected anything different. I need some time to sort out the mambo's message. Feel like some dinner? There is a lovely place over in the South Seventh Ward, Indian food."

"I think I'd better try to get rid of this headache, Miss Rebecca. Sorry." As if hypnotized, Michele stared at the long, floating curtains reaching into the room from the French doors like the stretching claws of a giant, white beast. They seemed to bring a sense of foreboding along with the night breeze from the square.

***

The Jewel in the Crown featured the best curry in the city. Nestled up on North Dorgenois, it was also a favorite of many of the Inhabitants of Bengali Harlem, an old community of Indians, Pakistanis, and Burmese in the clothing industry who trace their origins as far back as the 1880s.

Despite the lateness of the hour, Rebecca lingered along the avenue's stores after parking her car. Handwoven silk was the neighborhood's cottage industry as far back as anyone could remember. She spoke with a few women and girls in shops near the restaurant. Three dark-eyed retailers became excited at the prospect of selecting a gold and blue pashmina to accent Rebecca's outfit. They invited her in holding up shimmering examples of their creativity.

"This one would complement your lovely skin tones, Miss. The gold does not overpower the blue, making it an exciting but relatively understated accent for your evening or day wear."

Rebecca passed her hand beneath the translucent cloth, feeling its luxurious texture. Different styles and colors were offered for her consideration.

The store was filled with Eastern creations made from hand-woven materials. Objects of art and ornamentation filled walls and shelves, elephants, divinities, and jewelry. Here and there, one caught the perfume of exotic botanicals or the enticing scent of fresh spices in small, plastic-flapped bins. In the background, the cascading notes of a sitar were punctuated by the rollicking beat and overtones of a pair of tabla drums.

As Rebecca brought two scarves and a bracelet to the front counter, a woman looked up from late-night lessons with a girl no older than eleven or twelve who was fascinated by the contents of an old, blue-covered book, From the Mixed-Up Files of Mrs. Basil E. Frankweiler by E. L. Konigsburg.

Reaching for her credit card, Rebecca said, "That's a fantastic story. What do you think, gorgeous one?"

The blue-black eyes of the child framed by long, dark lashes looked up from her book. She said, "Yeah, it's good. I like reading about mighty girls and their adventures. Girl hero stories are sometimes hard to find. This is my second time through this one. Have you read it, Miss?"

“Long time ago, sweetie. Probably when I was your age. I wanted to be like Claudia in the book, live in a museum and all.”

“I want to be like her.” The child held up her bookmark with the face of Neelam Ibrar Chattan, a Pakistani campaigner for children’s rights.

Chapter Fifteen: WhatsApp from the Horn of Africa

NEW ORLEANS, LOUISANA AND DJIBOUTI CITY, DJIBOUTI

A bit of loneliness seemed to catch her off guard as she stepped into the almost deserted street and headed to the restaurant. Something about the muted sounds, the soft lights, and the darkness piled in the corners and alleys of the neighborhood brought a chill of isolation as she made her way. Off to the side, a few of the dispossessed vagrants kept to the shadows.

Her cell phone vibrated.

"Hello, Beautiful. How is my one and only? Ya miss me?"

"Mark, you are like water in the desert. I so needed to hear your voice, Darling. Did you arrive safely?"

"Clear flying all the way. Only two connections, Rome and Alexandria. Djibouti City is very cosmopolitan and crazy diverse. I am getting by on my French – so gonna need to perfect my Arabic one of these days."

He continued, "Just sent you a video of the beaches and the Gulf of Tadjoura from my hotel room. CBN has us at the Sheraton on the waterfront – incredible shipping lanes out there."

"If I know you, you are not hanging with the tourists. Too pedantic, no local flavors."

"Woman, I am at the confluence of Asia and Africa on the freaking Red Sea. No way I am interested in the monuments, architecture, and the shopping districts."

"And that means…."

"A hotshot journalist goes where the story is. Europeans and Americans abound, but I want to dirty up with the Africans and the Asians. So freaking interesting."

"Please be careful, Darling."

How is NOLA? Remy keep his Cajun paws off of you? He is the devil in tight jeans, my girl."

"He's fine and sends his love. Suggestive as a rent boy but not inappropriate. He kept it casual."

"Good, 'cause you know, I'd kick his ass."

"Ohhh, so caveman, Darling. Why my hand just fluttered to my dainty throat."

They both laughed.

"Did you get any information, Rebecca?"

"Lots of magic and mystery, warnings and veiled clues to the whereabouts of Arva's opera singer friend. Rather complicated."

Mark quickly interrupted, "Yeah, yeah, yeah. Let's talk about that later, dollface."

Odd, he doesn't usually shut me down. What gives, Gadarn?

"Hey, Rebecca, check it out."

Rebecca opened another video on the app. This one showed a man in Arabic dress – but a street Arab, very nomadic and lower class, smugged, tattered, and tough-looking. The cameleer waved and flashed dirty teeth. He alternated saluting and flicking a Bedouin fly wisk over his shoulder.

She said, "Your guide looks a bit... Wait a second. Hold on. Mark, is that you?"

"Yeah, yeah. It's me. How fuckin' cool is that? Bombing around the souks and bazaars, getting real with the locals. Ali Ga'darn. Do you fuckin' love it? FYI, the facial scar is makeup."

Rebecca heard the call to prayer in the background and a quieting of the background noise.

"You must be near a mosque."

"Yep, right across the square. I am meeting some Brits from the CBN squad. We are catching a football game at the *Stad du Ville*. Egypt plays one of the teams in the Djibouti Premier League– a bit of excitement, anyway. The city folks love their sports."

"Can you talk about the plan? Yemen, I mean."

Mark paused before responding.

"Becky, I'm in Djibouti, not Yemen."

When Mark called her "Becky," a nickname she absolutely abhorred, he was sending her a pre-arranged cipher that translated, *We cannot discuss that over this phone line. It's unsecured.* Mark's activities in dangerous situations came with cyber-surveillance tracking, for which he had to take security measures.

Rebecca sat on a bench, reached into her bag for a pen, and took notes on a loose envelope.

Mark said, "Forgot to tell you that before I left, I saw Sharon and Tim Chaplin, and they want to have dinner when I get back."

You need to check in with Caspar Haig and my techno-snoop, code-named Eris, for updates.

"So, I may get my ass over to the American Base in a few days and say hello to the fellows and gals. May find some of my buds from my previous work in this region and others. I will send you the contact information of one of my best buds at Camp Mongomery for you to say hello. OK, Rebecca? Send 'em some love. Those guys appreciate an American shoutout-- breaks the monotony."

Rebecca realized that Mark was setting her up with a contact at the American military base who would be essential should Mark get into trouble. She sensed that he was very quickly going rogue and blowing off any plans formulated by CBN to keep their journalists safe in a region of the world that was home to mortal danger for Americans.

"Mark. Please stay safe, OK? Caught the whiff of some weird warning about you and us when I was in New Orleans. I'm not sure what it means, but...."

"Hello? Hello? Think I am losing you, girl. I love you. Please don't worry...."

Rebecca spoke to the empty sound of the dropped call.

"I love you, Mark."

Chapter Sixteen: Potenza

TAMARIND, TCHOUPITOULAS STREET, NEW ORLEANS, LOUISIANA

"You have displeased me, Mr. Potenza."

"Sir. I dunno what happened. We made 'em coming outta those apartments around Jackson Square. They grab a couple of slices from Ilio's on Dumaine. Then, we're going down Bourbon Street, and we come to the part where all the gays hang out, and they are in the stripper bar getting frisky with the naked guys. Thought I was gonna puke. So we stepped outside."

The VIP's back dining suite at the Burmese restaurant, Tamarind, was on an open balcony overlooking the rest of the upscale venue. There were two staircases at either end that led up to the exclusive area. A third set of stairs behind a carved wall panel led to a street exit.

Patrons were not tourists. Staff cleverly turned them away. The club provided a refuge for those who required privacy and despised the plague of visitors that infested the streets of New Orleans. Consequently, the elite clientele paid big for the opportunity to conduct confidential business.

The staff of the executive dining room provided that extra layer of discretion, never obtrusive and almost invisible. The man known on the street as "The Chinaman" had the entire second-floor suite, and the staff quietly moved in a well-orchestrated ballet, making sure the businessman received the service he expected.

Ignacio Potenza stood. His boss sat. The gangster wiped his forehead and hands with a handkerchief as the conversation continued. The Triad leader held up one hand to silence the mobster as he nattered on about the failed assignment. The Chinaman turned to his beautiful dinner companion.

"Danella, Mr. Chantha, here…." He signaled to one of his guards, who came over and stood at the table, his strong features expressionless. "… finds you extremely attractive and would like to buy you a drink at the bar below. He is, my dear, extremely interested in …

how shall I say it... fucking you – a prospect that his physical endowments will make absolutely irresistible."

The young woman was unsure whether to be appalled, confused, or excited. Sean Chantha was notorious for his affairs with male porn stars as well as with women.

"I will send for you both when I require your attendance."

He waved them away.

"Continue."

"So, now they hop on to the next bar, and the guy with the dark hair, the artist – he's like real grabby on the street and all, but I make him for a cop."

"Mr. Remy Brasseaux is a hustler turned artist, Mr. Potenza, not a policeman. He is quite well known to at least one of my guards. You got that wrong, also. Your ineptitude is indeed record-breaking."

The mobster shrugged again.

"Better safe than sorry, Boss?"

"I don't pay you to be safe, Mr. Potenza. I pay you to get the job done. I am a businessman. Abduction, many times, serves my purposes. Rebecca Quinto is drawing close to an asset I require. Consequently, she has become an annoyance. I am also an impatient man, Mr. Potenza. I need to speed up the process here. Afraid my investors are very insistent."

"I get it, Boss, but this girl we're following, so she has this bodyguard chick that blindsides me in an alley, and that's when the police...."

"Yes, so I have been informed. And the lovely lady made off with your weapon. I am afraid your reputation when I hired you has been disproven over and over by your many... ahhh, how shall I put it... fuck-ups?"

"Boss, I know that it seems...."

"Mr. Potenza, I do not want excuses. I want results."

The crime boss continued. "You are boring me, and you are delaying my evening. And I cannot abide boredom or delay of any kind."

His eyes bored into his underling. His voice was like rustling silk as he said, "I want Ms. Quinto's threat to my operation terminated. Bring her to me. Then, we will decide if you are to continue in my organization as an operative. I am afraid my investors insist on quality performance or... shall we call it early retirement?"

He signaled that the discussion was at an end.

***

Standing at the bedroom window, Potenza blew smoke into the night air.

"This is bullshit, Loretta. I am fed up with the whole thing."

"Iggy, come back to bed. Just do what the guy wants."

"We're getting out, babe. I've had enough."

"No one leaves the corporation, Iggy. You, of anyone, should know that. I think your head wound is making you crazy. Come back to bed, Iggy."

She drew out the last word in a begging cadence that proposed continued lovemaking.

"I know stuff, babe. I'm turning for sure."

He thought as he smoked, translucent white curls from the cigarette wafting through the floor-to-ceiling windows. Lights from the street, filtered by the lace curtains, created intricate patterns on his naked body and the bedroom wall behind him.

"No police. I hate them fuckers. No, I will send them all a grand 'fuck you.' Turning evidence for the feds."

Loretta Potenza sat up in the bed, elbows on her knees, hands on either side of her face. *He is serious, and this is going to be very bad.*

He spoke the following words with much gravity.

“Quinto can get me to the FBI.”

He added, “And I know where I can find her.”

Chapter Seventeen: Red

PALADAR 511, THE FAUBOURG MARIGNY, NEW ORLEANS, LOUISANA

"I'd like the pappardelle with the sausage ragu and a small house salad, please." She tapped her glass of 2022 Tenuta Delle Terre Nere, Etna Rosso, indicating a refill.

Paladar's dining room was a trendy dining space located on the bottom floor of a former industrial space. The rest of the building at 511 Marigny Street was filled with fashionable apartments.

A mostly thirty-something clientele enjoyed the airy dining room where distressed brick descended from high ceilings and wrapped around tall windows. Where there were plaster walls, antique white melted into seafoam green to wrap around banquettes, and booths lining the space where sculptors once created with metal, fire, and light.

During the main course, the man at the table across from Rebecca slumped forward. A ruby-red puddle of blood began to seep from under his head and form a drip line off the edge of the immaculate golden oak tabletop after smattering a few centerpiece golden chrysanthemums. The thick outflow caught the glimmer of the candlelight as it puddled and dribbled to the floor.

There had been only a slight pop, and then a person quickly exited the noisy and very crowded restaurant through the kitchen. Therefore, the clientele was slow to react, mildly annoyed by the server whose tray of dirty dishes was upset by the fleeing killer. Gradually, diners became aware of the man with a hole in his head, bleeding into his empty dinner plate and blankly staring into the void of death-- the continued unfolding notes of an act of unspeakable, bloody horror.

Rebecca grabbed her purse and dashed through the kitchen doors in pursuit. Restaurant patrons stood up in wonderment. As she hit the doors, a woman behind her screamed. Rebecca slapped her Hermés clutch onto the chest of a young server who gasped with delight. "I'll be back for it, so don't get any ideas." Her voice trailed after her as she hurried through the crowded kitchen. She had removed the Baretta Px4 Storm Compact and her car keys.

Her target ducked and weaved around servers and chefs who blocked the path to the exit. Crashes of food, crockery, and rolling racks of kitchen supplies followed in his wake, making her chase next to impossible.

“Down, down, down.” She yelled and waved her gun at the ceiling as the kitchen crew ducked, rolled, and headed for cover. At the stoves, scrambling chefs collided with their assistants. As the staff dashed for cover, ruined entreés in delicate sauces tumbled to the floor. Rebecca’s quarry reached the exit doors, knocking down two entering servers returning from a smoking break.

Outside, she saw the black Viper with mud-spattered plates burn rubber in the parking lot and shoot out and up to the Rue Dauphine. A driver had been waiting. Rebecca scrambled for her car.

She opened the door, sat in the driver's seat, and was about to swivel her legs into the car when a sizeable black man, a homeless derelict so typical in the fringes of the ritzy neighborhood, grabbed the car door and yanked her from the vehicle. Before she could react, she was sprawled in the street, her gun yards away on the seat of her rental car.

The night creature gestured like a skitzo on dangerous drugs, mostly pointing to the driver’s seat. Rebecca stood up, very angry. The Viper was a loss, vanishing into the night. She slipped off her heels and was about to clobber the intruder, not quite sure of his motives, his mental state, or what the fuck he was trying to say. Rather than throw some offense, she pulled back her long chestnut hair and approached the hulking figure with what she hoped was a reasonable but determined attitude.

As she approached, the man ran to the passenger’s side and ramped up his raving. As she came around the back of the opened car, she read his fiercely flying fingers, “D-I-E.” Deaf and mute, the man pointed to her and the vehicle while fingerspelling the one-word message.

It was then that she saw it.

***

"So, I'm going to need some ID, Ma'am," As if on cue, the kitchen worker, leaving the backdoor of the restaurant, handed Rebecca her purse. She gave the police officer her wallet and her FBI Citizen's Academy registration while slipping her pumps on.

"Can you tell me what happened, Ms... ahhh... Quinto, is it?"

"Right."

Rebecca explained the scene inside The Jewel in the Crown and her aborted attempt to pursue the killer to the inquiring blond officer. A policewoman called the number on the card that Rebecca had offered as part of her ID. As she spoke to the reference, the officer signaled the tall blond detective that Rebecca was not one of the bad guys.

"Please step over here, Ms."

The male officer pointed to a colleague who delicately removed wires from the rental car's gas tank.

"Bad guy pries open your filler flap while you are inside. He shoves in these wires connecting your gas tank to the brake light on the passenger's side of the car." He pointed to the smashed rear light on the same side as the gas tank. "You put it in reverse and..." He made the explosion sign with both hands opening up on either side of his head while mouthing a silent "Boom!"

The big cop continued, "Let's start with why we're not scraping you off the sidewalk."

"Just lucky, I guess."

"Uh-huh." The officer was not buying it as Rebecca looked around for the deaf-mute.

"What suppose you and I go 'cross the street and have a cup, Ms. Quinto? Get to know each other a bit more."

They took two coffees to an empty outside table of the rundown shop. The police officer took out a small notebook and said, "Seems you have some friends in high places, Ms. Quinto. I'm gonna make this a bit easy for you, therefore. About the gun...."

"My associate, um… liberated it from a gent who was following us last night… make that this morning… over on Bourbon. It's all yours, Sargeant…."

Rebecca squinted in the dim light to pick out the officer's name from his nametag. "… McCullough."

"We have a homicide at The Jewel and an attempted murder on the street. Doesn't take much to see a connection. Why would anyone want you dead, Ma'am? And just what brought you to New Orleans?"

"I needed to see a fortune teller. Been having a streak of bad luck."

***

He was huddled under the I-10 interchange near Hunter's Field on Claiborne. A flattened cardboard box and three plastic crates crammed with various possessions and meager supplies seemed to total all his worldly possessions. The deaf-mute kept these close by and hidden when he went begging.

From the position of his space, it was easily seen that even among the small group of the forsaken claiming the asphalt hollows under the highway, he preferred to be alone. His jumble of meager possessions created a barrier. Even among his own, he was a pariah.

The desolate outcast was sitting on the ground, back to one of the massive highway pylons, when Rebecca's car rolled up. Above them, the sound of the night traffic on the highway created a constant din, one he could not hear.

Rebecca approached the disheveled man and smiled. He blinked but did not move from his spot. She handed him a sack of Po'Boys and a bottle of soda water from a nearby food shop. Tucked inside was also a monetary contribution.

Rebecca knelt on the edge of his cardboard and began to sign. She placed the fingers of her right hand near her lips, then moved her hand forward and down toward her companion.

Thank you.

She smiled again.

The man continued to look at her with wide eyes. Finally, he reached forward and slightly to the side with his hand, palm up, and brought it in toward his torso.

You're welcome.

Chapter Eighteen: The Little Death

ST. ANN STREET AND CHARTRES STREET, NEW ORLEANS, LOUISANA

Michele stretched out in her underwear on the tile floor of the guest room, a cold washcloth on her forehead. She had turned out all the lights in the condo. The migraine was intense this time. She practiced some meditation exercises to keep the stabbing pain behind her forehead at bay. The excitement of the last 24 hours had brought on a big one this time.

Become hyper-aware of your surroundings by focusing on the sounds around you. Remain as still as you can. Keep your breathing regular. Do what you can to lower your body temperature. Apply peppermint oil to the temples.

Michele resisted the use of painkillers. Chemicals in her body were not something she advocated– a personal thing. She shifted the cold compress to the back of her neck.

There it was again. The sound was like a deep humming. Closer this time. She picked it out from the soft sounds coming up from the square, the music, the voices, the soft rustle of the trees.

Quietly, she got to her feet, steadying herself against the tall bedpost. She waited for her blood pressure to equalize and for her sight to return from a blurry haze. Streetlife had sharpened her ability to keep still, observe her surroundings, and hide in the darkness of a bustling metropolis like Fort Lauderdale at night.

Someone had entered the living room from the balcony, but the intruder remained still. The vocal droning was almost imperceptible. Noiselessly, Michele slowly dropped back to the floor and slid under the antique plantation bed, moving aside the dust ruffle that reached within an inch of the ground.

Tiny, naked, black feet moved slowly across her line of vision – the space below the dust ruffle. Michele expected to be discovered instantly. Hiding under the bed was such a cliché. She fought back the head pain. Her night visitor, inches away, seemed to be sniffing the air.

The ginger powder and opened bottles of essential oils, her home remedies, wafted into the bedroom from the Jack and Jill bathroom that connected the flat's guest rooms. These were the burglar's destination, it would seem.

She slid out, crawled to the doorway, and stood as she entered the living room. Moving with the grace of a cat, she made for the darkest corner near the open kitchen space and the cluttered counter.

Some kind of weapon. Something...

The darkness of the great room, stirred by billowing curtains reaching into the space, caressed the air. Throughout the room, the shadow-tinged wall hangings and the furniture created a surreal and macabre effect. The light was minimal, but Michele felt the stare of tiny eyes in the darkened doorway of Rebecca's bedroom. The invader was scenting on the peppermint oil. A soft inhale, a slight, almost imperceptible change in the shadows—the young woman was in the crosshairs of danger.

Now, she sensed the stranger was in the room. There was a glint of metal as the phantom dropped into a deep shadow behind a chair. Was the burglar rising? Moving toward her or staying in hiding? Michele's vision was fading in and out. The guttural sounds started but were louder this time. Then, a soft clicking. She reached out.

The interior door opened. A silhouette stood in the doorway. Light from the hallway slanted into the great room. Michele covered her eyes with her left forearm, blinded. The figure in the middle of the room spun around, surprised by the trespasser. There was a slicing, whispering sound in the air.

Michele threw....

***

"Twice in the last hour, Ms. Quinto. How lucky can I get?"

Rebecca smiled at the 6'6', #225, blond cop. "When you gave me your business card, Officer McCullough, I had no idea this would be about you getting lucky."

Mike McCullough struggled to keep from returning the smile.

Rebecca went back to sweeping up the broken glass. Michele spoke from her place on the sofa, eyes closed.

"Yeah, so, when Rebecca opened the door, killer guy threw the hatchet, and I threw the vase...."

Rebecca said almost to herself, "And Remy gets a new Swarovski."

Puzzled expression from the hunk– "It's crystal, Officer."

Forensics worked on the small ax embedded in the door jamb, pictures, dusting for latent prints, etc. Michele continued, "Clipped him in the head with the vase, I think. Best I could see, anyway. The guy then vaults across the room, out the window and gone."

"You said he was dark-complexioned and short."

"Think so. My eyes are giving me problems."

Rebecca continued the narration, "Yes, he was very small. Climbed or jumped from the balcony. I saw him tear-assing across the square in the direction of the river. Not even 5 feet tall, I would say, wiry build and shoeless. The guy was very native-primitive, loose baggy pants and a sleeveless t-shirt, also drab. Has the whole hunter-gatherer vibe going on. He knocked over a flower cart in his escape."

Mike spoke into his mobile to an officer in the square.

"OK, my colleague's talking to the flower woman now."

"Mike, have we broken any laws?"

"Good question. This investigation will determine that. As I said back at the restaurant, I'm not quite sure what this is all about."

A woman with the forensics team said, "The metalwork and the carvings on the handle are from the Middle East, best I can tell right now. I'll have the lab folks do more in-depth research on it."

She asked Michele, "Were you hurt, Miss?"

"Naw, just a headache."

Detective Mike McCullough stood, stretching his tall, muscular frame. "I have the distinct feeling you two are not telling me everything. You have impressive friends, but it would appear you also have some very dangerous enemies. The stalker in the alley, the gun, the dead guy at The Jewel in the Crown, and now a potential murderer who climbs up on second-floor balconies, you seem to attract extreme danger, Ms. Quinto."

He looked at Rebecca with a gaze that combined professional interest with physical desirability as he continued. "I've doubled up beat cops in the square for a couple of days. You should be fine for a while. I have your contact information, Ms. Quinto and Ms. Larson. Do not leave town."

The police leFort

"Even with my eyes closed, I could tell Officer Beefcake was so into you, Ms. Rebecca."

"The curse of a pretty face. Let's go, girl."

"Where are we going?"

"Pack. We're leaving town."

Chapter Nineteen: Mike the Cop

NEW ORLEANS, LOUISANA

They didn't get far-- the Park and Lock on the Rue des Ursulines for the rental car. The police officer in the cruiser was a bit insistent in his demands.

"Detective McCullough would like to see you both, Ms. Quinto and Ms. Larson. How 'bout you follow me to the Metro 5th District over on North Claiborne?"

The police headquarters was at the intersection of three neighborhoods on the east side of town, the Florida area, St. Claude, and the Lower Ninth Ward, communities still coming back from the devastation of 2005's Hurricane Katrina.

"Making a quick get-away, women? Not looking good."

"Officer McCullough, allow me to repeat a previous question. Are we being charged with any crime? In this case, I need to contact my legal counsel. Otherwise, I am returning to Fort Lauderdale."

"Are you always this imperious, Ms. Quinto? And please call me Mike."

Rebecca did a hair flip, signaling, *That's not going to happen*. Michele raised her eyebrows and suppressed a smile. *This guy's got it bad.*

"Actually, I hoped you would help me with the identification of the man murdered at the table next to yours last night. Would you mind taking a look?"

Rebecca huffed with annoyance as she replied, "Lead the way, Officer."

***

The morgue was stainless steel tile and white lab coats everywhere. An assistant led the trio to a wall of stacked square lockers, two high. She rolled out their most recent corpse, a white male in his late thirties and in good shape.

Michele looked at the ash-grey body with the head wound and said, "That's the Clover Grill dude. He and his buddy started dogging us at Oz. The Baretta is his."

She pointed to a sizeable blue-purple bruise on his right eye and cheekbone. "I gave him that." The left side of the face was a gaping hole. "That one he got from someone else."

"Ignacio Dominic Potenza goes by 'Little Ig.' Low-level thug... mobster worked for a few *capos* in the "Little Palermo" section of the Quarter but recently on the payroll of a South Asian cartel headquartered in the St. Roch section. Did time in Angola-- Federal weapons charges."

The medical examiner rolled the head of the deceased mobster to the left, and McCullough pointed with a pencil to the hole in the back right side of the skull. He explained, "It was a gangland-style murder – a total *film noir* hit. Gun barrel pressed to the back of the skull, and the bullet exits out the left front. Blew his brains out on the beautiful damask."

Rebecca examined the entry wound and said, "Used a silencer... nothing but a soft pop-- barely heard in the noisy restaurant."

"We found a Smith M&P22 Compact outfitted for assassination with a suppressor behind The Jewel with no prints. The killer wore gloves. Still looking for the Viper. No sign of your protector, Ms. Quinto."

"Protector?"

"Deaf guy."

Rebecca said nothing.

Mike McCullough continued his analysis of the case. "Initially, Potenza was looking to do you some harm, we think. I'd say he loused up the operation in the Quarter thanks to Captain Marvel here." He nodded at Michele.

"Pretty sure his bosses were not impressed when he showed up without his gun. Anyway, tonight, someone took him out before he got to you. But what I don't understand is, if he were going to do a number on you, why didn't he make the hit in the street?

"And, if this was surveillance part two, why would his bosses put him on your tail if he fucked it up the first time? I think he wanted to make contact of a different sort. But why? And so the question remains, what are you up to, Ms. Quinto?"

As the query hung out there, Rebecca again chose not to respond.

McCullough signaled to the medical examiner, who covered the body and rolled the drawer back into the wall. Mike escorted them to a small interrogation room near the morgue.

"We're sending Little Ig to the County Coroner, but I wanted you to see him first."

"I never saw him, Mike. At the bars, I mean. Just heard the commotion on the street. So Michele's ID is it."

The detective came back with, "See, here's the deal. I need some answers. Arva St. Genevieve is dead, apparently murdered, and you are one of the last people to see her alive."

"Been talking to Fort Lauderdale Sheriff Dian Crawford, eh, Officer McCullough."

He nodded. "So, again, please call me Mike."

Rebecca said, "Pretty sure it had to do with the location of one of Ms. Arva's old friends who disappeared about forty years ago-- the opera diva Victoria Ricci. Arva was killed in a ruined attempt to find Ricci."

"Never heard of her."

"Gotta get you some culture, Mike, is it?" Rebecca did her best wry smile. She loved teasing with her splendid gift of flirtatious repartee.

The handsome detective smiled and nodded.

Michele broke in, "Check it out, you two, before we go way out on this thing. Let's the three of us talk to a friend of mine. But can we go outside? It's hottern hell in here."

The AC was pretty much on full blast, but Mike and Rebecca led the way to the street, where Michele continued by proposing the next step.

"Name's Nancy O'Brien, aka the Peeler. Buddy of mine from the streets and Covenant House down in South Florida. Went to Fort Lauderdale High with her until we both aged out of Children's Services. She got into some trouble and ended up here working in the exotic world of adult entertainment. Last I heard was she was trying to get straight. I can set up a meeting, but she can't know you are a cop. Street kids grow up hating you guys."

Mike's turn to sneer. "Well, let's see... hmmm... I can't be Rebecca's brother. 'Cause we ahhh...."

"Do not crack on my skin color, white boy. *Café au lait* Latinas rock, Wonder Bread."

"Easy, easy. Just strategizing our undercover. Merely police business... How about I go as your extra sexy boyfriend?"

He made as if he was going to put his arm around Rebecca.

Michele fumed. "Gimme a break."

Rebecca stepped away, turned to face the police officer, and did her best Aretha, index finger in his face and the other hand on her hip.

"You better think."

Chapter Twenty: The Peeler

THE NEW ORLEANS MUSEUM OF ART, CITY PARK, NEW ORLEANS, LOUISANA

The naked man braced one foot against a rocky outcrop and stretched the stringless bow across his well-muscled torso with rippling arms of steel. No, make that bronze. "Hercules the Archer" by Antoine Bourelle in the Sydney and Walda Besthoff Sculpture Garden at the New Orleans Museum of Art was a masterpiece of tension in balance. Surrounded by lush green lawns and a picturesque landscape of a magnolia grove and tall oaks dripping with blue-grey Spanish moss, the 8-foot high sculpture had been chosen as the meeting place with Nancy O'Brien-- ex-street urchin of South Florida and New Orleans B-girl.

Rebecca was doing her Head Museum Curator thing. "He is in the process of killing the monstrous Stymphalian birds of Greek mythology who fed on human flesh. There are a few copies of this work, but this is by far my favorite. I think the setting is what makes it unique. Bourelle was an assistant to Rodin, and you can see his influence – the impressionist style. The model was actually a military man who posed for him."

Mike nodded to the demigod's crotch. "Our boy musta been super popular with the ladies."

Rebecca rounded on the police officer.

"Seriously? Office McCullough, I need to say I find your switch from a professional member of the Louisiana law enforcement community to the realm of macho-Neanderthal-on-the-make a bit disturbing albeit rather humorous. And besides..."

Mike smiled and did a hands-up walk-back as Rebecca let loose.

Michele interrupted. "Hey folks, need to cool it... I think this might be her."

They were approached by a small, thin, young woman, dark-haired with aubergine highlights styled in a very current fashion.

"Peels! How you been, girl? Damn, you look great."

"Hey Mikey, so good to see you. I would not have recognized you – all spiffed up."

"Tell me about it. Landed me a super good job in the art world. This here is my boss, Rebecca Quinto, and her... ahhh... boyfriend, Mike."

Mike took Rebecca's hand in a casual but loving grasp.

O'Brien snapped, "Bullshit. This guy's a cop. McCollough, NOLA Metro, detective grade. You hauled me in off of Rampart more'n once for turning tricks. I never forget a dick face. Fuck you, pig."

The young woman looked around nervously and was about to walk off when Michele said, "Peels, this is not about you or any of all that."

"Good thing, and damn right. I've been clean and outta The Life for six months. Got me an excellent job at the museum bookstore – with benefits, and I volunteer three nights a week at the Acadia Addiction Center."

Rebecca said, "Ms. O'Brien. We have no intention of interfering with your career or your newfound financial security. We just need some information. I am the one who seems to be in trouble with the police." She realized that she was still holding Mike's hand and released it.

Nancy looked at Michele. "Is this for real? Your boss here looks like Prada royalty."

Her former gal-pal nodded and did a light back pat to try and reassure the reformed sex worker.

Mike said, "Couple of murders, and we are trying to tie them together. You are not implicated in any way."

Nancy thought about it and looked at the eyes of the three. "Let's go have a seat." She led them to a pair of benches, took a water bottle out of her bag for a swig, and said, "So, tell me what's going on and no more games."

Rebecca and Mike started with the eerie events surrounding Arva St. Genevieve's death, the conversation with Mambo Ondine, the killing of

Little Ig at the restaurant, and the tiny, dark, would-be assassin at the Jackson Square flat.

Nancy O'Brien does not have a poker face. She visibly balked at the names and descriptions of the principals except for Ms. Arva and the diva, Victoria Ricci, whom she apparently did not know.

Michele said, "Peels, this you tell no one. I need ya to promise."

Nancy looked around cautiously and said to Rebecca, "You are in hellacious deep shit. You need to disappear. I am so serious."

Mike said, "What's it all mean?"

"When I was in the... ahem... the adult services industry, my, um, manager... was crazy hot to get me some high-end customers. Turns out, I ended up with some pretty connected Johns, the criminal class, if you know what I mean. There was talk about the Asian."

She paused thoughtfully. After a beat, she said with intensity, "So, I tell you this. Stuff I never told anyone, and you stay the fuck away from me, McCullough. I'm respectable now and gonna stay that way."

Mike nodded.

When she continued, she spoke softly and carefully. "These guys would sometimes dress us up and parade us like we were their girlfriends or some shit. We were their whores. I mean, who's kidding who? On a few occasions, I would come in contact with some of the *capos*. You know, the made men.

"The boss dude in question has got to be 'The Chinaman.' He's not really from China. His drugs are. He is a Lao, I think. Crazy motherfucker."

Nancy looked at Mike and said, "You know this McCullough. The Fentanyl epidemic in NOLA is the new heroin scourage, and the cartels are bringing it in from China."

"Dao Luang Kham, the Red Spectre of the Ghost Hand – a huge Asian drug triad." Mike's words were like an ominous pronouncement of doom.

"No, seriously, this guy is batshit crazy. Jesus, I am so afraid just telling you all this."

No one said anything for a while as some art aficionados passed nearby, taking in the sculpture garden and snapping photos. Mike began to scan the immediate surroundings while listening to the young woman.

"Word on 'The Chinaman' is that his wife is a powerful influencer. She is big-time superstitious and has lived in New Orleans for a long time. There's your connection with the voodoo shit. I have seen Mrs. Chinaman with her fortuneteller turning those magic cards."

"The Spiritualist. Can you describe her?" Rebecca asked.

"Hard to say. Madame Lu uses a few different ones, a white girl and some old black woman with a cane. And some others. One's a guy. Creepy as shit."

"Ever see someone fitting the description of the little black guy we told you about – the one who broke into our flat," Michele asked as she stretched out prone on one of the benches.

"Shit, there she goes. You still got that medical issue, Mikey? Nothing they can do for you?"

"Just a matter of maintaining control most times. Some dizziness now, but I got it covered. Gimme some of your water, please. Go on. You were saying."

"The wife, Madame Lu, I think is her name – anyway, she has some strange agents who make an appearance once in a while. She is from somewhere in Africa or one of those islands in the Pacific. Not sure. But I've seen a few tiny, native-looking folks who they try to keep out of sight. I thought they were little native kids, but these little guys are adult men. One of my girlfriends told me they use them to get into places without being seen.

"Like you did, 'Mikey,' back in our street days. Wasn't a lock that could keep you out. 'Member the time you got up in that high rise on Las Olas for that gent you were working for? Fuckin' Spider-Man scaling those balconies. The highlight of your career."

"Um... trying to stay clean myself, Peels."

Michele threw a guilty look at the police officer.

Mike raised his eyebrows – *what fresh hell is this?* He didn't go there but said, "The Ghost Hand keeps the City in the grip of some real terror with all this occult stuff. Fear of crossing the Triad is pretty intense." He refrained from saying, *No one rats on these guys.*

He continued, "Lately, we hear that their funds are in decline. Law enforcement has been making strides to stop their supply at the ports and other contraband coming across state lines. Cooperation with Asian authorities has been proven to be effective. This makes things difficult for the Red Specter and his goons."

Michele said, "This one time, I was seeing this dude who was with the Triad. He let slip that 'the corporation,' as they call it, was in a bit of trouble. Thinking of defecting. I never got a second date. Disappeared. I mean, like without a trace."

Rebecca said, "My sources in the FBI talk about this cartel, the Ghost Hand. They have political aspirations in Southeast Asia. They represent a regional instability that threatens the dominance of the Chinese in that part of the world."

Mike said, "We thought that we have them on the run, but some of us figure they are just retrenching for an even bigger move, possibly worldwide."

Michele added. "The occult stuff is pretty freaky. Maybe we should circle back and talk to Madame Ondine and see what she has to say about this group."

Rebecca checked her phone.

"After our encounter in the Jackson Square Flat, I checked in with Remy. He said that both Benny and his aunt had disappeared. Said Benny texted him that he would be out of reach for a while."

Nancy O'Brien spoke up, "There was a rumor on the streets when I was hooking that the Ghost Hand was also running enslaved people. With all this immigration and war shit, there are huge numbers of displaced women and children. The Ghost has some pretty bad operations going down, here and elsewhere– you know, cheap labor in the illegal drug industry and the sex trade also."

Rebecca said, "So here's where we are. The Ghost Hand visits Arva St. Genevieve to get information on the diva, Victoria Ricci. Before they can find out anything, Arva dies. What I don't get is why they want to get their hands on an ancient woman who has been in hiding for more than forty years."

"You met with Arva a few hours before her death. The Hand had her under surveillance, and they figure she had passed information to you about this legendary woman." Mike said. "What did Ms. St. Genevieve tell you?"

"Not much. The trail led here. Michele and I are noticed around town asking questions about a famous voodoo mambo who was the spiritual advisor to my diva. All we come up with is what's in the cards, and I gotta tell you... I mean, what the fuck – supernatural forces out the ass. We are stalked with either the intent of eliminating us or finding out if we know where Ricci is hiding. I say it's the latter."

Nancy O'Brien interrupted. "OK, so here's the deal. Murder, voodoo, terror, and crimes against humanity shit – this girl's taking a pass. I am out of all this. I said too much to begin with. These assholes stop at nothing to get what they want. They lurk in the shadows and call on the devil himself to get over on their enemies. You are running around with a bull's eye on your back, Ms. Quinto, and I suspect so is anyone who helps you out."

She looked at Michele and said with finality, "Good luck and all that, but The Peeler is done. *Finito*."

No one spoke for about a minute. Then, Mike picked the narrative back up. "So Victoria Ricci, opera star, and what? She'd be about one hundred if she is even alive. She holds the key to bringing down the Ghost Hand. But how? What information does she have that a drug lord and human trafficker would want?"

Rebecca looked back at the statue of the gigantic hero resisting the forces of evil with all his might. She chose her words carefully.

"I guess we'll just have to ask her."

Chapter Twenty-One: Benny and the Snake

THE FRENCH QUARTER, NEW ORLEANS, LOUISANA

He was reminded of a cobra-- the green and yellow eyeshadow outlined in black, like the snake in the zoo that his Auntie had taken him to visit as a schoolboy. The evil beauty's head vacillated slightly from side to side, and she spoke with a soft, sibilant sound. He was a bird trapped by the hypnotic gaze of a beautiful but deadly predator.

"I am so disappointed that I cannot reach your aunt, Mr. Duplessis. I rely on her advice on both personal and professional matters."

Benny fidgeted a bit under the gaze of his interrogator. *This was big, powerful stuff here, Benny boy. Be careful. This one– she bites with the kiss of death.*

"I do not know what to tell you, ma'am. My Auntie hates the phone. She keeps all her clients regular by visiting them, and she keeps all that information in her head. She may be slipping – pushing 87, you know."

The woman known as Madame Lu favored modern Asian-style couture. Her delicate features bespoke a congress of human diversity – Chinese, African, and Pacific Islander. She wore her jet-black hair pulled into a tight knot at the base of her neck, held in place by an emerald green, imperial jade hairpin fashioned in the form of a hooded cobra. Her blood-red fingernails were deadly weapons.

The enigmatic woman looked down and slowly stirred her tea. Around them, the Black Scorpion Tea House staff made sure they stayed accessible but just out of sight.

Madame Lu repeated in her perfect English, "I am afraid you are in a grave situation, you see. It is vital that I contact her. I sent someone to her house, but there was no sign of her. The couple who live upstairs said she left. I insist you consider helping me to find Madame Ondine."

The accompanying gaze was direct and full of thinly disguised menace. The dark enchantress examined her fingernails and reached into her purse to remove a small vial. She cooly painted a chipped nail.

"My Auntie raised me, lady, but I do not live with her. She insists that we tend to our own affairs, as she puts it. I am not sure how much help I can be."

"And the last time you saw her?"

Benny shifted this coffee cup, keeping it between them like a defending chess piece. "Yesterday, early morning over in Tremé, the Amnesia Tea Shop. "

"Please be so kind as to tell me about that meeting – just you and Madame Ondine?"

Benny's "liar's tell" was very apparent. He looked to the left as he answered, "Yes, ma'am. Just the two of us. Catching up, you know. Think Madame told me she was planning on doing some visiting over near Baton Rouge."

"The Quinto woman, what of her? Tell me, and do not test my patience, Mr. Duplessis."

"Naw, naw, Mrs. I don't know anything about that."

The Cobra struck softly but insistently. The dagger-like nail of her right index finger bit into the back of Benny's hand like a fang.

She drew back her claws and inhaled softly.

"Please do not lie to me, Mr. Duplessis. You are well aware of who I am and that I am a fanatic for the truth. The dark-haired woman and your *Tata*– tell me about that conversation at Amnesia. Do not waste my time."

Benny rubbed the back of his hand and started to sweat. The tiny nick drew blood and stung sharply.

"Mrs., you gotta believe I don't know anything about that. My Aunt asked us to sit outside while she spoke to the woman in the shop."

"Us?"

"Yeah, um... a cop buddy, I see from time to time."

Benny hoped his lying reference to the "po po" would keep her away from Remy.

She wasn't buying it. "I find that your lack of information, your mendacious responses, and your feeble intelligence wearisome. I am not easily fooled, young man."

"Sorry, ma'am, but I got nothing here." *This shit was getting super scary.*

Benny looked around. *Exit... yeah... two of her goons between it and him. No likelihood I can make it from here... doubtful. Severe fuckin' shit, man....*

Madame Lu raised two fingers in an almost imperceptible gesture. One of her giant escorts came forward to stand behind her right side.

"I will drop you at your place now, Mr. Duplessis. Please come this way." She stood.

He bolted. He flipped his chair at the closest bodyguard and spun around to see the gangster's twin begin to charge forward. Benny jumped on the nearest table, tossing cups, plates, and tableware as he landed. He danced across tabletops like a frenetic Gene Kelly, scattering heaps of food, service items, and a few dazed customers, clawing his way to the door. Cries of fear, anger, and frustration accompanied him in his wake.

He grabbed a waiter and spun him into the dangerously close thug. Benny reached the shop's open door and looked down the street for his escape just as a sharp, short-bladed, and narrow-pointed dagger caught his pork-pie hat half an inch from his left temple, pinning it to the shop's sign.

He would remember the hilt of the weapon for a long time – an emerald-green, jade cobra with fangs exposed.

Chapter Twenty-Two: The Red Specter

THE FRENCH QUARTER, NEW ORLEANS, LOUISANA

"I am afraid, my dear, that your efforts are resulting in more confusion around the matter and continue to be ambiguous as to the rewards to be gained. Your nonsense creates a public spectacle, and we cannot risk drawing attention to our operations with your escapades in the tea shops of Metairie."

The restrained politeness and severity of his remarks underlined his concern as the crime boss continued, "My business is in the utmost peril. Both the drug operations and the sexual services we provide are, for many reasons, on the decline. Law enforcement is getting even bolder in preventing our operations, and the interference by our rivals threatens to move The Ghost Hand off the top position of the triads. Our honor continues to be besmirched."

A man of impeccable manners, the Asian businessman led his wife to a pair of chaise lounge chairs near the pool. The sounds of an urban oasis filled the grounds of their Garden District manse. They sipped dark red glasses of Penfolds Bin 95 Grange Hermitage.

A noisy family of green monk parakeets bolted from the branches of a magnolia tree, circled the garden, and headed off to the west. In the fountain, an assortment of doves, robins, and three goldfinches drank, bathed, and shook off beads of water. Along the perimeter of the property were the guards, one with a head injury from a recently thrown chair.

The woman met his gaze and said, "The defections among our soldiers do not help, and neither does the unfortunate embezzlement by the dearly departed Zhou family. My, my, even the children... You were ruthless in your response. Let's hope it has sent the message to our enemies. Though, I doubt it. Not cruel enough if you ask me."

The triad leader said, "The cash, however, is not yet recovered. And you cannot buy the allegiance of country militia in Southeast Asia with child prostitutes. They have plenty of their own, my dear."

She spoke firmly, "I have no intention of being the First Lady of a rubber plantation along the backwaters of the Mekong."

"You will be just exactly what I want you to be, Lucy."

"Louis, we have talked about this before. We need a transfusion of gold." She used her Americanized pet name for him.

Dao smiled, "Leave that to me. Just remember, my dear, we cannot have members of your opera guild overhear our conversation. Drugs, prostitution, political corruption-- how do you maintain your respectability as a New Orleans society flower and still inspire fear in the hearts of our followers and foes as the nefarious Madame Lu?

"Make-up change, high-class American fashion, and the persona of a Southern businessman's wife. It's all showbiz, my beloved, with a bloody streak." She examined one of her talons.

Lucy Pendragage's years of cheap theater roles in the clandestine establishments of the Far East allowed her to hone both her business and seduction skills. A series of near-discoveries by some of the sleaziest talent scouts in the Chinese film industry had been leveraged into many character roles, an asset for serving the greed and power lust she shared with her husband.

She reached for him, a man she idolized not just because of his physical beauty but also for his determination to do anything to get what he wanted. Dao had rescued her from the sex trade in Singapore and elevated her beyond the status of his tribe of whores. The Red Specter kissed the hand of his partner in criminal activity and in acquired respectability.

"Gold," she insisted. "The occult will bring the riches of past decades. That bitch in Florida knew the way. She died without revealing the secret of what we need to reach our destiny."

"And your pigmy minions destroyed that avenue completely. Keep those little monstrosities away from me before I decapitate one of them."

"Easy, my dear. My little death-dealers get the job done."

His anger quickly rose. "You continue to misrepresent your importance and have become a serious obstruction. St. Genevieve – dead and no information. The midnight raid on Jackson Square – two women– WOMEN! ... got the better of your best assassin. Such incompetence. You should be punished along with your black devils. I will take great pleasure in that, pleasure and amusement."

She tossed back his hand. "You are a pig among men. Keep your mind on the work. Lust will come later. And only if I say so." She tried to take a position of dominance but knew she could not. He downed the wine and, ignoring her empty glass, poured more for himself.

"I am going forward without your cards and magic, my supreme bitch. The Middle East contacts are ready to provide more resources for our trade. The militias are selling prisoners cheaply. My commissioners are completing the transactions in Yemen and in Syria. The corporation can expect the product soon.

The Specter continued, "You back off of your society parties and concentrate on serving me for a change. Considering your incessant nagging to become an equal partner, you have failed miserably."

The Cobra hissed, "And Little Ig. My, how you fucked that up. You are not the man your father was. He took what he wanted, Louis. Anything. He was a genuine man in so many ways, strong, virile, and irresistible. He would have never allowed...."

Her implication was obvious as she let her sentence drop.

Madame Lu stood and continued to admonish her husband with severe anger. "I can bring you the wealth you seek-- the treasure of empires as well as power beyond measure. It has been foretold, you imbecile. Do not try to stop me.

"Do not be premature, Louis, in ordering these killings. The Quinto woman can lead us to the ageless Diva. Do you lak the strength to make this happen?"

"Again, you are delusional, my dear. That woman knows nothing of your soprano, and she knows too much of my interests. My informants tell me she has enlisted the police in her little adventure. She needs to serve me immediately and then be removed."

Madame Lu pressed her point, saying, "Wait, my husband. I counsel patience, considering all circumstances. Allow her to lead us to the Diva. The Glorious One will provide, in unsurpassed measures, secrets that will pay off with power and cash. I have seen it in the spirit realm. Only then can your assassins wash both of their bodies in their own blood. It is what your father would have done. He truly appreciated my abilities and talents."

"You continue to anger me with your talk, my dear. Once this thing is done, I will replace you and your total ineptitude with one who is more compliant."

"Your lack of manliness disgusts me."

Dao Luang Kham stood to face the insulting and defiant woman. He held her by the front of her silk blouse and slapped her three times, raising red bruises on her delicate countenance and beating her into a haze.

"May I be of assistance, Sir?"

"Yes, Mr. Chantha." The Red Specter released his prisoner into the grip of his subordinate and quickly composed himself.

"Madame is having another of her nervous tension attacks. She requires another special session in the Devil's Chamber. You will take her there along with two of the other guards who have joined us in the past."

"Yes, Sir."

"I will follow along shortly to supervise. Then we may begin."

Chapter Twenty-Three: Secrets

FRITCHER MUSEUM OF ART, FORT LAUDERDALE, FLORIDA.

Micah Vélaz took the call. He stepped out on the sixth-floor terrace of the executive suite for some privacy.

The caller said, "Man, I guess I really fucked up."

"Good morning, Hud. So, not a good time. Work. My boss is due in any minute after being gone for three days, and the opening this weekend is in major trouble." Micah looked out over the dazzling city. *Best get this call over with. The guy won't stop leaving messages.*

"How's your stomach."

"Um, the trouble seems to have gone away. Hud, I didn't return your calls also because of the hoopla over the death of my neighbor and the Museum's board member, Ms. Arva."

"OK. Yeah, so I read about that. Messed up. Who would have thought, huh?"

"Yeah. So what's up?"

"Wave."

"Huh?"

"Look a bit to the north."

Micah saw the signaling figure in the glass tower across the river, on the balcony, one floor up. Hud's office. *Creepy? Not sure about this.* He waved, nonetheless.

"So, I wondered if I could get another chance?"

Micah thought about it for a bit but said nothing.

"It could be lunch. That's emotionally safe, and I promise I will not bore you with my talk of 'the man who got away.' Make that 'men.' I swear."

Hudson Ch'en was hot, very hot. Highly professional and respected in the not-for-profit and business community in South Florida. As a true sapiosexual, Micah liked guys with a brain. *Harvard grads with abs to the front of the line, please.*

Last year, Hud had gained some notoriety as part of a criminal investigation in Fort Lauderdale. The situation was unusual given that the foundation he headed was hyper about keeping a low profile. They met at last year's opening of *Seed Blood* at the museum. The guy Hud was with was a dick-- Roy, somebody, or other.

"So yeah, Royal Pig at, say, 1 PM?"

"Excellent. I'll be the one with the huge grin."

***

"Gonna need more brown drugs, M."

"Fresh pot on your credenza, Boss. Glad you survived the Big Easy."

"Barely escaped. Michele in yet?"

"Bright and early. She is working on canceling the next Saturday's opening and rescheduling.

"For your immediate attention: the press release... blah, blah blah... 'due to the untimely death of our Board Member'... etc. It's on your desk for your approval.

Rebecca said, "Switch 'untimely' to 'unfortunate,' please."

"Right. Michele and I will come up with the logistics plan for the rescheduled opening and...."

He thumbed through his tasks screen.

"The Ms. Arva memorial is tomorrow at the African-American Research Library and Cultural Center over on Sistrunk Boulevard. I typed up your remarks with a few changes – fact-checking mostly. A couple of media calls regarding the unexpected death – from tabloids to serious news."

"Thanks, M. I will get to all of that after the tour with the grade school kids. Chairman Billie and the Miccosukee Council are scheduled for 2 PM. I also need to speak to the installation crew. *The Aerie* statue in the last gallery is not lit correctly. It is one of the signature pieces of the *Tribal Blood* exhibit, and it needs to be just right."

"The team will be here at 1 PM. I told them about another walkthrough and a punch list with the CEO. You had something late afternoon, but I moved it. Let's see if we can get you out early after your travels."

"Not likely. I have so much to do, kiddo."

"Rebecca, may I take an extended lunch hour today, say an extra thirty minutes."

"Sure. Not my business, but a nooner?"

"I so wish. I need some no-strings sexing like you wouldn't believe, but this is most likely going nowhere."

"Hudson Ch'en?"

"Yep. A last Friday night reboot."

"Go easy on the boy, killer. He's had some tough times recently."

Micah shrugged and said, "Yeah, I guess I should be more patient. Break-ups, moving on, the rebound boyfriend– not easy to deal with."

"Hudson barely survived it all back about eight months or so."

Rebecca walked around her assistant, closed her office door, and turned around.

"Micah, how hard would it be for me to get into Ms. Arva's cottage?"

"Police took off the crime scene tape yesterday, but the place is locked."

Rebecca's tone was absolutely conspiratorial. She rolled her eyes up in an attempt at satire. "Too bad Arva didn't leave a key with a kindly neighbor who would look in on things from time to time or feed Rosie the cat."

Micah lowered his voice and said, “Text me later tonight, and let’s see what we can come up with.”

Michele knocked and was motioned in. She was carrying a large box.

Rebecca hooted, “Hot damn, the boots. The boots. Gimmie, gimmie.”

She put the box on the conference table and raised one hand. Micah slapped a sturdy letter opener into her palm with the force of a surgical nurse handing the doctor a scalpel. He went to her desk phone and punched in an international number. After a short time, amid the ripping and cutting, he directed the call to the hands-free conference line set on the table next to his hastily unpacking boss.

“You doing OK, Michele? Survive our New Orleans adventure?”

“Yes, Ms. Rebecca. One wild ride. Class tonight at the college will be so anticlimactic.

Michele turned to her co-worker. “Micah, I have a draft of the plan for the exhibit opening re-do and a report on who’s been contacted. I left it in your inbox for whenever you are ready.”

“Stéphane Rousteing.”

Rebecca was ecstatic as she pulled the last of the tissue paper from the calf-high, stiletto-heeled boots by the famous designer. She spoke to the caller.

“Stéphane, they are unbelievable. Darling, so gorgeous.”

The two staffers gasped as she stood the pair on the table. The exquisitely hand-beaded design in turquoise gold, orange, and brown featured the Native American Designer Jamie Okuma’s swallows, soaring and diving through intricate indigenous patterns. Black spike heels, blood-red soles, indeed a work of high fashion art.

The couturier said, “I am glad they arrived on time. Rebecca, my love, remember these are practically museum pieces. I absolutely forbid you to kill anyone with these.”

“You know me too well, my Darling. They so compliment the dress.”

"You're going with the Orlando Dugi on the gown for the opening of *Tribal Blood*, correct? His Navajo-inspired creations are breathtaking – all that desert wind and sun."

Rebecca sat and put on the boots. Micah took mobile phone shots of his devastating boss as she walked the imaginary runway. Michele observed and smiled broadly.

Rebecca said. "Stéphane, we are rescheduling the opening, so you must clear your calendar and get over here. The collection is mystical. Talking super-inspirational, my Darling, and not to be missed. We are planning a special showing for young designers."

"I will see what I can do, my love. My calendar is quite impossible. It all sounds entrancing."

"So you get here, you see all this fabulousness, and we create a fashion gala for your favorite charity at the museum."

"Something to think about, I will admit. Goodbye, my Darling. I will talk to you soon. Enjoy the Okumas."

***

The workday was a killer.

She texted Micah at 9 PM when she was just finishing the work of a museum CEO who had missed two days of work, hundreds of emails, and a dozen unfinished projects. The Miccosukee grade school children on their exclusive tour of the *Tribal Blood* exhibit were delightful.

Rebecca had three assistant curators and three graduate interns to field questions and explain the more fascinating parts of the exhibit on Native American Art. You could see the sense of pride growing in the conversations with the children. Consequently, Chairman Billie and his Miccosukee National Council members were pleased and promised additional sponsorship.

So, ready for some Nancy Drew?

Who is she?

God, you are so young

– iconic girl detective.

Ohhh Kayyy.

I'm here with the key and a flashlight.

Come on.

Rebecca stepped from her car and met her assistant in the gravel driveway, under the low-hanging branches in front of his cottage.

"Hey, M. Let's go around back. This is a criminal activity, I will admit."

Micah said, "Can always say I came over to get some of Ms. Rosie's cat food."

As if to add reassurance, Rosie rubbed against the closed screen door of Micah's place. She let forth a regal meow that could have only indicated disdain for her human subjects.

"No one ever comes down this street, although I did see a police cruiser late last night."

Rebecca looked into the overhanging trees and said, "No sign of tree-climbing small zombies, right?"

"Correct. I like this neighborhood on the river because it's so lush and wild, but that intruder last Friday really creeps me out."

They mounted the back porch steps, disturbing a curious opossum who dashed into the bushes. Micah opened the back door, and they stepped into the kitchen area.

He whispered, "What are we looking for?"

"Haven't the foggiest idea, to be honest, but here is what I am thinking: Ms. Arva knew something about the whereabouts of Victoria Ricci, and the killers want our Diva. I suspect the motives are greed, but that's as far as I go.

"Arva wanted me to know about her relationship with the reclusive, elderly opera star to protect Victoria or at least to contact her. So, I suspect there may be clues among her possessions about finding the Diva. That's what I'm thinking anyway."

They walked through the living room, the bedroom, the dining area, and the front foyer. The flashlight's light beam swept over the furniture, hardwood floors, window seats, and walls hung with personal memorabilia. Rebecca tapped for hidden partitions, snooped for attachments to the backs of framed photographs, and joggled for loose fireplace bricks in an attempt to find some clue to the Frozen Diva.

"A diary would be nice." She said aloud.

Micah said, "Might be one up there."

The living room of the cottage had a unique feature. It was actually two stories with an upper gallery. This long, open balcony lined with nine-foot overstuffed bookcases wrapped around three sides of the room. The fourth section held a small nook with windows facing the river. An iron circular stairway led up to the library space from the lower living area. Micah led the way.

"The woman certainly had an eclectic taste in literature. Some of these volumes are pretty old and on all sorts of topics."

"She also spoke French, Italian, and German," Rebecca said as she ran a finger over the titles. "Look for opera, a Ricci biography, or a photo album. A diary or journal notebooks would be ideal."

"Check it out." Micah pointed to a row of very old tomes with dark blue covers, all written by Carolyn Keene. He announced, "The Mystery at Lilac Inn, The Password to Larkspur Lane, The Message in the Hollow Oak, The Mystery....'"

"My favorite is the very first one."

An unexpected male voice came from beneath them. Micah dropped the flashlight, which fell to the rug one story below.

The silhouette, framed in the kitchen doorway, stepped forward to pick up the dropped light. The intruder shined the beam on the two startled sleuths on the upper balcony. Behind the shaft of hyper-illumination, he remained in darkness.

"The Secret of the Old Clock. Like the antique timepiece there just past your heads."

"Hud. Holy fuck. You scared the shit out of us."

"Sorry, Rebecca. I saw mysterious lights coming out through the windows. Then there's your car next door. I figured you would be among the snoopers. A little of the ole B and E, my friends?"

Micah said, "Hud, what brings you to this side of town?"

"My office is just across the river, as you know, but my gym is just to the South of here. I guess I wanted to see you one more time today, Mike."

Rebecca said to her fellow conspirator in a stage whisper, "Oh, Mike, is it? I see. Very interesting."

Micah did a do-not-embarrass-me face.

Hudson Ch'en moved the light to highlight a yellow and gold banjo clock that hung in a space between the bookcases.

There's your quarry, Nancy, my girl."

Micah said, who you calling a 'Nancy?'"

He lifted the timepiece from the wall. Rebecca took down the first volume of "The Nancy Drew Mysteries," The two of them descended the staircase guided by the beam Hud moved in front of them.

He was still in his gym togs, looked muscley, and smelled super man-sexy. His almond-shaped eyes almost glowed in the dark, complete with long black lashes. Hud gave each of them the European triple kiss, in part as a greeting and in part as an apology for frightening them.

"Umm, you're a nice scary guy." Micah placed a hand against Hud's cheek as they kissed. Rebecca thought, *Apparently, the lunch went well.*

She placed the antique timepiece on the dining room table. "I hate to interrupt you guys, but I need the light over here. Investigating, remember?"

The clock's case was wooden and featured a round, glass-covered, painted Roman numeral dial atop a long-waisted throat flanked by curved and pierced brass frets. A rectangular pendulum box, like the throat, was ornamented with reverse-painted glass panels. The illustration was of a knight standing next to a woman. The cavalier used a long spear to hold a second armored figure at bay. Musical notes climbed up the painted glass inserts of the neck, rising to the clock face. A finial mounted at the pinnacle of the case took the form of a golden chalice.

"Hey, can I see that?" The Asian American jock said. He examined the treasure up close.

"It's Parsifal. The story, I mean. The knight who sought the Holy Grail and the 'Spear of Destiny.' Wagner."

The opera buff pointed to the illustration on the pendulum box. "The Maestro's best composition and a complete spiritual revelation--spellbinding but highly controversial.

Micah said, "Such an intellect. What's the 'Spear of Destiny,' smart guy?"

"In the Gospel of St. John, it is the lance that pierced the side of Jesus on the cross." He hugged his buddy in the dark and did an ear lobe nuzzle.

Rebecca examined the piece and flew through Google on her phone. She said, "This is pretty valuable. Looks like it's from the studios of Simon Willard of Grafton, Massachusetts, near Boston-- late 18th century. They only made a limited number of them."

She turned it over and opened the door at the bottom. Nothing but clockwork.

"With apologies to Carolyn Keene, there seems to be no clue in this clock. No treasure maps or secret passwords or...." Micah did not finish.

"Look."

Rebecca's immaculately manicured blood-red index fingernail pointed to the back of the hinged door.

À Arva avec amour.

VR

15 rue Crespin du Gast 75011 Paris

"Jackpot."

Chapter Twenty-Four: Albert

PALAIS GARNIER, PARIS, AUGUST 1940

The opera star closed the dressing room door after her and called her maid.

"Astrid, do not let anyone in. I need some time to be alone."

"As you wish, *Fräulein*."

Astrid Cole had been Victoria Ricci's dresser and maid since the diva had come from Italy to Germany. They had become close friends and confidants since their collaboration began in 1935. The young woman traveled with her employer as the star's popularity continued to rise inside and outside Europe.

"Wagner, Wagner, Wagner. You would think no other great composers had ever seen the light of day." Victoria slammed her wig and headdress onto the dressing table. Her famous Italian temper erupted like a minor Vesuvius. "I am sick to death of these Teutonic heroes. Swords, spears, breastplates, helmets – how is one supposed to sing in all that metal?

"Give me a ballgown, a kimono, the trappings of an Egyptian princess... national music, my ass. My vocal cords feel like they have been through a cheese grater."

"I would not say that too loud, my dear. Keep your opinions to yourself."

Victoria threw an angry glance at her maid, who unbuttoned her Isolde gown.

"I am sorry, my lady, the Reichsminister insisted...."

Victoria threw up a hand at the handsome, uniformed government official.

"Albert, I need some time to myself. All this is much too much. If I am agitated, it affects my performance. I have six more nights of this

Germanic drivel. I cannot be expected to give a bravura performance night after night while being trotted out like a trophy for the Reich."

She stepped behind the dressing screen and struggled out of the cumbersome cape and heavy medieval dress.

"Victoria, you must keep negative comments about Hitler's much-loved composer to yourself if you are to remain his favorite soprano. He rarely embraces a non-German when choosing his artists.

And as for your popularity, the world must see the Führer as a patron of only the finest of the international artists. We are Germans, after all – Mozart, Hyden, Beethoven..."

"You all are German, Albert. I am Italian, and you know how he feels about my people. He thinks Mussolini is a buffon. He uses him to his advantage. And he is not wrong. Il Duce is an idiot, a monstrous thug. But the Italian leader commands a huge following."

"Victoria, do not upset yourself further, my dear."

"Ha! And I am Hitler's guinea pig, Albert, and you most of all know that. Those dreadful treatments are painful and interfere with my art. I must sing. I must act. It is my calling. There can be no impediments to my voice, my music."

"The Peter Pan Project is an essential work of science, my dear. Think of it as having the power to extend your career by generations. Your performances will last into the next century. *La Gloriosa*, has become *Der Herrliche* the German National Treasure."

"You heard him in there... using my stage for his Wagner and that hateful propaganda. I will not attend another post-performance reception if my art is to be twisted into supporting the racist programs of the Reich."

She emerged in a beautiful dressing gown and sat at her table. She pinned up her blonde hair and began to remove her makeup. The National Socialists' Chief Architect stood behind her and attempted to calm the enraged star by massaging her neck and shoulders. She looked at him in the mirror. *God, he was the most handsome and intelligent man she had ever met. Why did he have to be a fascist?*

They were quiet. Albert brought his face to the back of her neck and began to kiss Victoria, moving his mouth to her shoulder and parting the robe to expose more of her beauty. She raised a hand to his cheek.

"Is it true?"

He looked up at her reflection. He knew this was coming.

She turned to face him.

"Margarete."

"What about her?"

She erupted again. "You cad. You know perfectly well what I am talking about. Margarete, your wife. Rumor is the elite of the Reich have finally accepted her, and Hitler wants her at your side. He insists on putting an end to our affair. He wants you to part with your Neapolitan whore. Such hypocrisy – this complete sham of the inner circle to look respectable."

Speer felt himself losing his patience with this Italian firebrand. Many considered his marriage to Magarete Weber, including his family, as an alliance well below his social class, a step-down. The Webers were considered the epitome of the bourgeois in the days of the Weimar Republic.

"Hah! Am I to be packed off to Bavaria or some such? Imprisoned on a mountain top somewhere and preserved like a specimen with important medical value...."

"Victoria, I had no choice in this. You know...."

He attempted a tender caress, but she pushed him back in anger. "*Merde*, my love. You are one of the only ones that ever stands up to him. He adores you and your work. Be honest with him and demand he accept our relationship."

"Victoria, I cannot divorce her. It would reflect on the Reich. Furthermore, they would never accept my being married to an...."

"Italian? You all are pigs with your racial purity. I am sick to death of it. That man out there has raped Paris, the 'City of Light,' its people and its art. Tonight's German cacophony in the Paris Opera House is an outrageous insult."

Victoria slammed the objects on her dressing table to underscore her anger and outrage.

"National purity of music? Who is the racist now, my dear?"

He clenched his fists and continued, "I was going to say they would never accept my being married to an artist. And furthermore, your accusations are skewed. Paris surrendered. It was declared an open city."

She pulled him to her.

"Albert, take me away. Let's leave."

"*Meine Liebe*, what are you saying to me?"

"The Berlin Olympics brought you to the world stage, Albert. The Zeppelinfeld Stadium, your plans for the capital, all of that. You are known everywhere for your wonderful architecture and design. We could flee into exile. Look at Hesse."

Now it was the German's turn to contend, and he stepped back horrified. "I have no intention of spending my life in British incarceration."

"Well then, how about Marlene, Eric von Stroheim, Kurt Weil, the other artists, the scientists, the writers? Leaving by the hundreds... the world has accepted them as heroes."

The Diva continued, "Hitler's pogrom against any art that is considered degenerate is total megalomania. His personal taste in painting, music, theater, and film has become the law. Look at how your precious Führer has seduced Leni. Frau Riefenstahl is absolutely spellbound by Nazi power and glory."

The German lowered his voice. "You speak treason, Victoria. Hitler represents the fulfillment of everything I have dreamed of as a nations builder-- a glorious land of architectural monuments and public works that will remain for thousands upon thousands of years, rivaling Ancient Greece and Rome. We have projects throughout Germany in the making that will transform the empire of the Reich. Tonight, he spoke of a new vision for Paris. I cannot abandon this."

"Power and fame... at what cost? We are at war with the world, for heaven's sake. Many will die. So much will be destroyed. Men and women of conscience have left Europe in droves."

The passion in her voice was tempered with loving reasoning as she pleaded, "Albert, we are both gifted artists. You are the best architect in the entire world. We can go somewhere else and be recognized. Hitler's visions of glory are rotten from the inside. You know that, my love."

"Victoria. I urge you to reconsider or keep your opinions to yourself. There is much to be won if we have the patience to wait and believe in our leader. All of this is temporary. The vision of German glory goes far beyond Adolph Hitler. You will see. We can work out an arrangement to be together."

She said nothing.

He turned away, trying to control his own emotions and come to terms with this firebrand. "Will I see you at the *Musée du Louvre*? The reception is mostly in your honor."

Victoria Ricci looked at Albert Speer with deep sadness but made no immediate reply. Then she spoke.

"Won't you be ashamed to be seen with your harlot, Reichminister Speer? There will be talk." She brushed her hair emphatically.

Speer reached into his jacket, removed a flat case, and tossed it on the dressing table. The proud Reichsminister walked out of the star's dressing room.

The Diva collapsed onto her chair in heartbreaking tears and sobs. Astrid stepped back into the dressing room and tried to console her mistress.

There was a brisk but determined series of three knocks on the star's dressing room door. The SS officer and personal physician to Adolph

Hitler, Karl Brant, entered and got immediately to the point, opening his medical bag. Astrid went into the bathroom again.

"How are you feeling, my dear? Your performance tonight in *Tristan and Isolde* was magnificent. Finally, Wagner in Paris – a triumph in so many ways."

Doktor Brant continued, "Please roll up your sleeve."

"I am tired, Herr Doktor, but otherwise well."

The physician swabbed Victoria's arm and held the syringe to the light, flicking it with the opposite hand's fingers. "You are working too hard, my dear. You seem a bit overwrought with the stress of your artistry."

Victoria flipped open the flat jewel case left by Speer as the doctor plunged the syringe into her arm, administering the elixir.

The necklace was breathtaking. A jeweled, art deco peacock suspended between cords of emeralds, rubies, and lapis lazuli. The size of the masterpiece would allow it to sit just above the neckline of her most elaborate evening gowns.

"Ahh, *La Gloriosa*," Brant said as he took the piece from the case and held it up to the light. "The House of Fabergé-- you must wear this to the reception at the Louvre tonight. Each time Speer sees you in this, he will be assured of your undying love. You still belong to him, *Fräulein*."

Victoria sneered at the irony of the adjective– "undying" indeed.

Brant bowed. "I will leave you then, my dear, to finish your dressing. It pleases me to be your escort tonight."

After he left, Victoria said, "Reception in my honor, my ass. It is propaganda – The Nazi Party with its foot on the neck of the French." She wiped the tears and stood to select her gown for the evening.

"*Fräulein* Ricci, if I may speak frankly, you have been in much sadness for a long time. I may be able to help."

Victoria dropped her hands from her face and looked carefully at her friend and confidant. It was almost as if she saw this coming. Astrid was a woman of secrets. All those flimsy explanations when she was late for work and the sudden need to leave quickly, sometimes with a mysterious parcel of "laundry." Victoria's gaze was penetrating as if she were seeing the woman for the first time.

Astrid Cole took a deep breath and continued in hushed tones. "There is someone I would like you to meet privately. I will set it up. Her name is Elyesa Bergh. Please keep this between you and me."

Chapter Twenty-Five: Montgomery

DJIBOUTI, THE HORN OF AFRICA

"Absolutely no way, Mr. Gadarn. My advice is that you leave the area. The base is totally off-limits to you and any other journalists. There are operational security concerns."

"Major, It's important to let the American people know what goes on here. Camp Montgomery has been shrouded in secrecy for more than a decade. If the tax-payers back home are to support this new kind of warfare, they need to understand its full impact – drone warfare has been a game-changer."

"Not possible, young man. Members of the press need to understand that sensitive counterterrorism missions are just that – top secret. Our efforts are focused on the prevention of extremist footholds in the region. Leaks will result in complications and possible mission failure."

"Come on, Major. There is public skepticism from the get-go. For instance, the Pentagon has labeled Camp Montgomery a temporary facility. How is that possible with all of the expansion, infrastructure investment, and increase in personnel? Can you deny that this is the US military's first permanent drone war base? Montgomery's airborne systems are tasked with detecting, reporting, and tracking enemy aerial movements in the Horn. Everyone knows that."

"Mr. Gadarn, with all due respect, and I mean that. I follow your reporting. You take incredible risks, and your stories are about the civilians who suffer and die because of the continuing political crisis in this part of the world. Your reporting is fearless and very much needed in these times of lies and deception in politics and the media. But..."

Major Brian Anthony Porfilio looked at the dauntless reporter and sighed. "Mr. Gadarn, you just want to get into Yemen. I'm afraid we cannot embed any journalists right now in our monitoring forces as the conflict has recently heated up in the western part of the country. That's the long and short of it, Sir."

Mark held the gaze of the Camp Commander in an attempt to figure out his next move.

“Furthermore, we are attempting to warn all US nationals in the region to be on the alert for attempts at violence and abduction organized by any one of at least fifteen militias with hostility toward US citizens. Sir, you are in a dangerous part of the world and in grave personal danger.”

“Major, a few things here. My East African Bureau Chief can assure you that I can survive in combat and in situations of extreme uncertainty and high risk. Also, I excelled at my boot camp training before being inserted into the strike forces around Falluja and Aleppo in the Syrian conflict.

“Next, the only way to stop atrocities in the region is to allow the world to understand what is going on. Americans have attempted to be the champions of human rights, sometimes badly, but accurate information is critical to the effort. I’m talking about violent crime, torture, and murder directed against the innocents, like children.”

The major’s composure was slipping as he continued with the obstinate journalist. “Not gonna happen, Sir. You’d be a threat to your own safety and the security of my operations in the region. My advice is to stay with CBN’s media team, stay out of Yemen, or go home. With your reputation, you are gold for terrorists and pirates from Eritrea to Somalia and all the way to Nigeria. Huge price on your ass... sorry, I meant to say head.”

“Major Porfilio, I can assure you....”

“Mr. Gadarn, my staffer, will escort you to your vehicle.”

“And off the Base?”

“And off the Base. Please, for the sake of your loved ones, go home, young man.”

“Thank you, Commander.”

***

“Tough interview?”

"I always try the official channels first, Marine Corporal ..." Mark read the soldier's name off his nameplate. "Tersegno. Then pretty much go my own way."

The soldier escorting Mark said, "Yeah, 'Old Steel Balls' is pretty hard to deal with if he has already decided the issue. Maneuvering through all the armed conflict and terrorism in this part of the world calls for firm and unshakeable leadership."

Overhead jets circled the nearby landing strip while tarmacs and roadways were busy with the traffic of the most strategic US outpost in East Africa. The bright sun was unmerciful on the buildings and shelters, which housed personnel, base offices, service facilities, and weaponry. A fleet of various military aircraft was lined up in readiness. Off in the distance, the base's flotilla also stood in an advanced state of preparation on the bay.

The young Marine police officer turned the jeep into the visitor's parking area and headed to Mark's SUV. He pulled up and parked.

"Don't suppose you care to answer a few questions about the Base? I can keep your identity out of it."

The man grinned. "Negative, Sir. A journalist shows up at Base Camp Montgomery, talks to two people, and comes away with sensitive information. Hmm, now, who could have leaked this vital intelligence?

"Despite your well-earned respect for your bravery in saving those soldiers in Syria last year, still, I gotta say...." Jack Tersegno brought his face close to Mark's as he stopped the jeep. He smiled as he said, "Go fuck yourself."

Mark smiled at the soldier's frankness.

"Heard about you, Mr. Gadarn. An entire special briefing just about your activities and the concerns of the military over the controversies you create... You are a huge intelligence risk. Gotta say I admire your bravery, but no, I have applied for promotion, and talking to you could screw it up."

"OK. I took a shot. Thanks anyway. But Corporal, I have another favor to ask, man to man."

The Marine cocked an eyebrow and said, "And just would that be?"

"I have no family to speak of back in the US, and like your boss, CBN doesn't have the first idea on how to keep me in line." The journalist shrugged. "That's just the way it is."

"Go on."

"You hear anything about me... you know, of an unusual nature, my friend in Fort Lauderdale is Rebecca Quinto. Easy to find."

Jack reached for a pen and a scrap paper in his rucksack. "Naw, no paper, friend." Mark took the pen and wrote Rebecca's name on the heel of the soldier's right hand.

Mark swung his legs out of the passenger's side and was about to alight when Tersegno grabbed his arm.

"Listen, bud, *Ta Netjeru*."

"What?"

"It's a bar in Old Town. Ask in the *souk*. Gets interesting after midnight."

"Thanks, Corporal."

"It's Jack. You're welcome. And go native... shabby dirty. You show up looking like a fitness model on tour, and there will be trouble like you cannot imagine." The soldier's eyes lingered over the handsome journalist as they exchanged a departing handshake.

"Appreciate it, Jack."

"Stay alive, big guy. Shame to waste all of that."

Chapter Twenty-Six: God's Land

DJIBOUTI, THE HORN OF AFRICA

"Get the fuck out of here. God, you smell like camel shit."

The street ruffian opened a leather pouch, hung from shoulder to hip containing bazaar trinkets, and bowed in his stained, nomadic robes.

"Your pardon, *effendi*. I have some unusual gifts for your patrons. Please allow me to pass. You will receive my thanks and Allah's blessing for helping this poor unfortunate one."

The barman questioned the vagrant in Arabic, to which he received no response. The ragged man's French was too continental with few of the guttural idioms found in this part of the world – another recognizable fake.

"Whadda' you some sort of comic?" The big man shook his head while considering what he was dealing with. Finally, he nodded, understanding what was going on.

"Thought so," He hooked a thumb towards the rear of the bar. "Back behind the archway and find the darkest corner. Keep your eyes low and speak to no one. Phew. Some get up, Ali Baba."

Mark moved through the low-ceilinged, crowded tavern, which was extremely hard to find in the twisted alleys of the old city. He was jostled by a few folks who were clearly military despite their casual dress. Locals of every ethnicity mingled with Americans and Europeans, seeking an oasis from the anxieties associated with powderkeg sitting.

The alcove was dark, and the corner table was even more obscure. Someone brought him a bitter-tasting beer.

"Doing blackface, Champ? Pretty controversial these days, even over here."

Mark looked up at the woman who settled into the seat opposite him. She was in mufti but oozed military.

"It's dirt. I'm dirty. Been working hard."

"Ha. In that getup? Doing what? Mucking camel shit? Jack told you to hide your sexy. Good job, but go easy on the beast cologne next time."

Mark shrugged and looked over the figure before him as much as the low light would allow."

"I'm Sid Collins. I fly planes. Between jerking off over your pictures he found online, Jack Tersegno told me who you are and that you want some transport. The Seg-boy likes 'em fit, I will say that."

The aviator laughed heartily. Mark noticed the black woman's tribal tattoos snaking up her arms and in and out of her khaki tank top. Her hair was buzzed short. Lean and mean, she had the hard look of an inmate or a cast member of "Mad Max."

"Sid, can you get me inside? This fucking shit about reporting on the multi-ethnic tourism business in the 'French Hong Kong of Africa' is a waste of time and, God knows, not the story. I need some in-country time. Can you get me behind battle lines? Unofficially, I mean."

"The whole fuckin' country is behind battle lines. Famine, disease, death, and torture. You man enough to see the underbelly of what we got over here? The terrorists and religious zealots are the most extreme on the planet's surface. Public executions are as popular as Monday Night Football. Some fucked up evil shit in the desert. Makes the Vietnam War look like a Sunday picnic, Champ."

"You know as well as I that Porfilio wants to keep me out of Yemen because what I may find may impact world support for the Saudi coalition. He's a DC man through and through. He will prevent any reporting that presents the US side of the conflict in an unsympathetic light."

"Gadarn, you realize that you going into Yemen is tantamount to painting a red flag on your ass saying 'Kill me,' or worse, 'Kidnap me.' Talking captured, tried, and executed by some religious assholes.

"Embedded, you got the protection of the best troops on the globe. Non-embedded, you are a fuckin' target. Independent journalists get fucked every day in these times and places, wasted by the enemy and also by friendly fire."

Mark said, "Yeah, outrageous. Two-thousand-seven, Iraq War, those independent journalists were killed by U.S. troops when a helicopter gunship pilot mistook their camera for a grenade launcher. I know the risks, Sid."

"Hold on a sec."

The pilot switched her attention to someone lurking in the darkness.

"Something I can do for you, Youssouf? I thought you were told to stay outta my place."

Sid Collins addressed a shady-looking character who seemed to melt into the shadows of the candlelit recess. He nearly toppled an empty chair at the only other unoccupied table as he came forward. The man was tall and lean, dressed like a local. He said what sounded like a protest in Arabic.

Collins stood and snarled, "C'meer, you piece of crud."

She clocked him with a hard right to the jaw and side-kicked him into a crumpled heap as he crashed into a pillar, taking down a stack of chairs with him.

The commotion brought the barman Mark met at the entrance. Together, he and Sid Collins raised the fallen man and prepared to eject him out through the street door.

"Hold it, ass wipe."

The military woman reached into the belt of the stunned and struggling man to extract a deadly, curved dagger. She frisked him for additional weapons.

Inserting the tip of the blade into Youssouf's left nostril, she announced, "Never. You fuckin' hear me? *Never* come into my bar again. Hell, if I ever see you on the street, I will wipe the city walls with your blood. Got that, dick head?"

She turned to her employee and said, "Get him the fuck out of my sight, Frank." The barman yanked the spy out of the enclosure and in the direction of the street exit.

First Lieutenant Collins resumed her seat and slapped the dagger on the table.

"Little trick I learned from watching *Chinatown* about eight hundred times at the base cinema. Shoulda ripped some nose flesh from that prick."

"Pretty educated spy. Knows English."

Sid took a swig of her whiskey and assumed a world-weary expression. She shook her head and explained.

"Joseph Stapleton, aka Youssouf Kamil, is from East Orange, New Jersey. Affluent family to boot. Radicalized online by ISIL but fell off with them. Fucker's been selling information for a few years to any side that pays. He has a special gift for melting into the shadows of this asshole city. Step-daddy is retired army. Fuckin' rich boy traitor. That stinks, Champ. It really does."

"I wanna win one for our side, Sid."

"We all do, buddy. The question is, what side is that?"

"The side that says that a free people have the right to self-determination and the test of good government is how a country treats those most in need."

The pilot looked around and said nothing for a few minutes. She took a deep breath and went eye-to-eye with the journalist.

"Jesus. Just what I need: a fuckin' utopian. How soon can you be ready to leave?"

"Immediately."

"Good, no time for delays. You realize that Kamil knows who you are, and his masters have you in their sites – a shit-assed cell with your name on it. So, disappearing is a good thing."

Mark nodded.

"Meet me here tomorrow night at 11. Alley behind the bar. I'll bring an aircrew suit. We do some supply flights at night in certain locations when nobody's looking. You a jumper?"

Mark nodded.

"Good. We'll get you close to Ta'izz in the east. You hit the ground, and you're on your own. Getting out is another issue, Champ. Hope you can figure it out.

"I've been in tight spots before, Sid. I can do this."

She looked at the man in front of her with his high ideals all set to drop into a war-ravaged land.

"Yeah, Champ. I believe you can."

"See you tomorrow.

"Hold on. I have a request. You get over there and try to find someone for me."

"You got it. Who?"

My girlfriend, Susan Russell. She's a pediatrician with Doctors Without Borders. Her medical facility was bombed three months ago. She's alive but can't get out. Last I heard, she was helping out at an abandoned Red Cross facility in the port city of Mocha, which is near Ta'izz. You get out, she gets out. Deal?"

"I'll do what I can to get us both to safety, Lieutenant. Tell me, your bar... what does its name *Ta Netjeru* mean?"

"Ha! Yeah, I'm a part-owner with Frank of this little piece of trash. We like the B movie look of the place. Cut-throats, spies, and ladies of the evening tucked in the back alleys of danger and intrigue. All we need is a Marlene Dietrich perched on the bar singing with runs in her fishnets, Right?"

Mark laughed.

"*Ta Netjeru?* It means God's Land."

Chapter Twenty-Seven: Davia

TA'IZZ, YEMEN

The large canvas equipment bag stacked in the rear of the pile of supplies began to move. An index finger appeared from inside and eased the zipper opening. Then a hand, reaching out, finished the job. Mark crawled out.

He adjusted his red and white *keffiyeh* and the heavy black cord, the *agal*, that held it in place on his head. He draped the scarf from shoulder to shoulder to protect all but his eyes from the sand storm that whipped through the alleys and slammed into the highlands, cradling the city of Ta'izz. Sid Collins's helicopter disappeared into the night sky as figures moved quickly from the rural village of Al Misrakh to take possession of the supplies she left behind. Not recognizing Mark, they ran him off.

Rather than head right into the former Yemeni capital, Mark decided to tour the surrounding villages. There, he would find the story of the people's struggle to survive amid the chaos of "holy war."

In Ad Dimnah, he came upon a neighborhood where the people were being forced from their homes by the armed insurgents of the civil war. They escaped with only what they could carry. They fled to the countryside, where they found no food, water, or sources of income. He saw many children with swollen bellies from malnutrition. Charity and relief stations were quickly overwhelmed whenever supplies arrived. In some areas, many of the civilians staggered through the streets as if in a daze. One woman mourned her dead child on her knees in the square while family members urged her to prepare the body for burial.

The town of Al Abbed had been entirely wiped out by cholera. Warnings were posted in Arabic and French on wells and roadways throughout the village. He found no schools open, no police, and rarely a sign of government. He encountered brigades of workers carting loads of corpses into the desert to be buried.

Wandering into the brown-bricked city, Mark found a ruin near the Mudhaffar Mosque and tuckered in among a bedraggled group of the homeless. They filled the spaces of the bombed-out houses amid fallen roof beams and collapsed walls. The dark nooks were filled with many sad and desperate eyes. He checked under his robes for his man bag – some rations, water, first aid, and his mobile. He reached down to his ankle holster. The dagger was still there.

Sleep came after a restless and watchful hour.

In the morning, he wandered closer to the old citadel, which sat on a mountaintop near the Ta'izz City Center. He hunted for food and water. Mark needed to find his contact, Abdullah Nehan. The man was a former coffee grower from the mountains who now helped out in a clinic run by Doctors Without Borders. The fortress compound towered over the city. It was heavily armed and off-limits from its base to the soaring lookout.

There were violent outbursts day and night in and around the city. Bombings created panic and unrest. When the smoke and debris stopped, the dispersing battle smolderings revealed many dead and injured. Soldiers in a variety of uniforms under many insignias marched and fought in the streets, door to door, town to town. Whatever could burn was burning.

Near the Mosque of Al-Ashrafiya, he found Abdullah.

"No, you must go, *effendi*. Yemen is torn by deadly war. There is nothing here but death and destruction." Abdullah sat on a pile of rubble and tossed pebbles into the street.

"I have come from the hospital up the street. My daughter was in the isolation ward being treated for cholera. The bombs fell before I got there this morning. I searched through the fire and smoke, but she is gone."

The former CBN operative sat amid the ruins of his city with only a few scraggly palm trees, reminding observers that this square was once a tropical jewel of the now war-torn city. His grief was immense, and his loss seemed overpowering.

"Each day, I search amid the bricks and concrete in hopes of finding her remains. So many dead. So many to be buried."

Mark said, "Come, my friend. Come away from this place."

***

They ran and dodged, covering their heads. Bombs and gunfire raged all around. Abdulla and Mark took refuge in a wrecked house in the shadow of the ancient stronghold.

"I have lost all means of contact with the network, Mark. The reports I have sent them in the past have been a source of suspicion by the military in the city. This rebel group is opposed to the West."

In the gloom of the battered house, Mark saw a huddled group around a small fire.

Abdullah nodded to a woman in a dusty abaya and hijab. "This is my sister-in-law, Yasmin, and her children. My brother was killed two weeks ago. I have tried to get them to go up into the mountains or to the south, where the government still has a presence in Aden. Yasmin is much too afraid to leave this place."

The woman spoke in halting French peppered with Arabic, which her brother-in-law translated. "I have four boys, each over the age of twelve years, *effendi*. The militia will take them and make them soldiers to die in this ridiculous, endless war. And I fear for my daughters, also. In the mountains, they will raid us. On the roads, they will kill us for what little we have. They are godless dogs."

Her oldest, Davia, held one of her siblings on a low bench in the back of the hut. Her dark eyes were at once murderous and desperate. The family was covered by a pall of starvation that intensified daily.

"Hunger is ever-present. It brings weakness and disease. Why run and risk more suffering? My husband built this house. We will die together on our small plot of God's earth."

Mark said, "Abdullah. You stay here and protect your family. I will search for food."

Davia handed her little sister to one of her brothers and said, "I am coming with you." She began to pull on men's clothing, most likely her father's. Abdulla said, "One does not go out as a female in these times."

Mark looked at the girl. She appeared to be all of sixteen.

"You must stay with your family."

"No, you do not know Ta'izz. I can show you where the food is. They destroyed my school and killed my father, friends, and teachers. I must do this, sir. Our survival depends on what food we can steal. Come with me as an equal, or I will go alone."

As they left the hovel, they did not know they were being followed. A tall man in a black cotton *galabieh*, the robe of a peasant, kept them in view as they made their way into the city, ducking in and out of the buildings and piles of rubble.

***

"The soldiers in the fort of Ta'izz have food, but the supply trucks are guarded once they make it up the mountain road in the space that used to be the governor's garden. At this time of the evening prayers, only one guard can be found watching the trucks. You must do as I say, *effendi*. Use this sack to get as much as you can, and get back down the mountainside by this goat trail."

They climbed into the walled garden, and Davia pointed to the guard just ahead, relieving himself not far from a supply container, recently hauled up the mountain behind a tractor-trailer from the port of Mocha on the Red Sea.

Davia grabbed at the dried shrubs that remained in the garden and managed to pull together what appeared to be a pile of kindling. She stepped from behind the broken wall and gathered more sticks as she approached the guard. As she came closer, he ordered her to stop. The girl shook her head and pleaded to be allowed nearer.

She seemed to stumble and drop her parcel. Mark could see that her robe was open. The soldier approached and removed Davia's headscarf. Her long black hair cascaded to her waist. As the soldier pulled her into a rough embrace, Davia pretended to enjoy their contact. She turned the soldier, limiting his line of vision, and motioned to Mark.

He found very little inside the storage container but began to fill the shoulder bag with whatever he could. He tightened and tied the drawstring after cramming in two loaves of hard bread and whatever other supplies would fit. As he stepped from the chamber, he drew his knife.

Davia was against the nearest garden wall and was hoisted up against the soldier's body as Mark emerged. The rapist looked in Mark's direction and then cried out as Davia plunged her dagger into his midsection and pushed him off her. He fell into the dirt.

They ran.

In a mad dash, they went up over the wall and down the winding path that led to the city below. The alleys twisted before them as they dashed over rubble and bundles of ragged people. Near a cross street, three soldiers stepped out of a doorway and blocked their escape.

"He is an American. He will bring much in ransom. Take him." Youssef Kamil, the stalker in black robes from *Ta Netjeru*, cried out from behind the soldiers.

Mark swung the heavy bag and took out two of the militiamen. A well-placed maneuver sent one soldier careening into a mangled metal beam. He flopped on the ground, struggling to get up and recover his rifle.

Davia ran in a crazed frenzy at the third, slashing with her bloodied knife. Kamil stepped back and seemed to contemplate his next move. Mark did the best he could in the cumbersome robes definitely not made for martial arts street fighting.

The food bag tumbled away, and both Kamil and Davia made a grab for it.

The fierce young woman thought, *It means the life of my family.*

Youssef managed to retrieve the bundle, but the determined Davia jumped on his back with the knife at his throat. He swung the satchel of provisions, and his attacker dove for it.

Mark yelled, "Go, go, go."

The girl wrested the sack from the spy and raced up the street. Gunfire followed her. She stumbled, righted herself, and dashed away.

Pigs who cannot shoot to save their miserable lives.

Mark faced each of his three attackers as they circled him. Kamil held back. "Do not shoot him. He is valuable."

A deep voice barked in Arabic, and the soldiers came to attention. An officer exchanged words with the spy and waved him back with palpable disdain. The ends of the officer's headscarf were tucked at each shoulder of his uniform, hiding his lower face. He now turned to his comrades who were preventing Mark's escape. He had their undivided attention. The man spoke to Mark in English.

"This is not good. I have one stabbed soldier. He is dead. And I am missing some vital rations, Mr. Gadarn. I am very displeased with you. You violate the hospitality rules of my country with much disrespect. Extremely bad, I am afraid."

The man oozed danger, and death cloaked his ice-cold demeanor. "What is one to make of this? American journalists who fight like ... um. Who is it?" The officer looked perplexed at his colleagues.

Youssef said, "*'Abtal khariqin*, my General."

"Yes, yes, a superhero. You are a comic book guy? What is this world coming to?

He was larger and evidently more experienced than his young recruits. Mark could see from his bearing that this was no grunt. He spoke with authority and moved with the measured grace of an athlete.

"American, I invite you to be the guest of the Scourge of God. You will find the accommodations at the citadel quite disappointing, I am afraid, Mr. Gadarn. But, you will not be with us for too long a time, my friend. What do you say, hero guy?"

He took a step toward Mark, who brandished his knife.

The General turned his back, saying, "Come, come, Captain America. This will never...."

He handed his rifle to one of his subordinates, approached Mark, and stopped. He turned his back to the journalist, spun, and slammed a roundhouse kick to the side of Mark's head, completing his sentence through clenched teeth.

"... do."

An unconscious Mark hit the ground.

Chapter Twenty-Eight: Captives

THE CITADEL OF TA'IZZ, YEMEN

Darkness.

Mark struggled to regain consciousness but failed to reach any visual clarity. He realized that he was restrained and hooded. The floor and the wall of his confinement were hard. He could hear the soft moaning and chatter from other prisoners around him. The voices were female comforters and weeping children.

"Sir, are you awake?" A whisper. Close.

"Who are you? Can you get this hood off me?"

"No sir, I am restrained, likewise. It would appear you have been treated harshly."

Mark felt the return of pain in his torso and face. Yeah, he remembered the three guards, the spy, the General, and the kick. Fuck!

I hope Davia got back to her family.

My name is Amat Al Kindi. I am a school teacher from Sana'a. The rebels captured me, my fellow teachers, and forty-seven of our students. We will be sold as slaves."

Jesus, what a fuckin' nightmare.

The woman continued, "You are an American. You will be ransomed."

Mark heard movement in the space around him, murmuring and the soft rattle of chains. Somewhere, a clanking door moved on hinges. He felt a boot in his ribs. "Stand up, unholy dog."

He struggled and then was pulled to his feet. The wall shackles clanked as they dropped to the floor. He heard Amat Al Kindi whisper.

"Cooperate and live, Sir."

Chapter Twenty-Nine: The Chieftan

THE CITADEL OF TA'IZZ, YEMEN

"First, the interrogation, then we film. Afterward, keeping the American alive is imperative until this scum is ransomed." He lifted the bowed head of the kneeling Mark Gadarn and spat into his face.

The leader spoke to his henchmen in a situation room tucked into the rounded brick arches and boarded-up windows of the mountaintop garrison and former governor's palace. Parts of the roof were gone; starlight poured in. Many walls were broken and had tumbled down the mountain during the seemingly endless conflict. Ali Ibn Zalid's escarpment camp looked down on some of the poorest sections of the third-largest metropolis in Yemen on the west coast of the war-ravaged country.

Below, the clamor of street fighting could be heard in the city. On certain days, the smells of the Red Sea floated past the port town of Mocha all the way to the slums of Ta'izz and up the slopes of the mountain fort. Around the streets and alleyways of the city, the creeping sands of the desert made their own relentless war on civilization as they had for millennia. *The plight of humankind is futile. You will all go back to the earth, under the sands.*

Armed guards were everywhere in the city. Large trucks formed a barrier at the lowest end of the access road to the fortress. Access to the central command of the insurgent band was through one set of guarded gates.

In the Chieftan's headquarters, a young man spoke to Ali Ibn Zalid. He was no more than fifteen but dressed like a rebel fighter. He pointed to the captive journalist and said, "CBN will pay much for his release, but there is another possible very rich connection. Look, please, Sharif."

The monitor of the desk computer brought up the face of Rebecca Quinto, head of the Fritcher Museum in Florida, USA.

"The reporter has no family but is romantically linked to this woman. Also, I have found out that Mr. Gadarn is a notorious reporter in the

American media. He fought in Syria and Afghanistan and has caused trouble wherever he goes. The Turkish pigs almost jailed him last year." He tapped Rebecca's image. "This one will definitely buy him. She is a rich American." He grinned at his commander and made a gesture indicating wealth by rubbing his thumb and index finger together.

A man with the build of a soccer defender moved forward from the obscured parts of the room. He addressed the Chieftain with the title of respect. "This one is a spy, *Qayid Baladiin.* All American journalists are agents and allies of the Saudis. We must find out what he knows of our operations and to whom he reports."

The speaker was dressed in a drab t-shirt with his camo pants tucked into military boots. Without a head covering, he looked like a Western soldier. Dropping onto a bench, he placed his assault weapon across his lap as he spoke to the leader. Yasser Abdulkhalek was the Chieftan's Number One, head of staff, and commanding general of the rebel militia. Mark had met him in the alley in the city below. The journalist rubbed the side of his head in remembrance – one ruthless fucker.

"I will take over the interrogation, my Sharif. Leave him to me. He will tell us anything we need to know."

***

"I have heard much of the General since coming to Yemen. My sources, however, were mistaken."

Mark was being tied to a chair in a deadly-looking interrogation room. The General supervised but kept silent. His piercing black eyes took in every detail of his prisoner. Around them were the instruments of torture.

The captive journalist continued, "They said the People's General was a man of honor. They called him brave, strong, fearless, and sound of intelligence, as he was when his football team won the World Cup. I am saddened to find out otherwise. That he is not a man but a coward."

The General caught his underling's upraised fist before he could smash it into Mark's face. The powerful officer grunted and gestured for the soldier to stand down. He delivered the blow himself, splitting Mark's lip.

"You will die painfully, American dog. You may be assured of that. Ransom or no ransom."

Mark shook his head, fighting off the darkness of unconsciousness. "So, prove me wrong. Fight me, General, unbound and free. If you have the courage. If you are indeed a man of honor.

"The airways are full of videos of savage beatings of prisoners by thugs from your country. The world despises you as gangsters devoid of decency and not worthy of respect. Your provisionary government will never get the esteem it demands if your public image is that of savage torturers, religious fanatics, and sellers of women and children."

Mark spit blood as he went on, "Fight me if you are still the brave hero of the Helsinki football games. If you win, I will tell you everything you want to know. Where is the courage and integrity in Yemen, General?"

"Untie him and bring him outside."

The citadel's courtyard was quickly ringed with soldiers cheering their football star/general. They waved assault weapons and chanted for victory. Some positioned cell phones to record the bout.

Abdulkhalek had about 2 inches and 20 pounds on Mark. Still, the reporter was in excellent shape and had learned a lot from CEPOL combat training in Eastern Europe last summer. The shirtless warriors circled each other as the match began.

The General had the power, but the journalist had the speed and the expert MMA moves. At first, Mark was dazed by the body slams and the roundhouse kicks. The former footballer relied on a self-assumed superiority but was sloppy in his form and had little tactical sense. He fought like a street brawler with brutal force and the punishing blows of a juggernaut.

The journalist, on the other hand, moved with athletic grace, all ease and lightness. He concentrated on his opponent's hips, anticipating the direction the General would move. Mark saved his energy with defensive moves, allowing his opponent to exhaust himself with showboat attack moves.

"Come to me, little American dog. After I kill you, I will find your woman and use her for my amusement."

The journalist resisted his opponent's mental assault-- thoughts that broke his concentration. *This asshole is starving women and children with his bullshit war.*

Too late. The cost of this distraction was a power twist takedown from the General that spun Mark to the perimeter and brought him to the ground.

As the General advanced, Mark came up and clasped his opponent's torso around the middle. Using the man's momentum, Mark stepped back, pulled down, and flipped the General over his left shoulder into the dirt. The two fighters lay chest to chest. Mark pushed up and off into a standing position, fists raised with Abulkhalek looking up at him. The speed of the takedown allowed the American to clear his vision and focus his thoughts.

Once he took the offense, Mark spun, struck, ducked, jabbed, and kicked with speed and intensity. His counterattacks caught the General off guard before the soldier could pull back and regroup. As Mark got the better of him, Abdulkhalek fought with increased rage, further diminishing his skill level and precision.

Twenty minutes into the match, each battered and a bit broken, the warriors circled each other. A failed series of jabs by a faltering Abdulkhalek allowed Mark to transition to a new strategy. He came in close and grappled the soldier into a dominant clinch. Mark had both hands on the back of his opponent's head with both arms inside the General's. The American now had the physical and psychological advantage as the soldier fought to break the hold.

He pulled his partner's torso down, attempting to beat his opponent with a series of knees to the head, but Abdulkhalek's defense was strong. Using his legs and upper body, he steered the American off balance in the clinch. Feigning a break in the hold, Mark loosened his grip on his opponent. He suddenly stepped back and came in with a straight left knee shot to the General's liver, pulling the man into the full force of the blow. The strength of his attack brought the officer to his knees, coughing and gasping for breath.

The cheering of the rebels came to a dead stop as Mark again shot his stance above the reeling General who attempted to rise. As Mark stepped back and was about to deliver the *coup de grace*, with a spin kick to the head when a soldier smashed him at the back of the thighs with a club. The American collapsed.

"No!"

The Chieftan called off the attacker, responding to the cry of his number one.

The defeated General spoke between heavy panting and staggering. He split blood as he said, "This was an honor match, my Sharif. I accepted the challenge. I ask that it end honorably." He stood, pulled Mark to his feet, and handed him one of the spectator's sidearms.

The American was bruised and battered but better balanced on his feet than the Yemeni athlete-turned-soldier despite the knock to the ground. He met the gaze of the defeated warrior and handed the firearm back to the defeated rebel General.

"I guess we negotiate, huh?"

The Chieftain gave sharp orders to remove both fighters and see to the General. He commanded that the captive be put back into his cell, but not until his cuts and scrapes were cleaned and bandaged. The two fighters locked eyes as they were taken away in opposite directions.

Chapter Thirty: The Trial

THE CITADEL OF TA'IZZ, YEMEN

Mark was returned to the barred enclosure adjacent to the women and children. Food was very scarce. The students and the adults were showing signs of weakness.

Amat Al Kindi spoke softly in the dark. "I praise Allah that you have survived your ordeal, American Sir. Be warned, however, that the leadership of the Sharif is tenuous at best. Ibn Zalid is very much unpredictable and an egomaniac. He trusts no one and suspects treason in his ranks."

Mark tried to find a comfortable position against the hard surfaces of the cell. His wounds were clean, but he longed for the numbness of large doses of ibuprofen. A sympathetic soldier had given him a swig of something vile but potent from a canteen-like vessel when no one was looking.

Al Kindi continued, "There are many groups at war in this country. Our captors are Ali Ibn Zalid's forces, The Scourge of God. They are part of a multi-ethnic militia belonging to the Supreme Political Council connected to the Houthis, who now control the capital, Sana'a. Some of Zalid's men are Yemeni. Most are not – privateers from throughout the region."

Mark closed his eyes and said, "Tell me about the war."

"The Houthis are an Islamic religious-political-armed movement which started right here in Ta'izz. The group assassinated the former President of the Republic. The Houthi advance on the capital in 2015 ousted the Hadi government, claiming sole legitimacy. The Hadis fled south and set up the provisional government's headquarters in Aden. They are supported by a Saudi-led international coalition."

Mark said, "Here is what the world sees: Insurgents and loyalists fighting back and forth across the country with territories changing hands and back again. The accusations of war crimes, especially against the Hadi supporters, have reached levels never seen in war. Civilians are targeted and killed by the tens of thousands, whether by mass killings, fighting, bombings, famine, or disease."

He continued, "The UN has appealed for international aid for Yemen. It claims 7.5 million people have been affected by the conflict. So we are talking about requests for medical supplies, potable water, food, shelter, and other forms of support to the international community by the UN."

A few older students sat closer and listened to the discussion with large, sad eyes. Other teachers cradled the young ones and settled in close for warmth as the chilly mountain night crept into the partially bombed-out medieval fortress.

Amat Al Kindi pulled her veil closer, covering more of her face. She said, "Our families can verify that the airstrikes in the north destroyed medical facilities and used excessive force against civilians, journalists, and humanitarian aid workers. Demonstrations are not allowed, and both sides are preventing supplies from getting through to the war-ravaged populations. I heard a report that a Doctors Without Borders facility was bombed by the Hadi supporters in Ta'izẓ. Some of their staff are here among us."

A young woman said, "In my village, they bombed a center for the blind."

A voice in the dark said, "There are reports in my village of cholera. The water is bad, and many are dead or will die. I fear that my entire family is gone or dead."

Another said, "I volunteered for a while at a neighborhood clinic and food pantry. Before the war, I studied medicine abroad. I came back here to help my country's people. It is said that one thousand children are dying every week from preventable killers like diarrhea, malnutrition, and respiratory tract infections."

One teacher remarked, "The International Committee of the Red Cross fled across the sea to Djibouti last year after one of their workers was killed by a gunman not half a kilometer from here."

Mark remembered some of the information from his orientation for the mission. In November 2017, U.S. Senator Chris Murphy accused the

United States of complicity in war crimes and the humanitarian crisis in Yemen. The Senate Chamber became the stage for debating US support for a humanitarian catastrophe inside Yemen of epic proportions. The United States of America has taken two years to condemn the atrocities and consider withdrawing support. Up to now, the White House has refused to condemn the crimes of the Saudis. As a result, many had died.

He looked at the hungry, dirty, and bedraggled adults and children that he could see in the darkness surrounding him. Ms. Al Kindi spoke with much sadness, saying, "Mr. Gadarn, the people of the world should know that they are using poison gas to mutilate and destroy Yemen's people-- bombs from the sky in violation of international law."

She lowered her veil. Three nearby students uncovered an arm or a leg. A young man raised the back of his shirt.

Mark could see the burns on the teacher and her students in the dim light.

***

Mark stood outside the door to the Chieftan's quarters. He was guarded and shackled. There was shouting from the inside. The soldier who had given Mark the whiskey stood very close and murmured a translation of what was happening behind the closed door. The other guard remained silent. It seems there was no agreement on what would be done with the American journalist.

The Chieftan pounded the desk. "We need American dollars if we are to continue. We lack soldiers, supplies, and arms. My army will soon desert and join one of the other factions fighting the Aden government and the international coalition unless we increase our holdings."

A young soldier could be heard. "My Sharif, the video equipment being sent from the capital has been delayed. There has been fighting on the roads."

Another voice, "Our transport of the prisoners will also be delayed, Sir, but not by much. There is fighting to our west as well."

Mark could hear the voice of his fighting opponent, “Prisoners, you call them? They are women and school children, my Lord. Let us serve Allah in truth.” Yasser Abdulkhalek‘s voice was passionate but restrained. His disgust, however, was apparent even on the other side of the door.

He continued, “Are we slavers? These are Yemeni people you hold in the dungeons. The American knows nothing. He wants the story of the misery you and your fellow leaders bring to your own people. Let us go back to fighting for justice for our people. We have lost sight of our divine purpose.”

“I am the Scourge of Allah. Where is your loyalty to me, General? How many agree with you on this? I insist you follow my orders regarding the prisoners without question.”

It was rage and frustration that fired the leader’s outburst. Silence followed.

“Enough. Bring in the journalist.”

Mark was brought in and forced to kneel before Chieftan Ali Ibn Zalid. The Commander of the rebels was dressed in his army fatigues. Medals of valor adorned his uniform. His keffiyeh was white and held in place by a black cord. Behind him, General Abulkhalek looked at the prisoner with a mixture of defiance and disgust.

The Sharif spoke in English. A soldier held a mobile phone, taping the sentence of the Commander.

“Mr. Gadarn, you have been tried by the Court of the Sacred Coalition of the People’s Committee and found guilty of espionage. Your sentence is death by beheading to be carried out at a future date but in no less than three weeks. Remove the prisoner.”

Mark traded looks with General Yasser Abdulkhalek. Each of them sported a black eye and additional facial bruising. The Yemeni officer’s gaze bore into the American journalist with a conflicted and unreadable stare.

Chapter Thirty-One: Elyesa

15 RUE CRESPIN DU GAST, 11TH ARRONDISSEMENT, PARIS

The petite woman was in her mid-60s, very spry with dazzling eyes and a bright smile. She spoke English and was very affable.

"So you came here all the way from America? It is so good to meet you. Ms. Quinto. Please sit. We will have tea, yes?" The French woman dashed into the kitchen to put on the kettle.

Rebecca, entranced by the apartment's surroundings, called after her hostess, "Madame Géroux, I am sorry to arrive unannounced. I am the head curator at the Fritcher Museum of Art in Fort Lauderdale."

"That is in Florida. I know that. I once traveled to Montreal in Canada but have not yet been to the United States."

"Very nice. I am here to study the life of the opera singer, Victoria Ricci. Have you heard of her?"

The woman stepped from the kitchen with two empty tea mugs in her hand and a somewhat surprised expression on her face.

"I cannot lie. You can see the Diva all around you. This was *La Gloriosa*'s apartment for many years in Paris." She set the cups on the table.

"Ms. Quinto, may I be so bold as to request to see your identification?" Rebecca obliged, reaching into her purse for her passport. She also gave Elyesa Géroux her business card.

"Thank you."

"Madame, how are you connected to Ms. Ricci, please?"

"My other last name is Bergh. My mother worked with Victoria through her dresser, Astrid Cole, during the war. The first Elyesa Bergh, my mother, served in the French Resistance, as did my father. He was captured and killed by the Germans.

"Ms. Ricci took us in because of her connection to the Resistance and, through them, her association with the British espionage network that had infiltrated the highest ranks of the Nazi High Command. The Diva was an important agent for the British and the Allies. My mother and Astrid recruited her."

"So, this is a collection of her memorabilia. You have created a private museum of her life."

"Yes. My family is grateful to her for so many things. When she left Paris, never to return, her fame seemed to dwindle on the world stage. We kept her things in excellent condition. We gave some of her clothing to people experiencing poverty. In our little way, my family does not want the world to forget her. Here, allow me to show you. Please bring your tea."

The memorabilia had been arranged in chronological order throughout the flat. Old, faded pictures of the Diva hung in frames near the flat entrance.

"Italy, yes?"

"Correct, she grew up in the south of that country. She was relocated as an infant and raised in a church-run orphanage near Ravenna. She used to say that her parents could not afford to keep her after the hard times that followed the Great War. See, here she is with a few of the other children and the nuns."

As she spoke, Elyesa moved through the photographs, pointing and explaining. "Apparently, the sisters recognized her vocal talents at an early age. An orphanage patron sent her to work at the Milan Conservatory as a kitchen maid. Someone was impressed when she was caught singing while washing the pots and pans.

"She took vocal training there and became a junior member of the school's opera company at fifteen. Gradually, she was cast in some minor roles, as you see here."

She pointed to a framed program and a series of vintage pictures. "Her La Scala debut was in the role of Gilda in Verdi's *Rigoletto*. The reviews were excellent, and she began to appear in many of the leading roles in the company's repertoire. This is the original costume of her opening at the Paris Opera in *La Traviata* in the role of Violetta. So small and delicate…"

A mannequin was draped with a vintage, white, sheer nightgown from the death scene of Verdi's famous courtesan. Next to it, a wood and canvas head held a well-preserved geisha wig adorned with metal sticks bedecked with flowers and jewels. It was easily recognized as part of the stage regalia of Cio-Cio San, Puccini's *Madama Butterfly*.

As they toured the spacious apartment, performance mementos were displayed from a dazzling career that spanned close to fifty years on operatic and concert stages worldwide. Photos of Victoria with historical figures and ordinary folk from the many international communities she toured were interspersed with the Diva's awards and letters of commendation.

"She so loved children. Victoria encouraged girls everywhere to stop at nothing to achieve greatness. She believed that education was the right of every child."

Rebecca read aloud from a framed plaque above a mounted blue and gold cross on a red ribbon hanging in one of the front rooms. "It reads, 'Dame Commander of the Most Excellent Order of the British Empire,' so she became Dame Victoria Ricci."

Elyesa said, "Yes, for her espionage work during the war. It was awarded in 1945 as part of the Allies' acknowledgment that she was one of their best informants. Providing information on troop movements, sabotage strategies, and the rescue of those fleeing Nazi arrest– yes, yes, she played a vital part. The German High Command never knew. Her Ordre National de la Légion d'Honneur from General Charles De Gaulle is on the other wall."

Against an overflowing set of bookshelves, four mannequins were bunched together, dressed head-to-toe in costumery from some of the soprano's most famous roles.

"Do you recognize these characters, Ms. Quinto?"

Rebecca scrutinized them, starting with the closest. She pointed as she spoke.

A midnight blue and silver masterpiece with an elegant crescent moon headpiece was dubbed by the visitor as Mozart's Queen of the Night from *The Magic Flute*.

"Am I looking at a design by the legendary Paul-René Larthe?"

"Correct. Madame was one of the only sopranos in her day who could take on the role."

"Exquise!"

Elyesa fingered the gown of shining stars made of semi-precious stones embedded in layers of shimmering satin and tule. The train was more than twenty feet long.

The Parisian continued, "The ovations lifted the roof of the opera house each time she performed. You see, the Queen of the Night's Act II aria is full of virtuosic vocal fireworks and peppered with rare high Fs. La Gloriosa had a stratospheric range."

A Chinese fantasy in ornate ice-blue and white, strings of faux jewels from the ostentatious headpiece fell onto draping, silk sleeves–*"Turandot."*

The French woman said, "The Frozen Diva as Puccini's born-again Ice Princess. She ruthlessly traps and kills any man who would seek her hand. That is one of my favorites."

The third ensemble was a short, low-cut, cream-colored flapper's dress. The wig was a jet-black bob cut with 1920s spit curls. A monocle and a silver cigarette holder completed the jeweled accessories.

Rebecca turned to her host. "I need some help with this one."

"The title role in Alban Berg's *Lulu*, the 1950 Zurich production. Her first opera role after the war. Desire, eroticism, and obsession—the rise and fall of a woman who captivated all who crossed her path. No one gets that one."

The fourth figure was arranged behind the first three and nearest the door. It sported a cowgirl's hat pulled low on the mannequin's face. Rebecca reached over to adjust it higher on the head while saying, "I think I know this one, but the outfit is all wrong."

As the hat went up. The figure spoke.

"*La Fanciulla del West*-- The Girl of the West."

***

"You scared the shit out of me."

The three laughed and gave their orders to the waiter at the café on the street across from Madame Géroux's apartment.

"My grandson, Loic, loves to play the joke on our guests," Elyesa said. The strong-featured young man with the military cut laughed again. "Yes. I apologize for giving you a start. My sense of humor is a bit on the teasing side. It gets me in a great deal of trouble, I will confess. Remember the woman who fainted, Grandmother?"

"You are altogether too much, my boy. He gets it from his father, a roguish devil if there ever was one."

The "kid" was all of 24 and very buff. Dark eyes that darted everywhere with mischievous intent, especially over Rebecca's body, a killer smile, and 6'3", 215# of man-muscle, Lieutenant Loic Antoine Theriault leaned forward on the table on arms that were sculpted from military training and hours in the gym.

"Is that..."

He answered in a soft baritone as he rolled up his right T-shirt sleeve, bedroom eyes on full. "Got this when I was fourteen. One of my all-time heroes."

Spider-Man swung on webs drawn onto an impressive shoulder. He winked and said, "Got others, but I do not know you well enough, Mademoiselle, to show you everything, and anyway, not in front of my grand-mère."

Elyesa swatted her frisky grandson. "You behave now, my rascal. Be respectful."

Loic ripped off a chunk of a crusty baguette and passed the basket to his grandmother. He raised his glass of deep red wine and said, "This is soldier's wine. Named, *Pinard de Guerré*. A couple of glasses of this, and I go back upstairs and nap for hours. Try some?"

"I'm good, thanks." Rebecca raised her Perrier.

The hunky lad said, "That was my duffle bag in the hallway upstairs. I'm just getting back from maneuvers in Pakistan, part training and part of a humanitarian relief effort on the part of NATO."

The soldier's grandmother said, "Loic's enlistment in the NATO Response Force was a blessing. He fell into a rough crowd a few years back and was looking at some serious trouble with the police. A law enforcement officer took him under his wing, kicked his delinquent ass, and got him into the NRF."

Elyesa added, "We are a small family now. There's just us. Everyone else is gone."

Loic took his grandmother's hand and kissed it softly. She caressed his handsome cheek gently and briefly.

The food arrived.

"Grand-mère..."

There was an unspoken question in the word that Elyesa understood in the telepathic way close people have.

The French woman placed Rebecca's business card before the soldier. "She also showed me her passport, my boy."

As Loic examined the card, turning it repeatedly, he looked over Rebecca with interest.

She asked, "What's with the high-security, folks?"

"Grandmother had some trouble last week while I was in Pakistan. Some rough *mecs*, strong-arming the doorman and demanding to see the place and her. Many questions about our Diva. I suspect they will be back. Requested a guard in the downstairs foyer. Takes time, I guess."

Elyesa said, "I told them she had died in an uprising in Istanbul in 1993, but they did not believe me."

The woman continued, "Why would anyone use violence to get at *La Gloriosa*?"

"I'll tell you why, but my story has a lot of gaps."

Rebecca started with the death of Arva St. Genieve and brought the woman and her grandson up to speed on her search for the Frozen Diva. She included the warning from Madame Ondine to secure the safety of her love, journalist Mark Gardarn.

"*Le baiseur* got major balls going into Yemen. That place is bat-shit crazy, as the Americans say. Sorry, Grand-mère."

"Loic, your language."

Rebecca looked with entreaty at her tablemates. "I know she is alive. Please believe me when I say that lives may depend on finding her."

Elyesa said, "We consider her a member of our family and will prevent any danger from coming to her. You realize that she is a super-centenarian. This year, she will be a hundred and nine years old."

"Elyesa, I promise that I will not allow any harm to come to Ms. Riccci. She provided information to the Allies that saved many and helped bring about the end of one of the most evil regimes that ever walked the face of the earth. There is still great suffering, crime, and terror, and Victoria is somehow the key to stopping it and safeguarding the lives of innocents. She still has importance, I am convinced."

The woman exchanged another near-telepathic look with her grandson as she sat back and folded her hands.

Rebecca looked from man to woman. "Do you know where she is?"

After a brief silence, Loic said, "Yes, and so do you."

"What? If I did, do you think I would be here questioning the two of you?"

He gently took her hand. He lifted it to the level of his eyes and examined it as if it were a specimen.

"What did the Voodoo priestess say to you about the location of the Diva? Tell it again."

Rebecca responded, “Madame Ondine said that the Diva was embedded in ice, in a cage of steel. Something about swords and daggers. ‘The swords and daggers of kings protect her.’ Then there was something about the saints and the three faiths safeguarding her from the world.”

She let the young man toy with her hand. He said, “And where is this place of royal steel? From medieval times, nowhere else in the world has produced the swords of kings.”

Rebecca retrieved her hand with a yank. She knew.

“Toledo. The steel of Toledo.”

Loic said, “Making hard steel weapons since 500 BC. It is said that Hannibal’s arms were made there when he fought with Rome in the Punic Wars.”

“How do you know so much? Are you a history buff?”

Elyesa said, “My grandson has made the study of weaponry a hobby.”

Rebecca had another moment of sudden realization.”

“The three faiths-- Judaism, Christianity, and Islam; Andalusia, and Toledo have been home to the three monotheistic faiths since ancient times, mostly living together peacefully. The city has many churches, mosques, and synagogues. Ricci’s secret is surrounded by saints.”

“Yes.” Loic retook Rebecca’s hand, this time more tenderly. His other hand went exploring as he looked into her eyes and said, “Let’s go and find her, you and I together, my sweet. You need a soldier for protection and a man for other things. I am on leave for a month. I will accompany you to Spain. Together, we will explore the secrets you crave.”

Rebecca sighed and pushed him away. “Ohhh, brother. Get a load of you.” She looked at the older woman. “Elyesa, that is some line your grandson has. Listen, Lancelot. I need you to make this caper all man-strong like I need a hole in the head. Haven’t you been paying attention, Lochinvar? The days of the male-dominated sexual hierarchy are so over.”

She removed his wandering hand from her butt, adding, “Also, you need to know, I have been seeing a man, and we are equals-- very much in love.”

Loic looked at her with soulful, brown-black eyes and said, “Yes, Mark Gadarn. And where is he? He stands on the precipice of catastrophe in the hellish land of death and great destruction-- Yemen.”

Chapter Thirty-Two: The Goddess of Discord

PARIS TO BRUSSELS

"Rebecca, you can be in Brussels in under an hour. I have a CBN corporate jet at Charles de Gaulle waiting to bring you directly to NATO Headquarters. Make it fast."

Rebecca felt her blood turn to ice. *They got Mark. Shit.*

Caspar Haig, European Bureau Chief for CBN and former Assistant Communications Director for the Obama White House, was direct in his instructions and cautiously brief. He could not tell her over the phone what was going on.

"I'm on my way."

She turned to Elyesa and Loic. "I have to go, folks. Something's come up."

She stood and looked at Loic. "Trip to Toledo on hold, soldier."

"We go together to Brussels."

"What makes you think so?"

Elyesa said, "It is easy to tell from the few words you spoke that your man is in trouble. If my Diva is involved, Loic needs to accompany you. She is family."

She handed Rebecca a napkin. "Look to your face, my dear."

Rebecca touched her cheek and realized that a tear had found its way over her lower eyelid and was slowly making its way down her face. She was surprised at how hot her face felt.

Loic said, "Your expression during the call was that of a person receiving very bad news. Charles de Gaulle to Brussels, ASAP? Gotta be NATO/OTAN. He's been kidnapped, and his company has reached out to the best military organization charged with safeguarding freedom in this part of the world to get him out. One puts two and two together."

"Lieutenant, I appreciate your offer, but until I know...."

"This has the potential of becoming what you Americans call a shit storm, Rebecca. Getting him out the usual way has about a one-in-ten chance of success. You need to do this by unorthodox methods. I am your man for that."

Elyesa said, "My Loic is in counterintelligence, my dear. He is the best. Speaks eight languages, four of them are cyber. "

Rebecca looked at the two with uncertainty. Elyesa added, gently cuffing her grandson. "And he will be a total gentleman at all times."

The handsome soldier looked at his new friend with assurance. "I have nothing to do for a month as my unit is on rotation. Let's kick some terrorist ass."

Rebecca pointed to the apartment building across the street and said one word.

"Pack."

***

"Gentlemen, your information on this is way too sketchy. Give me a minute. I need someone else on this."

Commander of NATO Intelligence, General Patrick S. McGrath, was not pleased. "Who?"

Rebecca continued, "I don't know her name, General. Mark calls her 'Eris.' She provides him with information by hacking into sources all over the cyber universe. I can get her on a web call. Your people can help me do this. I have the contact information."

Haig mused, "Eris was the Greek goddess who was snubbed and not invited to a big wedding. She came anyway and tossed in a golden apple inscribed with, 'For the Fairest.' The result was the Judgement of Paris and the Trojan War. This hacker means business, and it sounds like they thrive on chaos."

The Commander frowned as he said, "I cannot approve of what is coming together as a very unconventional plan to rescue an American hostage taken by some of the most ruthless mercenaries in the Middle East."

Caspar Haig said, "With all due respect, Pat. I came to you because we are friends. Media corporations worldwide are losing journalists left and right because we are attempting their rescue by the book, by negotiation. We have to go guerilla with this, or they are gonna snuff that boy.

McGrath was not agreeable. "Caz, we have been friends for years. You know I cannot break protocol and approved procedures. NATO Command is accountable to the twenty-nine member nations that implement the North Atlantic Treaty. We are verging here on threatening the security of our intelligence and overall engagement objectives."

The CBN chief said, "So, just look the other way – support what you can but officially acknowledge nothing, CYA. I get it.

Haig continued to make his point, "Pat, it's a new world out there. World leaders despise the media because it continually exposes their duplicity, ignorance, and lack of conscience. Journalist lives are cheap. No one gives a shit until they have been beheaded publically or assassinated by being cut to pieces in a foreign embassy.

"The rise of ISIL brought a new level of evil to global terrorism. The bad guys are insane, General. They stop at nothing to get cash, power, and media attention. We need to do this another way. Old strategies are not working anymore, especially with Gadarn. He believes in breaking all the rules to get at the truth."

Commander McGrath responded, "Caz, I do not need a lecture on terrorism and the media in the 21st century. Your boy was not embedded, right? Big mistake – bullshit gonzo reporter, and now he is gonna...."

The General stopped as everyone looked at Rebecca. She was pale but firm in her resolve to get Mark home safely. General McGrath looked away and shook his head in frustration.

Loic spoke up, "Begging the general's pardon, Sir. Gadarn may have acted foolishly, but he had put in place a few precautionary strategies to ensure his safety."

The hotshot Lieutenant continued, "A hacker is one who has valuable information, disguised, hidden, and able to be disseminated for critical reasons. I believe we can engage Mr. Gadarn's Eris without compromising NATO intelligence. I have done it before. May I?"

The young officer took the seat vacated by one of the General's tech officers. She looked at the general, who shrugged and raised his palms up. The officer watched over Loic's shoulder.

"Look, if we go this way...." He typed and clicked. "This is what we call a Zooch-Job VPN– a secured door to the outside. Quite complicated to explain but a combination of a Medusa and a Proteus program."

Loic looked at the non-techies in the room and said, "It changes if you attempt to fuck with it. Turns the shit birds to stone."

The brash Frenchman quickly said, "Begging the Commander's pardon, Sir."

He typed as he said to the NATO technology officer observing over his shoulder, "See the indicators... we are clean and able to receive – to talk with Eris with no risk."

He turned to the keyboard next to him, instructing the soldier to enter some test data that would verify the security of the programs he had quickly set in place. The young techie confirmed, "Very cool, Lieutenant. We are outside, and no portals to our intelligence are exposed or in danger of breach."

Loic beamed. *Can I cook, or can I cook?*

Rebecca handed him her phone. "Get Eris for me."

Loic opened the 'door' to the sanctuary of the Goddess of Discord. The splash page on the monitor was full of tribal images and notifications stating that all contact was subject to approved protocols. Images from movies and literature skated across the page, warning, whispering, and giving secret signs. Apparently, this hacker was a specialist at being elusive and invisible. It looked, at the same time, deadly and comic.

Swirling text announced, "Abandon all hope ye that enter here."

After a short time, an image of Agnes Morehead from her *Hush, Hush, Sweet Charlotte* role as Velma Cruthers, the crazy housekeeper, came on the screen. Music from the film's theme song played softly in the background.

General McGrath said, "What in heaven's name...."

Casper Haig laid a hand on the shoulder of his concerned friend.

On Loic's monitor, the mouth of the freaky image was animated by the hacker as audio came across.

"Knock, knock. Who's there?"

***

A green screen replaced the splash page, and a cursor flashed on the upper left-hand corner. When engaged, it moved across to the right, one letter at a time.

"Inquirer's identification: Please respond to the following questions."

Eris was aping the old computer screens of the 80s. The cursor flashed again.

"With whom are you requesting contact?"

Rebecca spoke, and Loic typed, but the letters were hidden.

"The Goddess of Discord"

"Who seeks the counsel of the Goddess?"

Loic typed, "Rebecca Quinto."

"This individual is not known to Eris."

Rebecca said, "Try Becky." *Leave it to Mark to use a name I loathe.* Eris was satisfied with the response.

"Who or what is this in reference to?"

"Mark Gadarn."

The cursor flashed for a significant amount of time with no response. Eris was thinking it over.

"You have entered a miserable response. That individual is not known to the Goddess. #24601 One last attempt."

Shit! He uses a code name. It could be fuckin' anything. Rebecca stared at the screen. Loic turned to her with an enigmatic look. He ran a finger under the digits and then the adjective, 'miserable.' He raised his eyebrows. *Well?*

He said, "Rebecca, this is the prisoner's number."

She leaned over him and typed the name of the protagonist of Les Misérables.

"Jean Valjean."

The vintage screen shattered into glass-like shards and was replaced by a blue and black image of a hooded figure in dark monk's robes typing on a laptop as viewed from the side. When Eris turned to look at her subjects, there was no face in the cowl, only a dark void inside the hood.

Soft, sinister strains of music highlighted the eerie image. It appeared that the Goddess of Discord was immersed in a sea of data and code washing from left to right. As she spoke, she typed, and the blue letters floating across the ghostly image coalesced into sentences.

A weird female voice spoke.

"I am Eris. I am the essence and substance from which your artists and scientists build beauty. I am the spirit with which your children and clowns laugh in happy anarchy. I am creative chaos. I am alive, and I tell you that you are free.

"How may I help you?"

***

Loic said, "She has switched to vocal recognition."

Rebecca said, "Intel on Valjean."

The phantom spoke her response, and the corresponding text appeared.

"This is the most current information on the subject Valjean from his conversation with the Goddess four days ago. He has supplied Eris with the following information relative to his movements in eastern Africa and the anticipated relocation to Yemen:

One: The unit, Becky, is the point of contact during the possible detention of Valjean or in a hostage situation.

Two: Becky and Valjean will create proof-of-life protocol questions to verify that Valjean is alive. Questions and answers are not known to Eris at this time.

Three: The unit, Valjean, has given his medical provider DNA samples to be used for identification, if needed, as of January 1 of the current year."

The communication with Eris stopped for a few minutes. The monitor image sputtered. A bolt of lightning split the screen, and the roar of thunder could be heard with a screech of lost souls. The hooded image looked away from her computer and peered into the eyes of her supplicants. Even without a face, one could tell she was super pissed.

The Goddess raged, accompanied by a roar of thunder.

"Take your tracers off the Goddess, Irish Boy. I have been in and outta your intel hole like an ass pirate on 'Grindr.' Got news for you. A few of my kind have. Fix your security some other time. You are causing me to lose contact and provide complicated avoidance maneuvers. Desist or pay the penalty."

Caz observed, "Irish Boy? This cyber bitch is good. She knows you, Pat."

Loic muted the microphone and looked at General Patrick S. McGrath, who gave an order to his tech officer. The French NATO Lieutenant added, "By the way, you do realize that Eris is AI, correct? I am able to detect that she is Artificial Intelligence. Part of her disguise is to come across as human. I would say she is a top-grade program.

"So this last exchange... using something called lureware, 'Eris' can anticipate trackers and breaches to her security system and morphs her defenses with incredible speed. It will be almost impossible to stop her, General, Sir."

General McGrath said, "Lieutenant Theriault, please assure me again that this hacker is not a threat to NATO Security."

Loic leaned over and pointed to his colleague's screen. "Firewalls and security nets have not been breached, Sir. No alarms or system shutdowns. She is outside, and we are talking to her outside NATO's infobahn."

McGrath's security officer confirmed, "Sir, I have set up a cybercage so that if there is an attempt to breach our defenses, the hacker will be sucked into a program of misinformation and destructive cipher. She gets thrown to the monsters – worms, holes, chimeras, the whole virtual zoo, and she becomes fresh meat."

Loic thought, *Fuckin' love these geeks. Welcome to 21st-century warfare.*

He unmuted, and the communication with Eris continued.

Rebecca said, "Eris, please interpret the feed we are sending. We are uploading the kidnappers' video."

"Unnecessary. The Goddess already has the ransom note."

Loic said. "She will not accept files and attachments. She has what CBN was sent due to her abilities to hack in almost anywhere, it would seem."

McGrath said to Haig almost imperceptibly, "She's up your ass also, Caz – reading your transmissions and mail."

After a few minutes, Eris responded.

"The subject in the film clip is the unit known to the Goddess as Jean Valjean. Face recognition confirmed. Eris will not comment on the audio as the message is quite understandable by the Becky unit. Eris will decode the unspoken communication. You will wait."

A message repeatedly flashed, "Divination in Progress." The Goddess came back.

"Observe the subject in the video. Valjean is mixing sign language, Morse Code, and semaphore to communicate his location and some details of his incarceration. The movement of his fingers over parts of his body, eyes, arms, and forehead is purposeful. Valjean is coding his location.

"The Goddess is concerned that his information is nonspecific. Conclusion: Valjean has a general idea of where he is but cannot pinpoint more than Ta'izz, western Yemen. Eris confirms that that location has the global coordinates 13°34′44″N 44°01′19″E."

General McGrath said, "Helpful, but we will need to get in closer. We will need a GPS signal from the ground if a rescue crew is to reach him. In my estimation, that is highly unlikely."

Eris sounded a bit confused as she continued.

"Additional: School? School? Hold on, please... Expected time for response is one minute and fifty-three seconds... You will wait."

There was a pause in the communication as the mad hacker practiced her "divination." Rebecca was amazed that Eris was a machine. Her somewhat emotional responses and cussing created an image of a 21st-century cyberpunk gearhead surrounded by pizza boxes and whose other avocation was being a gamer– kicking ass with Halo 2.

"It appears that the subject is being held with a group of school teachers and children from a destroyed *madrasa*. Coalition forces reported bombing a school and a medical facility... four days ago... north of that location. Militia forces swept in to gather up the refugees. The coordinates given by Valjean coincide."

"Checking my sources... there was chatter about teachers and minors up for sale. Shit, these fucks are cyber amateurs – so fucking easy... ever heard of a firewall, bitch? Such jerkwads. Fuckin' losers."

Another pause. Then Eris continued.

"You will wait... wait, wait... continuing. This Divinity is working..."

Within seconds, the program responded with more information.

"Although the Goddess cannot pinpoint the location of the feed, the captors have a buyer for their hostages. The Red Specter – drug and human trafficking triad first identified in Laos in 2000. The triad has a global reach... massive and very dangerous. The Goddess advises Becky to confer with her FBI connections on this.

"Hold it… Eris is sorting out her data… Fuck me. The Red Spector's recent transactions for human properties are being reviewed. Details can be made available. Damn... the juvenile units will be sent to Russia through Southeast Asia."

The Goddess will now speak the prophecy--

"Valjean is totally fucked."

Chapter Thirty-Three: In the Intestine of the Leviathan

PALAIS GARNIER, PARIS, SEPTEMBER 1940

"The backstage manager, he will wonder why I have not left the theater, Astrid."

"He has been taken care of, Madame. He left twenty minutes ago, well paid. There will be no observers."

The dresser took up a drawstring canvas bag and led the way out of the star's dressing room.

"Follow me, please."

Astrid Cole led Victoria to the back, right corner of the stage of the Paris Opera House. The sets for the fall repertory loomed in the darkness around them as they made their way past scenery wagons, turntables, and lifts. Astrid brought them to an opening and took the stairs down five levels to the base of the sub-stage rigging, only occasionally lit by caged light bulbs in the massive stone walls.

The arbor pits, an array of ropes and chains resembling the strings of a mammoth harp, descended into a vast abyss of counterweights. The sets that rose from the stage floor and dropped from the ceiling depended on the operations of this complicated wall of hemp stringers and steel weights, which seemed to connect the earth to hell.

One set of imposing cables vertically bisected a sign on the wall: *Le Lustre.* This was the rigging for raising and lowering the Paris Opera House's famous chandelier, cantilevered down here from the dome above the audience. A formidable padlock prevented access and any threat of another disaster.

Near the bottom of the stairwell, Astrid unlocked a large metal door whose surface announced, "No Admittance." They were greeted by the smell of stagnant water and sewage. Astrid removed a flashlight from the bag and indicated the garments inside.

"You must change your clothes, Madame. It is now well past curfew, and you will be moving below ground for the rest of the journey."

Victoria exchanged her suit, shoes, and hat for a man's pants, jacket, and overcoat. Clunky oxfords and a fedora completed the disguise. The band of the hat sported a green stripe. The waters of the underground lake below them glistened in the light from the open doorway and the hand torch.

As she stuffed Victoria's evening clothes in the satchel, Astrid reached over. She turned up the collar on her employer's overcoat. The woman said, "The Elyesa Bergh you will meet tonight may be somewhat unrecognizable compared to the society maven you met at the Café Luxembourg on Thursday afternoon. She will approach you with a companion. They will appear to be a couple of the abandoned ones who live in the sewers. They will be arguing about a loaf of bread.

Victoria nodded. She pulled her coat against the dampness.

"You may take the light. Please follow the tunnel to the right, away from the underground lake. The passageway opens to a catwalk. Take the third opening and then the second stairway down. You will be quite close to the Seine, so be careful not to slip in the muck. Do you have any questions?"

"No, Astrid. I will see you tomorrow night."

"Good night, Madame."

***

Victoria held her right hand against the crumbling tunnel wall as she walked into a vast vaulted space. A river of sewage and runoff water flowed below the iron catwalk toward the waste treatment plants outside the city. The only light came from her flashlight, and the sounds of creatures scuttling away from the human intruder scratched softly, mixing with the murmur of the sloshing water.

The first opening was partially barricaded. The second had only a ladder going up. Victoria found the third tunnel and, after a space of about a kilometer, took the second stairway down.

Odors of the river seem to replace the rotten smell of garbage and offal. Here and there, water descended in a spray that almost blocked the walkway. Victoria moved against the far wall and lifted the collar of her coat even tighter around her face and neck.

The catwalk ended at the confluence of what appeared to be three underground streams pouring into a large swirling cistern. Ancillary tunnels grouped around the waterways with platforms jutting out over the domed space holding serpentine conduits and massive shut-off wheels. Fires burned on some levels, and dark phantoms moved singly or in groups. Four massive pillars held up the roof of this underground cathedral. Now, Victoria observed shapes coming out of the darkness to view the newest visitor to their hidden city.

"It's the Bastille, Monsieur." A pile of rags had crept into her path and was pointing up to the brick pylons. "They disposed of many prisoners in this hell hole-- from up there. Cut their heads off and tossed them through a trap door into the waters. Above us, the prison's gone, but the bones of centuries of the dead are under us."

Victoria felt a tug on her coat. "What have you brought us, lamby pie? I very much like that coat." A crone reached into the pockets as Victoria attempted to pull away.

"Here, back off, Tonette. This un's a gentleman. We need to be respectful. His type's got money." The decrepit man pushed the woman away and held Victoria by the lapels of her coat.

His breath was rank as he said, "What are you doing here in the sewer? What ya got for us, Monsieur? That torch is a starter. How about that nice watch for Tomás here?"

Victoria slid in the muck dangerously close to the edge. The groping ruffian, Tomás, pulled her back from falling and being sucked into the whirlpool below.

"Here, puke face, I am sick of you muscling in on my things. You swiped my nice loaf of bread this morning. Didn't even get a taste."

"Wasn't me. You old whore. Was your brother, and ya knows it. Moldy shit, anyway."

Tonette said, "Listen, this *mec* can judge us up fair and square. C'mon back here. Mister and I'll explain the situation about the bread."

They entered a tunnel that ascended up by way of ramps and stairs. Victoria could smell fresher air at this level. Some ambient light seemed to shimmer at the end of their trail through the grates above. Tomás and Tonette pulled her down on a bench in a dark alcove.

"Sorry about all of that, Madame. The Nazis are making it extremely difficult for above-ground meetings, especially with the curfew. You can be sure their agents are also in the sewers.

"This here is Victor. He works for the Resistance.

She could not tell but was pretty sure that Tomás/Victor nodded politely.

"Please tell me what you want me to do."

Elyesa Berg, aka the hag, Tonette, said, "You told me when we met at the Luxembourg that you have access to Herr Speer's office in the Reichstag."

Victoria hesitated, unsure of revealing more about her affair with one of the highest members of the Hitler elite. *I will hold nothing back in this.*

"Yes, I have access to his suite. It is a workroom and a private living area."

"Bedroom?"

"Yes."

"I apologize if this is uncomfortable for you, Madame Ricci. So much depends on your help."

Victoria said, "I understand and will do what I can."

Elyesa continued, "The Reichsminister's office has a secret chamber that he uses as an archive for copies of the plans he and his architects draw up for the government. We have reason to believe he also has been entrusted with a variety of plans for armaments, troop movements, and war strategies. He saves everything in his personal archive."

"Yes, I have seen the files and have worked in the archive."

Victor Bergh said, "There is only a single lock on the door. You could make an impression for a copy from Speer's keys."

Elyesa started to say, "I presume...."

"Yes. Reichsminister Speer removes them from his pants when we are intimate."

Elyesa said, "Victoria, we know that Speer has made you a clerical assistant in his office so that you may come and go without his wife or any of his associates from becoming suspicious."

"Yes, Madame Bergh. During the war, my travel to perform on international stages has been severely limited, so I have become a secret courtesan. Reichsminister Speer has devised it so that I do not interact with any office personnel but work in his office, only coming and going through a private entrance to his rooms. I am familiar with the chamber of which you speak and the files there. He has charged me with organizing them. He is planning a memoir."

"We are interested in munitions plans, current and future in the German-occupied territories."

Victor spoke up, "We also need construction information, rail, and access road information for the concentration camps.

"Is it possible for you to pass these files along to us? We will copy and return them in a matter of hours. I have compiled a list, but you must commit it to memory, no paper."

"I suppose we could...."

She stopped and thought.

"Albert is a man of passion. His work comes first, but he has a few extravagances of a more sensual nature. One of those is a love of alcohol – French wines, actually. The other is making love.

"After each of these foibles, he sleeps, and he sleeps soundly."

"That enables this arrangement to pass documents. If at any time you have a concern for your safety, leave a five-mark note with the newspaperman in the kiosk just outside the Chancellery."

Victoria stood up. "You can depend on me. I am a well-trained actress in addition to being a musician. "

She continued, "I am tired of the Nazis. It is time for the world to be rid of them. Their atrocities are many, and each one of us must do what we can to bring them down, regardless of one's self-interest."

"Here is the media for the impression of the key. When you are able, pass it to Herr Biermann, the newspaperman. He will also take the files. Wearing the peacock necklace will signal that you have something or need something from him. He will ask you for your newspaper for the trash as you leave the Chancelry each evening. Put the files in the folds of the paper. Buy the *Völkischer Beobachter* in the morning and *Der Angriff* in the afternoon. Returning documents will be in the next day's newspaper purchase from Biermann. Remember, if you are suspicious at any time, a five-mark note, and we will get you out of harm's way."

"How will I recognize Herr Biermann?"

"You are looking at him, Madame Ricci. I will never be far from you."

"I will do my best. My friends. May God watch over us all."

Chapter Thirty-Four: Caught

THE REICHSTAG, BERLIN. JANUARY 1942

Victoria turned from the files in Speer's archival chamber. She noticed an ornate wooden box in a cloth bag on a shelf near the back. It was about a half meter in length and seemed to have jewels covering the top. As she moved towards it, she heard noises in the suite's entrance foyer. She quickly exited the closet and took a position in front of the Reichsminister's desk. She picked up his leather work folder.

"What are you doing in here?"

"Oh, Albert, you startled me. I thought you had gone home."

"I did, but not home. Dinner with the Führer... I called for my car. I wanted my portfolio for a meeting in the morning."

He waved a hand at what she was holding.

The Nazi Party's Minister of Armaments and War Production silently closed the door behind him and moved into the office. He tossed his winter coat on a chair and walked toward her. Speer's face was hidden in shadow.

He unsnapped the holster flap, removed his Luger, and held the pistol at his side. His uniform shirt was partially unbuttoned. "Unkempt" was never an adjective to be applied to Albert Speer. Unless...

He had been drinking. A shock of black hair cascaded over his forehead and into his eyes as he moved into the firelight.

"You have not answered my question, Victoria." He looked around the room.

"Albert, in addition to my clerical work, I am preparing for my return to te stage, and the light in here is better. I worked on my correspondence until past curfew. I did not realize how late it was, to be honest."

He raised the gun.

She continued, "I am very excited that the Reich is allowing my trip to Scandinavia. So, I decided to stay here for the evening. I love lounging in your bed even when you are not...." She attempted to look enticing as the initial shock of being discovered left her.

"Lies."

"Albert. You don't know what you are saying."

"You are a spy, and I have caught you in the act."

Holy Mother, I am about to be killed or jailed, and I am terrified.

They said nothing but stared at each other. The fire, the only light in the room, cast surreal light and shadow throughout the office. Victoria touched her peacock pendant and wondered if there was any chance of escape.

She followed his gaze. It was then she realized that the panel to the hidden room was slightly ajar. She stepped forward so that she was close to him and blocked his view. Victoria reached up and took his face in her hands.

"My Darling, I would never betray our love. We mean so much to each other."

She slipped a hand between the buttons of his tunic. His chest was warm. Albert wavered a bit on his feet. He gestured ridiculously with the gun and pushed her away.

"Remove your dress and underclothes. Do it now."

Victoria could not believe what she was witnessing. She disrobed. The Reichsminister removed his Sam Browne belt, a symbol of his authority in the Nazi regime, and his uniform jacket.

"I have been appointed by the Führer to be the torturer of every slutty female spy who we capture, and you are mine for the night until I am satisfied."

His hand roamed roughly over her naked body, causing her to submit to his eager fondling. She tried to push him off, but he would not be deterred.

He caught her by the hair and growled, "This is going to hurt…." He rocked on his feet. "… and I am not going to stop." She caught him as he almost fell flat on the floor.

She managed to break out of her panic, and then, she remembered. She said, "Please, Herr General, I will do anything, and I mean anything, to make this right." Guiding another of his hands' journeys over her body, she added, "Sometimes I am very reckless when you are away, and I fear I cannot satisfy you. I get into your bed and imagine your hands. Then I must… "

She moved his hand down her abdomen.

He set the Luger on his desk and roughly turned her around, winding his belt around her wrists at the small of her back.

"You are an insatiable Italian whore and will stop at nothing to gratify your lust, including using your body to serve your Russian masters. How many have you had today?"

Albert loved roleplaying, made-up scenarios of romantic, fantastical, and sometimes near-brutal episodes of pure pagan sex play. His favorite was the repressed, virginal nun and the passionate gardener. They acted it out many times. In some of their lust fiction, he even played the submissive role. He enjoyed eroticizing her theatrical and physical gifts.

His attempts to bind her proved too much for his liquor-soaked mind. Speer stumbled and draped himself over her. As she nearly carried her very intoxicated lover into the bedroom, she had one thought.

I must remember my newspaper in the morning.

Chapter Thirty-Five: La Niña de las Camelias.

CASTILLA-LA MANCHA, SPAIN

Rebecca raced the Ducati Multistrada 1200 S touring bike down the *autovia* to the east of Madrid. They took the ring road around the Capital after picking up the motorcycle at Madrid-Barajas Adolfo Suárez Airport. Loic held on behind her and leaned into the turns. He spoke over the helmet's communicator.

"I would have gone west and south, but you are the driver."

"The countryside to the east is so much more inspiring, my friend, and actually a lot quicker. You get a feel of the Castilla-La Mancha of Miguel de Cervantes and his knight errant. So, beautiful."

As if by evoking the fabled Don Quixote, the famous windmills appeared on the southern horizon. The land rolled out as a broad plain, flat, dry, and filled with sleepy farms and pasturelands. They slowed for quaint villages seemingly frozen in time.

The bright sun revealed livestock, vineyards, and fields for row crops at every turn of the road. Here and there, a goat herder led his flock along the roadside. Farmers had winterized their fields and now were anticipating springtime planting. A range of mountains stretched off in the distance like an ancient barricade from east to west.

"We used to come down here on holiday when I was an undergrad at the University of Salamanca. That's in the other direction." For Rebecca, the plains of La Mancha and the area around Toledo brought many memories of art, culture, and romance.

They pulled off just as the road to the south took a turn to the west. A small farmhouse nestled amid a grove of olive trees looked inviting. Lines of bare posts and wire raced along the countryside. The pruned stumps of grapevines huddled below their supports. An older man and his daughter waved them over to a wooden table near a twisted olive tree that had to be 200 years old. The lowing of cattle and bleating of the famous La Mancha goats replaced the roar of the motorcycle as they dismounted. Rebecca pulled her hair out as she removed her helmet. Their hosts tried not to look surprised that a woman was the sleek-suited driver of the slick machine.

She spoke to the Spaniards, and they nodded before hurrying to the house to prepare a refreshing lunch for their visitors. A little boy leaned out of the doorway with big brown eyes and an open mouth. He pointed to the "aliens" who appeared at their farm in black helmets and aero suits-- totally science fiction.

The boy came closer, still pointing and wrapped in wonder.

¿Eres superhéroes?

Loic pulled off his helmet and unzipped his jacket. He dropped to one knee before the youngster and said, "No, my little friend, we are only tourists."

Despite Loic's French accent and the boy's rural Castillian dialect, their exchange in Spanish was understandable by both. After a 360-degree inspection of the tall soldier and his female companion, the youngster moved over to the Ducati. The soldier lifted his new buddy, Mateo, onto the motorcycle seat. The boy was in heaven.

The family came out of the house with wine, bread, olives, and cheese. The youngest of two girls clapped her hands and ran around her motorcycled brother, uttering cries of joy. Loic lifted her behind the little guy who was holding the handle grips and making motor sounds. The shyer elder sister stayed close to her mother and prepared the table for *el almuerzo*, lunch.

In the breezy afternoon, the adults exchanged pleasantries. Keeping to the tourist persona, Loic and Rebecca asked questions about life in La Mancha.

"We get many visitors being so close to Toledo and the road. When we are not busy with the farm, we have time to welcome them and provide some local food."

The farmer added to his wife's comments, "We even have some simple accommodations for those who would like to stay. Out here, one can enjoy the country and not be bothered by the crowds in the city." He gestured through the trees to the silhouette of the metropolis on the hillside, slowly being revealed through the low clouds in the west.

"Toledo is less than an hour away and the capital...." He pointed in the other direction. " ... is about 70 kilometers up to the north."

Rebecca said, "You are at the crossroads here, then."

The mother spoke, "Yes. We get the tourists from the south also. Last week, we had two autobuses come through. I had my cousins and sisters from the next farm to help. We did well, and the folks were happy."

The farmer introduced his brother, who came from the ramshackle barn wiping his hands to investigate the new arrivals and their exotic driving machine. The young man's niece and nephew were still chatting about the bike.

"He is the family tour guide, a scholar, and a musician." The farmer made a guitar-strumming motion with his hands. He tells our visitors stories from the land, a history of this country.

The young Spaniard said, "My brother loves to brag about my schooling. It was good, but I prefer the sun, the earth, and my music."

Loic said, "Castilla-La Mancha has a rich history." It was almost a question.

"Oh yes, this is bloody soil going back thousands of years. They say that is why the earth here is so rich for crops and the feed for the animals." He dropped easily onto the bench, a dark male beauty with a sensitive face and the sparkling eyes of an artist.

"This land was once the center of Spain during the *Reconquista* when the Christian King and his Queen sent their troops to drive out the Moors from Africa who had lived here for seven hundred years. Toledo was once the capital for the Catholic monarchs."

The farmer's wife added as she passed the dishes, "So much killing. My grandfather fought in the Civil War. Such terrible stories he had." She pondered the sadness of her words, shaking her head. "Yes, all the way back to ancient times. Yes, La Mancha is a crossroads with many travelers and battles throughout its history. But there will always be a need for farmers, and so, we farm."

Her husband spoke. “We know the day is coming when developers will want to buy our land as the city continues to grow. They say industrialization is headed out here. It will be a good opportunity for my family. Farm life is hard.”

The brother said, “It would be excellent if we got some technology companies interested in this region or even factories to build motorcycles and cars.”

Rebecca watched as the older girl walked off quietly to find a shady spot near the horse corral and open a book. A young colt stretched its head through the wooden fence, and she patted his muzzle as she read. Excusing herself from the table, Rebecca approached the teenager and settled in next to her. They spoke in Spanish.

The girl told her a bit about her life and her aspirations to go to the city one day and become a teacher. Mostly homeschooled, the young woman was eager to continue her education.

“What are you reading?”

The girl turned the cover so that Rebecca could read the title, La Dama de las Camelias. She traced a finger under the last word of the title. “That is my name, Camila.”

“I am Rebecca. It is good to meet you and your family.”

They both looked up to see Loic giving the children motorcycle rides as the table was cleared, and the men laughed and drank wine.

“Rebecca, is America wonderful? I have heard so.”

“Yes, it is an exciting place, Camila.”

“I would like to go there someday, but my family needs me here. My father and mother want me to make a good marriage.”

“May I ask you where you get your books?”

Camila closed the volume and looked out toward the city in the distance. She spoke with the simple dreaminess of one who longs for more life.

"She drives a blue and white truck, like a lorry thing, from Toledo out into the countryside. Every few weeks, she comes this way. She has books and stops to tell stories and do some lessons, the maths and such. Young people from nearby farms come here and spend the day with the old teacher. She assigns readings and leads discussions with the older folks. She even brings my Uncle Hugo some sheet music for his guitar. I think she was once beautiful like you. Now she is very old, ancient."

In a nearby pasture, Loic was teaching the young farmhand how to ride the Ducati. The parents were calling in the excited children.

"What is your teacher's name?"

"I do not know. We call her *La Profesora.* She once told me she has many names. I am grateful for her visits to our farm."

Rebecca pulled up a picture of Victoria Ricci, a theater shot taken toward the end of her career. She handed Camile her phone.

"No, Miss, that is a picture of a great lady. *La Professora* is a peasant like me... wait... The eyes are a bit familiar, deep, and knowing. Anyway, the teacher is not Spanish. She has a slight accent. She is not from this region."

As if anticipating the next question, the girl said, "We never know when she will come by this way. I hope it will be soon. We have not seen her in a while."

"How old would you say your teacher is, Camila?"

"Oh, she is very old, Miss. Like the same sage as my Papa."

Rebecca thought for a moment as the girl spoke once more.

"Yes, very old, at least 60."

Chapter Thirty-Six: The Imperial City

TOLEDO, SPAIN

Toledo crawled up the hill like a white and russet panther glistening in the afternoon sun and slowly growing its deep shadows, building by building. The ancient town seemed to dangle its hind paws in the craggy gorges of the Tagus, flowing in a semi-circle around the venerable metropolis. Verdant green fields and rocky outcroppings spread out like a richly patterned apron from beyond the river and seemed to leap over the walls of this city, twisting up to form castles, fortresses, and cathedrals.

On the outskirts, the riders paused at the bend of the road that led to the Roman arches of the Puente de Alcántara, the pilgrim's bridge across the Tagus River on the eastern side of old Toledo. They took in the view that inspired many famous artists like El Greco and Van Gogh. The Castle of San Servando guarded the eastern slopes behind them. The stone fortifications of the Alcázar crowned the highest hill across the bridge. An assortment of church spires reached to the heavens, some the converted minarets of ancient mosques.

They entered the city and ascended the steep side streets to the imposing fortress with its bloody history, the Alcázar of Toledo. Pulling into a parking lot near the impressive cream-colored walls of the citadel, they surveyed the landmark with its quartet of signature towers topped by gray-black roofs complete with ornate spires.

Loic said, "This is an incredible monument. This castle played a huge part in the Spanish Civil War, one of the first battles between the Nationalists and the Republicans – the Siege of *El Alcázar*. By the end of September 1936, only four sections of the walls were left standing. Can you see the difference between the original and the restored stonework? And there in the uneven roofline, see? Fact: Himmler visited here in 1940."

Rebecca shivered, "Ick, Nazis. How come you know so much?"

His black eyes flashed. "Just handsome and smart, I guess. A winning combination." Loic's killer smile sparkled. He slipped an arm around her shoulders as they passed through security and entered the inner courtyard of the citadel. Rebecca politely moved out of the boy's very familiar, casual embrace.

"Besides, the military and its history are my stock in trade. Love studying up on this stuff."

"When you're not putting the make on women of all nationalities." She noticed the stares from the other tourists as they advanced through the fortress.

He said in French, "Just young and frisky, I guess."

"Behave, my French Romeo. You agreed to gentlemanly behavior."

Loic did a mock, courtly bow and then continued his lesson.

"The Alcázar of Toledo is now a military museum and a library. Ahhh, my sweet. Now I know why we are here."

"Right, you can explore the museum. I want to see some of the folks at the... " Rebecca read from a blue and white sign,"... the Castilla-La Mancha Regional Library."

"OK, meet you back here in a few." The young soldier strode toward the entrance of the Museum of the Army.

***

Rebecca flipped through her phone while sitting on a bench under the arched arcade of the inner courtyard. Without looking up, she said to her approaching buddy. "WiFi here is for shit-- these massive walls."

She glanced up and asked, "How were the guns and cannons?"

"Very cool. I learned a lot. Many sacrifices by so many. Years of struggle and death. Any leads as to our Diva?"

"I met with some of the higher-ups in the world of Toledo's bibliography. They have no information on a mobile library that serves the rural communities of La Mancha that fit my description. Their mobile units are of a different color, green and yellow, not blue and white. They suggested inquiring at schools and educational not-for-profits. I thought of bookstores also."

He flopped down next to her, pulling out his mobile. "We got the ride. I got us some rooms. We can continue the search." He showed her his screen and the outside of their hotel. "Albergue Los Pascuales-- very nearby."

She cocked an eyebrow.

He stood and held out a hand and said with a mocking grin.

"Don't give me that look, my virgin. Two rooms. I'll drive. You ride bitch for a while."

She swatted his behind while taking his hand. They headed to the exit.

***

Rebecca and Loic checked in and went for a stroll as the night came on, coaxing the street lamps in the winding passageways and boulevards to deepen their soft glow. The discussion over partridge braised in wine accompanied by assorted cheeses and savory tapas concerned the history of the arms industry in Toledo.

Rebecca commented, "Knives and guns are everywhere in this town."

"The old Royal Arms Factory is gone, but the armaments legacy remains in many workshops around the city. In these times, they deal mainly in ceremonial weapons, spears, and swords with the traditional Toledo blades, " Loic said.

Here and there, they asked locals about possible leads to Victoria Ricci, inquiring about old teachers and librarians. Weariness seemed to settle over them, enhanced by the wine and comfort food. Looks and innocent touches seemed to take on a more intimate meaning. They returned to the inn.

Rebecca was sitting on the bed when the knock came on the door that connected their rooms. She was updating both Haig and McGrath on their progress. Rebecca was also planning to communicate with Eris for additional advice and a status report on Mark.

"Yes, Loic. C'mon in."

The young man came into her room. He was shirtless, and in the slacks he had worn for the evening's dinner and walkabout. The sexy lad was barefoot. His sexual marketing strategy, using his magnificent young warrior's body, was top-grade, and the wine bottle with the two glasses removed any confusion about his intentions.

Through the open windows of Rebecca's balcony came the soft night sounds of strollers, occasional dog barks, and the sighing of the night breezes through the trees. Someone in the courtyard below played a soft flamenco, accompanying the muffled cries and rhythmic cadences of a few spectators and dancers.

Loic quietly inquired about her welfare. "I thought you would be interested in a nightcap and perhaps...." His seduction vibes were in full gear as he put the wine and glasses on the side table. He seemed to unconsciously palm his chiseled abdominals.

Rebecca sighed, closed her laptop, smiled, and said, "Hey, bud. Look at you and all that sexiness-- all muscle and Latin romance. Pour us out a glass and have a seat. I want to tell you something." She motioned to the club chairs and stood up from the bed and her work.

The hot soldier poured out the wine and eased back. His long legs stretched invitingly into the space between them. His handsome face was smiling in anticipation of a night of expected and intense passion. Loic was one of those men who was well aware of his masculine, good looks and was frisky as the day was long.

She came off the bed and slowly walked the room as she talked.

"Loic, I have a healthy sexual preference for fit, young men, and you definitely check all the boxes of my lust profile. Yeah, you are definitely a hunk."

Loic blinked. Sex partners usually responded with less of an analytical discussion and more intimate body action. *C'mere, big boy...* He attempted to rise and take her into his arms. She held her glass and gestured for him to remain seated as she continued.

"You know. I am crazy-assed, head over heels in love with Mark."

Shit. You gotta be kidding me. I hope there is a 'but' in here someplace. I want this woman tonight.

She faced him, settling back down on the edge of the bed.

"I meant it in Paris, kiddo, when I said no sexin' on this little escapade."

She sipped.

He raked one hand through his close-cropped black hair and stretched. He smiled, totally sure that the shot of his bicep peak and torso ripple would cause Rebecca to lower her defenses.

She waved at the half-naked male animal, voguing in the chair with lust on his mind.

"Yeah, yeah, yeah, with all of that.

"And frankly, I am a little pissed off that, despite your agreement, you think you can wear this woman down with all that man-lust, muscle posing, and testosterone. Yeah, it would be a hot and amazing ride, but sometimes, ya gotta be true to the ones you love, my friend."

"Rebecca...."

"One last thing, Loic. You are a soldier, top of your game, respected in your profession, a man of might and integrity. I checked.

"There is much honor in the military. You respect the profession you have chosen and aspire to be a man of principle, I am sure. Otherwise, I would not have agreed to share this mission. And the bottom line is, I can do this with you or without you, and you know I am very capable of either option."

The Frenchman shrugged and said, "I just thought...."

"Yeah, I get it. Thinking with the little head as opposed to the big one. I suspect you rarely get a turndown."

Silence.

He drank, stood, and gazed out the window, his heart reaching for the solace of the *cante jondo* vocals wafting up from the flamenco musicians in the street. After a bit, he turned back to her.

"I apologize, Rebecca. I will live up to our agreement and see this thing through. You have my word."

"Good. So, let's just talk. A conversation is a way for us to know each other better."

He grinned as he came back to his seat. Loic said with just a tad of sarcasm, "Conversation with a beautiful woman. Now, there's a novel idea. Sure, why not?"

She hiked a pillow at him.

They talked for a few hours about life, family, art, the military, history – many things. When the wine was gone, he stood to leave.

Rebecca said, "Sleep well, my friend."

As the young man left her suite, Rebecca noticed the tattoo on his broad back, dead center below the nape of his neck.

A star.

***

On the second day in the Royal City, Loic and Rebecca hit the markets and many churches in the city. Devote seniors and shop proprietors had no information on the elusive teacher, artist, and legendary beauty. Beneath the ornate facades of cathedrals and intricately carved city gates, Rebecca and Loic sought *La Gloriosa,* looking for folks who best knew both the public life and the *demimonde* side of Toledo. No luck.

In the afternoon, they drove the motorcycle along the roads that ran close to the ancient, encircling walls. Turning into a cozy neighborhood, Rebecca pointed to a cream-colored building with a sloping tile roof that seemed to have a slapped-on, cross-mounted façade. The structure dominated the small plaza. Loic parked the motorcycle in a space near a corner bookshop.

"So much history in one building," Rebecca said as they stepped inside. "This baby was built by the Castillian King in the 14th century to apologize for the slaughter of the Jews whom the Catholics blamed for an outbreak of the black death. Originally a synagogue, it became the

Church of the Transit of the Virgin. It is now a Sephardi Museum, the Jews of Toledo and southern Europe."

She continued her historical review of the national monument as they passed walls of Nasrid-style polychrome stucco work bearing Hebrew inscriptions from the Book of Psalms. Arabic inscriptions were intertwined with the floral patterns in the plaster. Stylized calligraphy, combined with intricate geometric and vegetal forms, ornamented the spaces between the horseshoe and multifoil arches.

Loic was amazed at her knowledge, for which she offered the following explanation: "Museums are *my* stock in trade, friend. This one is a favorite."

Rebecca went on to expand on the Islamic influence reflected in the women's gallery, the lace-like wall that held the recess for the Torah's Holy Ark, and the windows atop the delicately carved reliefs of the upper story. Thinking that the woman in the black leather and Kevlar aero suit was a tour guide, a handful of tourists began to edge closer to listen to her impromptu lecture.

Rebecca pointed up at the massive *Mudéjar Artesonado* ceiling. "This is a Spanish masterpiece, a style found throughout Moorish Spain and North Africa co-opted by the Christians during the *Reconquista*. You see it everywhere in Spain."

She pointed up to the intricate tracery and added, "The ceiling is entirely wood lathing, interlaced in delicate geometric patterns between the rafters. Many times, they painted or gilded the wood. *Artesonado* comes from the Spanish word *artesa*, a shallow basin used in breadmaking. The *Mudéjars* were the Muslims of Castile given special status by the Crown as artisans. They were the builders of this synagogue."

Loic said, "Rebecca, the three faiths...."

"Yes, Darling. Jews, Christians, and Muslims. Our elusive superstar is somewhere near."

Chapter Thirty-Seven: The Woman of La Mancha

TOLEDO, SPAIN

The Ducati was gone.

"Rebecca, I know I locked it."

"Holy fuck, this is for shit, Loic."

"Let's see if anyone knows something." He strode into the bookstore/souvenir shop.

"Yes, you locked it, but vandals can hurt your machine, sir. It is in the alley behind the gate on the side of the store." The speaker was a young woman in her early 20s who read a large book as she sat behind the counter, The Siege of Numantia by Miguel de Cervantes.

Loic headed out with the key to the locked gate in the alley.

"How..."

"There are few locks that she cannot open." The woman nodded to the back of the shop.

Surrounded by stacks of books and bookcases, Rebecca found an older woman playing solitaire. She did not look up but nodded to the empty seat. As she settled opposite, Rebecca noticed that what she thought were playing cards was actually a Tarot deck.

The woman looked up and said, "I saw that you were coming."

Then she saw the eyes, and Rebecca knew.

The back alcove's occupant resembled a well-cared woman in her 60s in stylish jeans and a Ralph Lauren top. Modest earrings, a necklace, and tennis shoes completed the look. A winter shawl was draped over the back of her chair.

The woman's skin was relatively wrinkle-free, and her face showed little evidence of cosmetic surgery and sparse makeup. She wore her long blonde/brown touched with grey hair up and off her neck. The entire effect was that of a retired film star with a preference for the rejuvenation spas of Rodeo Drive.

Impossible. Victoria Ricci would be over one hundred, stooped, and without muscle tone. Gotta be a daughter or granddaughter.

As if reading Rebecca's mind, the elderly woman said, "In Spain, the dead are more alive than the dead of any other country in the world. Federico García Lorca."

She dealt 5 cards face down. She turned one, The Priestess, and placed it in front of Rebecca. "You have come from a long way searching through time for...?" Rebecca turned over a second card, The Empress. She placed it in front of the older woman.

Rebecca answered, "You. If you are the Frozen Diva."

No response. They were interrupted by Loic's return. He was excited as he said, "Rebecca, the bike... the alley ... a blue and white lorry...."

He noticed the woman.

"Holy shit."

Loic pointed at the elderly woman and began to stammer, "You... you... you're the... the.... "

Open-mouthed, he dropped into an empty chair just as the woman turned the third card and placed it in front of him, The Star.

The woman in question tapped the card and looked up at the soldier. "You are the bright and strong guide for the journey."

"Thank you, ma'am." The young man was mesmerized. He continued to have perceptible trouble speaking.

She looked at him closely as her eyes filled with tears. "How is your mother?"

Loic stammered, "She is well, thank you, ma'am, and... and... she sends her love."

She placed one hand on Loic's as she turned the fourth card. No one said anything at the appearance of The Hermit. The woman picked up the card and seemed to look at it lovingly. She then looked intently at Rebecca before asking, “She has crossed over, yes?”

“Yes, Miss Arva is dead. It was she who led me to you before and after she died.”

“After? Ahhh. Through Madame Ondine?”

“She provided the best of the clues. Her power is real and true.”

She flipped the last card-- The Lovers reversed.

“Tell me.”

Rebecca took the free hand of Victoria Ricci as she tapped the image of the naked man and asked, “That is Mark. He is in much trouble.

“Please, can you help me rescue him? He is everything to me.”

Chapter Thirty-Eight: Parsifal

THE BAYREUTH FESTSPIELHAUS, BAVARIA, SEPTEMBER 1944

"But you must take it, my dear. So much depends on the safety and proper use of the artifact."

The Reichsminister drank deeply from the whiskey flask. He was unsteady on his feet. Victoria suspected he would fall from the grid deck, high in the flies of the Festival Hall, a favorite trysting space for Hitler's Architect and his beloved *La Gloriosa* when they were in Bavaria, despite his bad knee.

Now, his words of love were replaced by torment. "Germany is losing the war. This horrible opera of nation against nation is drawing to a close, and I have come to realize the monstrosity of Hitler's ambitions. I will not play my part much longer."

She held the handsome German close to her. Below, a few workers secured the empty stage, turning out the lights, removing props, and placing the safety lamp center stage. The theater would be bunkered against the bombing and ravages of Germany's enemies. The war had come to Wagner's Bavarian paradise.

The intoxicated soldier whispered, "The spies among us have stolen Germany's war strategies, tearing them to pieces like the ripping shots of machine guns. The agents of the Allies are inside the Circle, and the destruction of the so-called Thousand Year Reich is written in blood. We are doomed."

She settled him against the catwalk supports as he continued, "You must realize what it is I have hidden among the regalia of this production of *Parsifal* and am now entrusting to you. This is no gaudy, theatrical prop, Victoria. It has a terrible divine power. In the wrong hands, it will bring about the destruction of many. Take it. Hide it in some secret place, my ageless beauty. Only you can do this."

Speer clung desperately to her as he continued, "Since the artifact has come into my hands, I have become a distraught and terrified man.

I can not hold it in my hands without seeing the blood – blood covering these hands, the blood of innocents."

He held them before his face and shook with agitation.

Victoria attempted to calm him. She reached for him and drew him close as she said, "Albert, my love, you are filled with a terror that reaches into your soul. Whatever this object conjures in your mind, I will do what I can to remove it and keep it secure."

His fear began to subside.

"But, now, you must help me get you down. Your driver will be waiting."

After a few settling breaths, Speer attempted to change the subject and manipulate the walkway in the fly loft to the stairs.

"Your Kundry was magnificent tonight, my dear. The members of the High Command were singing your praises. The Chancellor told me that this would be the last of the Wagner Festivals in Bayreuth for a while but that Reichsminister Joseph Goebbels has approved your tour of "The Ring" to Copenhagen, Stockholm, and Oslo. He is always so moved by our national saga. If the devil has a spiritual side, Hitler finds his rejuvenation in Wagner."

"Yes, I know. Der Führer sees himself as the Wagnerian hero of the New Order-- art as propaganda."

They gained the circular stairway and descended to the stage floor. Before departing, the lovers spoke briefly of her medical treatments.

"You are well, my love? No side effects from this?"

"None, Albert. It would appear that the Chancellor's doctors have perfected the treatment. Has the Führer begun the transfusions?"

"Not yet. Since the Allied Invasion of Normandy, Hitler has become extremely paranoid and very preoccupied with finding the traitors in his government as well as the defense of the nation and the occupied territories. He suspects everyone of feeding the Allies important information-- even me. Even you."

He stroked her flawless beauty. Victoria embraced him and led him to the stage door and his waiting car. The soldier stopped and kissed his mistress but kept one hand on her throat.

"You are innocent of such suspicions. Yes, my dear?"

She escaped his grip and stepped back. The Nazi's hand remained outstretched for her. His intentions seemed to change from a grasp of warning to a yearning lover's reach. He lowered his hand, past his holstered pistol, to his hip flask. The single stage light glinted on its silver surface as he took another deep pull of the fiery liquid it held. She saw in his thirst a desperation for an obliviating forgetfulness.

Victoria said, "Albert, I am an artist, not a politician. And now it seems I am a high-classed Nazi courtesan, despised by the virtuous wives of the Third Reich. Should Germany lose the war, my fate will be one of total humiliation and, most likely, execution. Yet, suppose we are to be victorious. In that case, I will no doubt be subjected to intense scrutiny and hidden away-- a price I am willing to pay for sharing your bed and being your lover."

She stepped back into his embrace and remembered how attracted she was to this handsome man. But now, all was pretense. She was performing in her most challenging role. This man... no longer her heart's obsession. Victoria was playing with fire and had been for a long time.

He was so very powerful, and their relationship was indeed star-crossed. A man who lost his way little by little and beginning long ago, was now facing the consequences of his compromises, promotion after promotion, all in the name of his art. Her Albert was a dark Byronic hero tragically evil, torn by an internal rebellion, always arrogant, becoming supremely anti-social and yet enticingly romantic.

"Do not forget, Victoria, the... the ...." His eyes again were large and full of fear as he gestured backstage.

She covered his mouth with hers and kept him from speaking more about their secret, whispered on the broad space of the Festspielhaus stage. She was well aware that the auditorium was not empty. They were being observed from the darkness of the arena. There, in a darkened row of seats or in a shadowed alcove – searching eyes. In the deep shadows behind the sets or high above in the lofts, the informants of the Reich lurked in the night.

Victoria whispered softly, “I will do as you have instructed.”

Albert Speer’s driver snapped to attention as he arrived. The officer saluted and assisted the Reichsminister out of the theater by the stage door. Victoria turned in the direction of her dressing room, where Astrid, her maid, waited, holding her robe.

As she passed the prop room, Victoria remembered where the stage manager kept the key.

She would return.

Chapter Thirty-Nine: The Spear of Destiny

TOLEDO, SPAIN

"In the opera of *Parsifal*, the knights search for the Holy Grail, the cup Jesus used for the sacred wine during his Last Supper. But, the libretto includes another holy artifact. The spear that pierced the side of Jesus as he hung on the cross."

Following the encounter at the bookstore, the woman asked Rebecca and Loic to go for a stroll with her along the Calle de los Reyes Cathólicos. They found a shady table at the Café Restaurant Scorpions in the shadow of the Monasterio de San Juan de los Reyes, away from intruding eyes and ears.

Victoria continued, "The Lance of Longinus is a relic steeped in more than two thousand years of Christian legend from gospel times to the adventures of the Jerusalem Crusaders and beyond. It was claimed that it was part of Charlemagne's regalia for the Holy Roman Empire. Wagner's sources for his masterpiece, *Parsifal,* drew on those stories. In the opera, the spear is the conduit of divine power and carries with it the judgment of God."

Loic said, "When I was a boy, my mother and I visited St. Peter's in Rome. I remember hearing that the spear was in the Vatican. There is even a mammoth statue of Longinus in the transept of the Basilica."

Victoria corrected, "Not so, my friend. The Catholic Church has a spear relic but makes no claim to its authenticity."

The Diva looked off into the trees and the winter garden as if remembering a painful time in her life. "Hitler was obsessed with sacred mysteries and the occult. He wanted eternal life both physically and spiritually. His agents scoured the earth for holy artifacts and medical treatments that would both extend his life and secure divine approbation for his ambitions. I am a living example of both those fixations.

"The secret medical experiments of the Third Reich included research into extending human life naturally and artificially. How ironic from a regime responsible for the slaughter of countless millions across Europe and the East."

She shook her head as she continued, "Primitive by today's standards, I was part of the experiments with undifferentiated cells, now known as stem cells. My body was capable of resisting the aging process associated with the body's production of free radicals that lower the life span of organs and tissues. The chemistry and biology were not as sophisticated in 1940, but they were on to something. It was a beginning, and I am a living example of agelessness– or at least curtailed senescence.

"After ten years, my treatments stopped in 1945. Hitler ended up a burned corpse outside his bunker in Berlin, and Albert Speer was sent to Spandau Prison by the Allies. It would seem that a healthy and active lifestyle has continued to keep me 'frozen in time,' if you will, an artifact myself."

Loic jumped in. "But you are a hero of the War, Ms. Ricci. Your espionage for the Allies secured important information that resulted in the bombing of Nazi armaments in Europe and Russia. You were honored and acclaimed after the war."

La Gloriosa patted the Frenchman's hand. "Your great-grandmother-- now there was a brave woman, together with your great-grandfather, Victor, they were the real heroes. The French Resistance benefitted from our snuggling up to those Nazi murderers. Women throughout history use the only strategies left to us by our masculine overlords, sexual seduction, romance, and beauty. But we succeed."

The Diva plucked at her shawl as she said, "In the end, Hitler's agents were close, but we got out. My dear Astrid and I were in Paris for a production of "Butterfly" in July 1945. I remember we could hear the canons on the frontier.

"It was during that tour that the suspicions of the Nazis brought them to my door. They planned to arrest me after the final curtain call. I managed by a prearranged signal to tip off our friends in the Resistance. Your great-grandparents showed up in my dressing room during the intermission. They were disguised as stagehands. They spoke softly but firmly as they said, 'We are leaving now.' I had very little time."

Victoria pulled her shawl closer as if the memory of her near capture brought chills. She continued, "Act Three played with an understudy, but Butterfly's geisha makeup is so heavy, they never suspected until the performance was over. The Resistance got us to Allied-occupied territory in western France and safety."

Rebecca asked, "And the relic?"

"Sounds like that movie... um... Raiders of the Lost Ark, does it not, my dear? Yes, I took it with me. The Sacred Spearhead has always been close to me. Because of its power, I am reluctant to part with it."

The Diva spoke with a slightly mysterious tone disguised as an invitation.

"Come, my friends, you must see the winter garden in the cloisters of the Monastery."

***

The lower courtyard of the Monasterio de San Juan de los Reyes features a small, enclosed garden. Rebecca and Loic accompanied Victoria through the beautiful monument built by Ferdinand and Isabella in the 15th century to the sunny, green space tended by friars. They settled on a bench in the afternoon sun, watching the monks pull the winter mulch from the flower beds.

"See, the baby green shoots anticipating spring and rebirth."

Rebecca asked, "Please tell us more about the relic, Madame."

"In 1938, with the Anschluss...."

"The annexation of Austria into Nazi Germany."

"Correct, young man. Hitler had the Imperial Regalia of the Holy Roman Empire brought from the Hofburg in Vienna to Nuremberg Castle for safekeeping. The Spear was among the treasurers. Goering or Himmler, I forget which one, had a special bunker built under the Castle to protect some of the Nazi's stolen art.

"After the war, Patton's Monuments, Fine Arts, and Archives Program claimed to have the Spear among the recovered Austrian treasures, but there were many stories of copies, theft, and substitution. It came into my hands in Bavaria near the end of 1944. The War would last until September of the following year with the defeat of Nazi Germany."

An elderly monk greeted the Diva and exchanged a few words with her.

Rebecca said, "The legends say it has the power to heal drawn from its contact with the blood of Christ."

"Yes, *la Sangre de Cristo*." The Diva rose and indicated that they should follow her. Public access to the Monastery was dwindling. As they walked into the shade of the cloister, the elderly monk instructed four of his novices to scrub the slate stones of the passageway on their hands and knees. As Loic, Victoria, and Rebecca stepped into the middle of the walkway, the clerics cordoned off the ambulatory at each end to prevent traffic. On either side, ornate Gothic arches contained statues of holy men and women who peered down on believers from both sides of the beautiful passageway.

... saints of the Three Faiths look down on her and guard her....

Victoria pointed and said, "That is San Juan, St. John the Evangelist, for whom this monastery is named. Of the four gospel writers, he alone mentions the spear."

She motioned to Loic and continued. "I think the statue of the saint is coming loose, my strong friend. What do you think?"

Loic stepped to the stone image which stood just above their heads. The powerful soldier reached up to the base with both hands. The statue of St. John pivoted forward and to the side, revealing a recess behind it, encased in shadow.

The old friar interrupted. He said nothing but placed a small wooden stool at the soldier's feet, part of his crew's floor washing implements. He slipped his hands into his oversized sleeves, bowed his head, and walked to the other set of novices on their hands and knees, spreading soapy water on slates that were worn from the tread of hundreds of years of holy monks and devout visitors.

Loic withdrew the package.

Chapter Forty: Flight

TOLEDO AND LA MANCHA, SPAIN

Loic sprinted down the exterior stairs from the second floor and crashed through the shop's door. Rebecca and Victoria took the back stairs from the upper level, which served as the residence. The American raced around the alley and re-entered the bookshop. She yanked a fire extinguisher from behind the desk and dashed to the rear of the first floor. The blaze was small, but the smell of the accelerant was heavy in the burning alcove. Flames licked at the bookshelves.

Victoria pulled a carpet runner from behind the desk and followed. She took the extinguisher from Rebecca. Together, they beat and doused the flames in a cloud of smoke and CO_2. Despite the lateness of the hour, neighbors arrived to help.

It was over in a few minutes. They stumbled, coughing, into the plaza. Victoria leaned on the arm of a formidable-looking woman who spoke excitedly in Spanish. Nearby, the cry of a wounded animal came from the front recesses of the synagogue.

Loic staggered as he backed into the dim lights of the plaza from the portico. His t-shirt was torn and bloodied. A hunting knife of Toledo steel clattered to the pavers. He turned and went down on one knee.

Rebecca hurried to the side of the wounded man, who raised a hand to indicate he was not seriously injured. A police cruiser and a fire engine screeched into the plaza. Loic surrendered to a ministering neighbor who checked him for wounds and sponged off the blood using the water from the plaza fountain. He spoke to a grave-looking police officer who used a flashlight to examine Loic's wallet and credentials.

"Two. There were two, Both dead. Back there." He waved to the porch of the synagogue. Rebecca asked him again if he was OK. Victoria walked the small distance to the group around the fountain.

"Is the boy all right? The fighters assure me that the damage is minor, that it is safe to return upstairs, and that we are lucky." She took the hands of the NATO soldier, seeking assurance of his safety.

Loic leaned close to both of them.

"As soon as we can, we are leaving."

***

"You have improved, dear boy. Flamenco guitar is not an easy style, but you have the talent. As you play, let your instrument convey the deep emotions of death, anguish, despair, and religious doubt. Think of your audience and draw them into your art. Entice their hearts and touch their very souls with your art."

Victoria Ricci smiled at the young man and turned back to the lessons with Camila. The family crowded into the small room, ensuring that their guests were comfortable with the simple accommodations.

In the middle of the night, back in Toledo, a greengrocer's truck had backed into the alley between the bookshop and the small market next door, its bulk completely filling the space. Thirty minutes later, the driver headed out of town to the countryside of La Mancha to pick up produce from local farmers. Onboard were Victoria, Loic, and Rebecca.

After the family left them, and Loic argued. "Let me contact my people. They will get us out of Spain."

"Yes. Do that. The Ghost Hand is close. We are in much danger. I am turning in." Rebecca made as if to settle in for the night.

Loic said, "Whoa, whoa. This is a switch. How did you get so agreeable all of a sudden? What's happened?"

"Nothing, Darling. We need to get Ms. Ricci to safety. I am just tired of all this."

Victoria said, "I have a tendency to agree with our French colleague, Ms. Quinto. Something is going on, and I believe you are considering going alone. Surely, your concerns for Mr. Gadarn have not changed. I believe that you are having concerns about me and you are reconsidering your options."

Rebecca said nothing but could not meet the Diva's gaze. Victoria took a deep breath and continued.

"I have left the bookshop in the hands of my heavy-set friend, Carmen, and her family. No harm will come while I am gone. Her brother-in-law will return the Ducati. Carmen will see to it that the book van and the lessons for the children in the country will continue."

She pointed in the direction of the departing guitarist. "I have given instructions to my financial manager that Hugo is to go to the music conservatory in Granada when the time is right. The Delgados will receive an annual stipend to cover the wages of a replacement worker while he is away at school. When Camila gets older, there is a scholarship for her at the University of Toledo.

"I tell you this not to brag about my financial security but to assure you that I am in an excellent state of mind. Your concerns about my ability to continue in this rescue mission are unfounded. I also tell you all this to let you know I have my affairs in order."

Rebecca said, "But your health, Madame. You are more than one hundred...."

"Rebecca, in my life, I have faced the Nazi High Command, enraged wives, dastardly critics, disappointed audiences, impotent lovers, and the strain, and honor, of fighting for the French Resistance. Whatever Hitler's doctors did to my body has worked for a long time."

She stood up and gestured with sincerity seasoned with operatic gusto and heart-wrenching pathos.

"There are children in captivity, and we must, we <u>must</u> free them."

She spoke with genuine sincerity as she continued, "I am a diva, after all. I am used to the most extraordinary challenges. And I conquer. In my profession, I reign as the undisputed queen.

"And, my dear, I continually insist on having things go my way. You both must believe in the spiritual connections I have had all my life. We can use them to help those who cry out for help."

She continued, "Rebecca, I say all of this in humility. And finally, you must realize that I will accompany you in this to the end. I can do no other."

Her audience of two was speechless.

The woman who many times had channeled the conviction, passion, and strength of any one of a host of opera heroines continued.

"And neither can you."

Silence.

Victoria added, "I assure you, Rebecca, you will not be saddled with an invalid old woman. Do not fear. I am a wonder of physical and spiritual power. You have the Empress, my dear, and...."

She pointed to Loic. "... the Star."

Loic looked at Rebecca. "What is it, my friend? There is more you are not telling. Take us into your confidence."

"Before we left Toledo. Eris sent me another communication. She was able to intercept communication that the sale of the hostages had been speeded up. Agents of the Red Specter are moving in place for the deal."

Loic said. "Then, we must intercept them quickly."

Rebecca said, "Loic, my concern is we need fast action and cannot be hamstrung by international bureaucracies and politics. We need the big dogs to back off a bit. We have to do this by the back door. Trouble is, how do we get into the war zone and confirm that these coordinates are legit? Could be a trap."

The young soldier said, "Leave that to me. Either of you get seasick?"

In the end, it would be the macho Frenchman who puked his guts up over the side of the fishing boat crossing the Red Sea to Western Yemen.

Chapter Forty-One: The Refugees

FORT LAUDERDALE, FLORIDA

"Victoria Ricca would have to be one hundred and nine years old. Rebecca said the woman looked and acted sixty. That is impossible, Hud. The Fountain of Youth is a myth."

"Sixteenth Century, Ponce de León – right here in Florida. You, my friend, Micah, need no youth elixir. You have enough vitality for four men. How about another round?"

"You and your insatiable homosexuality. I am appalled." Micah joked at the man whose bed he shared. "Besides, I have the Museum exhibit plans to finalize and need to get some sleep."

"Some opening. Your CEO is missing in action-- off in Spain somewhere."

"Dude, that's top secret. There are evil elements around that would give anything to find her. Anyway, she will be here for the opening. There is a lot at stake. Board members are calling for her resignation even as we speak."

Hud stroked the face of his new friend. "So let's not talk, let's just...."

Micah swatted his frisky bud. Their relationship was still in its early stages. Micah liked to call it "The Wonder of Me" phase – intimate moments of long and sincere conversations that lasted well into the night, gestures filled with romance, and sex-ups like they invented man-on-man copulation. This included frequent sleepovers at Hudson Ch'en's spacious condo in an ultra-modern high-rise in Fort Lauderdale's trendy Las Olas district.

My neighborhood in the New River Bayou creeps me out, man, ever since the death of Arva St. Genevieve.

"Micah, you are never going to get some rest. Your mind is like a steel trap. You get hold of something and cannot let it go. Something is bothering you."

"Yep, Hud. You are right. You know, this long-life thing from the World War II era, I just don't get it."

"OK. Prop the pillows and listen to your Hud. I had a down day at the foundation, so I did some web surfing on the topic."

The young executive continued, "So, we are talking about the 1930s and forbidden experimental medical treatments to ensure longevity. Looking back on what we know now, there are two ways Hitler's mad scientists could have gone."

Hud reached for his phone, and Micah repositioned his new crush so that Hud's head lay on his chest as he scrolled. A red, black, and gold dragon tattoo coursed up the right thigh and onto the butt and back of the elegant Asian American, peeking in and out as he settled against Micah. The executive assistant played with Hud's jet-black and super-straight hair.

So gorgeous.

"Back then, the scientific understanding of genes and chromosomes was pretty primitive, although the discovery of DNA and chromosomes goes back to the middle of the 19th century by German and Swiss scientists-- big surprise. They knew of hereditary mechanisms in the thirties.

"Breakthrough would come after the War in 1953 with the structure of DNA proposed by Watson, Crick, and others like Maurice Wilkins and Rosalind Franklin.

"A woman – don't hear much about that. Very cool."

"Don't look at me, sexy. You caucasian dudes have been writing Western history for millennia and leaving a bunch of us out."

Micah lightly punched his friend's muscled shoulder and said, "Hud, I'm Latino. Brown people have been passed over too as the white guys wrote the history books."

"Yeah, whatevah… so then came the human genome project of the mid-20th century. But the point here is the Nazis had been fiddling around with cell theory and tissue culture for a while. So, they injected La Ricci with undifferentiated cells or enzyme extracts that acted like the body's substances that naturally repair DNA in cells. It talks about the Hayflick number… yadda, yadda. The stem cells extend the life of replicating cells by… blah, blah, blah….

Hud left off, set down his mobile, and turned to Micah. "Boring, boring, boring… Mike, let's play."

"Talk about a one-track mind." Micah tickled the trim abs of the sexy man. Hud rolled over and looked at Micah. The dragon raced across the naked man's flanks.

Hud said, "Anyway, they stumbled on a scientific accident, and it worked. Ricci is a living example. Science is full of that serendipitous shit – Fleming and penicillin, Curie and radium. Glad they never used the Ricci protocol on Hitler."

He set the phone aside and said, "Lesson over, my man." Hud pulled his boyfriend on top of him and kissed him passionately. Arms and legs began to move with carnal determination, positions changing slowly with lust-filled energy.

"I gotta tell you, Museum Boy, you have one amazing ass."

Micah's phone went off.

"Seriously? You are not going to take this call now… I was just about to…"

"Hey, Michele… Downstairs? Hold on."

Micah looked at his buddy. "Feel like visitors? This sounds important."

Hud smiled ruefully and reached for his robe.

"Sure, but you owe me one mindless shag. This man is boy butt hungry."

"Only one? Such an amateur."

***

Michele apologized for the intrusion and led three strangers into the condo, a young man, an attractive Bradley Cooper look-alike, and an ancient black woman.

Hud asked, “Tea, Madame? I only have oolong.”

“Oh, yes, my angel child, I need the black dragon’s brew. We have come very far.”

Micah held up a bottle of bourbon and caught the eyes of the men.

“Ahh, so fine, my friend. Remy takes it on the rocks. Gimme da ‘gay pour’ *mon amie*.”

The other man said, “I’m Benny, and I would like one of those also, please.” He was fascinated by the beautiful condo and its Eastern motifs.

Reaching for water for Michele, Micah said as he served the hefty cocktails, “Rebecca and Michele in New Orleans, right? Wow, I heard about your adventure.” He poured a “vodka, rocks, twist,” one for Hud and one for himself.

Everyone settled on the large sectional. The night view of ‘the Venice of the South’ sparkled through the large windows.

“Dey come into my town and cause all such trouble, Remy is here to say. Now we are on da run. We are hunted by dangerous criminals at every turn. Nowhere to go.”

Hud returned with Madame Ondine’s tea and a plate of sandwiches, provisions intended for holding up in the condo and making love for hours. The guests helped themselves while explaining their run from the Ghost Hand, including Benny’s encounter with the Jade Cobra and her minions.

“Gimme a sec, folks.” Hud exited into the Primary bedroom and returned in jeans, a t-shirt, and tennis shoes.

Ever the man in charge, Hud said, “So, here’s the plan. Micah will call Rebecca’s contact at the FBI, Special Agent Mary Chaffee. These folks need a meeting with her.”

He held up a set of keys. "This is a house in Wilton Manors. I am supposed to be looking after it for my ex. He moved away, but it is furnished. No one will find you. They will be looking for connections with Ms. Arva and Rebecca Quinto. This address is not connected to either of them. It's a safe place in a sleepy neighborhood."

Michele said, "I know the house. I will take them there. Grocery store close by. Bit of an Airbnb. All good."

Micah said to Michele, "Park the rental car here in Las Olas and Uber over to that address. Change the rental car as soon as you can. Put it on the museum's card. Stay and help them get used to the place. I will cover your desk tomorrow until you think they are comfortable. I will let you know what the FBI says about a meeting."

Remy said, "I will remain a few days, my friends, but no one scares Remy from his beautiful Nawlins. You understand? Anyways, Remy will stay close to da blonde po po man, McCullough, until this is over."

Michele sighed. "Jesus, are there no more straight men? No offense, guys."

"Naw, naw naw, 'lil *cherè*, Remy means for safety."

He took her hand and kissed it.

"You say da word, *ma belle,* and all of this Remy is yours."

She pushed him off with a laugh.

Micah said, "Please rest a bit, Madame. When you are ready, we will get you to your accommodations. All will be well."

Madame Ondine took the hands of her hosts and examined their palms. "Your spirits are forceful and very generous. You will receive many blessings for your kindness, each of you."

She pointed to Hud. "You…."

"You have reached a turning point of the heart. Follow and be true to it. Dark times have passed, my angel."

She turned to Micah, placing her hand on his chest. "You are wise beyond your years. Lift up from the many tasks you take on and enjoy love where you find it. Your work is not who you are. Cast off fear, my young friend. You have a friend close by on the other side. She watches over you."

Benny said, "Come, Auntie. Our journey has been long and tiring. Again, we apologize for interrupting your... um, evening. Thank you, gentlemen."

The older woman took her nephew's arm as they rose to leave. She spoke a final departing word.

"Please extend our thanks to Ms. Quinto. She faces grave danger at this time. I pray very hard for her and for the Frozen Diva."

Chapter Forty-Two: The Penitent

TA'IZZ, YEMEN

The sound of fighting was everywhere. The enclave of Ali Ibn Zalid's militia had been under siege for the last three days. The hostages had been moved deeper into the undercrofts of the castle. Food, water sanitation, and medical supplies were in short supply, with the soldiers receiving most of the rations. There was little to spare.

The children and women were separated from the American journalist, but not by much in the cramped spaces. A dark figure approached the imprisoned Mark Gadarn.

"Fuckin' Judas. What do you want?"

The penitent replied, "Atonement, redemption, the chance to sleep for just one night with an untroubled conscience. There is much blood on my hands."

Youssouf Kamil hid in the recesses close to Mark's cell and spoke softly. Mark's response was not polite.

"You crud. I am supposed to believe you. You change sides faster than a whore turns tricks during Fleet Week. Who are you working for today, Judas? Back to Al Shabab?"

Mark had a hard time speaking. His lips were dry, his throat hoarse, and he had not eaten in two days.

"I want to go home."

Mark spat, "Rot, fucker."

Joseph Stapleton, aka Youssouf Kamil, from East Orange, New Jersey, pushed a flat canvas sack of food and water under the bars.

Mark felt primal instincts kick in but held back.

"The kids..." he rasped. "Give it to the kids and the women.

The shadow moved off in their direction with another satchel.

***

He whispered into the darkness. "They are planning to punish you again, Mister Gardarn. You may not survive the beating that is coming. This squad is losing men, munitions, and supplies every day. Their insurgency is in a total death spiral unless they can get funds and get them soon. They take out their frustrations on their hostages. Your friends will not be able to find you."

Mark said nothing.

"They are leaving the women and children unmolested for religious reasons, but faith will soon give way to more sinful needs. These are savage men, Sir."

Now, the journalist mocked, "Unlike you."

The spy ignored the rebuff.

"Their contacts are arranging for the transport of the women and children. They are being sold as slaves to international human traffickers. I am trying to tell you there is not much time. Soon, the trucks will arrive at the foot of the mountain, and the hostages will be marched down under guard. They will be as good as dead."

Mark thought for an interval. "What's your story, man? You are a long way from New Jersey."

"I thought the Islamic radical movement was my calling, I guess. I never really fit in at school. I had no friends to speak of. Spent a lot of time reading materials on conservative Muslim sects on the web. Talked to some folks. Bastard for a stepfather who threw me out. Changed my name and my religion – I guess, anyway. Not sure I believe in God or ever really did.

"It was only once I got into the movement, ISIL in Syria and all, that I realized that the violence was totally fucked up. There was no road to God, no righteous Utopia in all the killing and atrocities. I was even more of an outsider."

Mark listened to the voice in the dark alcove. There seemed to be a fraction of sincerity in the man's story.

"I was trained not as a soldier but as one who gathers information, espionage. There was tons of indoctrination and lousy religion. Just a fuckin' mess. I tried to make friends, but no one trusted anybody. Three of my buddies were killed by the group.

"After my training in Syria, I began to listen for a way out. You do not just walk away from these crazies, man. I tried to align myself with other radical groups, hoping for protection. I just got deeper and deeper into the shit. I was selling out people left and right for money, for food – sometimes just for the hell of it. It became addictive."

Youssouf Kamil's voice caught as he attempted to continue.

"I don't know if you believe me, Mr. Gadarn, but I wanted to be a soldier, a fighter for something good. My family and the few friends I had in America thought I was a big loser, and it appears that I am proving them right. There is no honor among these devils. I wanted to be a good man committed to something. I believed that in the *jihad,* I would eventually come to see the face of God. The god I have come to see drips with blood, poison, and hatred. All I have come to know is a horror beyond comprehension."

"What was the tipping point, Youssouf? What made you lose faith?"

The spy choked back a sob and took a deep breath. He spoke so softly that Mark had to strain to hear him.

"I was a fuckin' fool, man. I saw what they did to the kids, abused them, sold them, killed them. These guys over here." He indicated the captured school children. "Are better off dead. What's gonna happen to them is nuts, man, insane."

Neither spoke for a few minutes.

"Yeah, so, I continued to have some regrets, you know? Then, about a year ago, I was ordered to take out a family with eight kids in Fallujah. Just fuckin' waste them all."

"And?"

Now, the man moved so that he was partially in the light. He lowered the hood of his thawb. The scar began just above his left ear and cut back through the side of his skull.

"My hand shook too much. I even fucked up killing myself."

How old are you, Youssouf?"

"I am twenty-three, sir."

Youssef continued, "Before I go any further with this, Mr. Gadarn, I apologize for betraying you to the Scourge. After your capture, I went back to see if Davia had made it. Apparently, she did, and the uncle got them on the road to a safer location."

Mark thought, *Thank heaven.*

The shadowy figure moved back into the darkness. "I want to help get you and the other hostages out of here, but I do not know how. I need to do this to get right with myself."

Mark thought for a moment. Then he asked, "Can you get to a mobile phone or a computer?"

"Yes. With all the fighting and desertions, their tech room is often left unguarded."

"How good is your memory?"

"I am a spy, sir. I have been trained to memorize."

"Listen carefully and remember. Much depends on you right now."

Chapter Forty-Three: Sid

CAMP MONTGOMERY, DJIBOUTI

“Thank you for coming, Lieutenant. I would have thought that a request to meet with your commanding officer would predicate a bit more neatness in your uniform. Still, I am aware of your rather unconventional behavior.”

“And my citations for valor, Sir.” It was not a question.

“Yes, your decorations for bravery in the line of duty are well known to me and have been, in the past, cause for the administration to look beyond your, shall we say, eccentricities?”

“Thank you, Sir. What can I do for the Major?”

The commander of the base looked intently at his rogue flier.

“One word: Gadarn.”

"Major, I could say that I had no notion of the journalist in my last intelligence run across the Sea. Still, a lie is unworthy of our relationship, Sir. I caved, pure and simple, at his request, Sir.”

“This is very troublesome, Sid.” Major Porfilio waved the woman into a seat in front of his desk.

“Let’s talk about looking the other way.”

She thought, *Shit, this is going to be deeply fucked.*

“I allow you and your team to do unofficial forays into Yemen with humanitarian aid– I can only hope that is what you are flying in– and from God knows where you are getting this stuff….”

“Because the Pentagon’s bureaucracy will tie up efforts to help people who are dying by the thousands, right next door. And I have ways to get supplies to them. We are Americans, Major. We are supposed to care. We save people.”

“Excuse me for talking while you are interrupting, Lieutenant. I advise caution here.”

"Begging the Major's pardon, Sir."

The commander paused to gather his thoughts. There were always operations that went on that were not regulation. His own career was cluttered with some risky behavior to secure the safety of his troops and the civilian population. His thoughts went to his three tours of Afghanistan. You do the best you can, pray for a favorable turnout, and beg forgiveness. US engagement in the Middle East had changed the rules of war for good.

"Lieutenant Collins, I am afraid the Gadarn operation has gone to shit, big time. He was advised not to go in-country and get his ass out of the Horn. He has been captured by a rebel group in the western part of the country, The Scourge of God. NATO has approached us to assist in his rescue as there are other civilians, mostly Yemeni, being held with him."

"Why doesn't his bureau, CBN, I think it is, pony up for his release?"

Brian Anthony Porfilio shook his head. "The likelihood that this particular group will play fair is zero, Sid."

They were interrupted by Corporal Jack Tersegno.

"Excuse me, Major, but the others are here."

"Please send them in, Corporal. We will use the conference table. Do you have Brussels on the line?"

"Yes, Sir."

Jack Tersegno led seven soldiers into the Major's office. Each of them exchanged a nod or a knowing glance at Lieutenant Collins. They were her rogue team and frequenters of her God's Land bar. Everyone sat at the table as Corporal Tersegno lowered a video screen and cued up the video from NATO headquarters in Brussels.

Porfilio said, "General McGrath, good morning, Sir. How may we at Camp Montgomery assist NATO at this time?"

"Thank you, Major. I am accompanied by Caspar Haig from CBN. He is Mr. Gadarn's supervisor. Let's begin with the challenge before us.

"We are in receipt of information that Mr. Gadarn is somewhere near Ta'izz and is being held by religious extremists known as The Scourge of God. There are some thirty members of a destroyed health facility and school bombed out by the Houthis in that region of the country. The intention is to sell the hostages and ransom the journalist.

"In the past, we have seen rescue and ransom operations like this one fail in about 60 percent of the cases. We are asking for an unconventional and covert operation with the cooperation of the United States Government. I have forwarded copies of my interactions with the Pentagon on this matter. Suffice it to say we have a green light on this one."

Haig interjected. "This one is so far under the radar, Major. It disappears if you know what I mean."

Sid Collins said, "Freakin' Mission Impossible."

Porfilio threw her a glance of warning. He said, "Sir, I have assembled my team of specialists on this one. I have their credentials on file if the General wishes…."

"No need, Major. The less known, the better. You say they are the best, Brian. We totally have your back. Just get it done and fast. We hope to avoid an international incident – the West against the East sort of bullshit… creates more terror in the world. This out-of-the-ordinary course of action is an attempt to avoid the violent repercussions that usually follow these forays into enemy territory."

"Thank you, General."

The soldiers around the table began to relax.

Haig added, "Complications, Major – the US Congress is trying to disengage with the Saudis in Yemen, but the politics on this appears to be a bit ambiguous. The Executive Branch seems to want Saudi friendship, while the legislature wants no part of this international atrocity. Folks, this has to remain a secret project. When the smoke clears, thirty more refugees turn up at Montgomery, and Gadarn is shipped back to the US with no one the wiser. I put him on reporting the weather in the Midwest."

Major Porfilio asked, "What intelligence do we have on their location?"

"Here is where the logistics get a bit complicated, Major. I have a NATO operative working with Gadarn's partner, Rebecca Quinto. Ms. Quinto has strong ties with the FBI and CEPOL. They have received some intel, albeit very little, from the prisoner. I will forward it to you."

McGrath continued, "NATO's operative working with Ms. Quinto is Lieutenant Loic Antoine Theriault, Special Forces – total hotshot, Brian." The Commander put up a picture of both Rebecca and Loic.

Porfilio thought, *Just what we need, another risk-taker who believes his own press.*

Corporal Tersegno thought, *Holy shit. Look at that guy.*

The Commander of Camp Montgomery said, "General McGrath, Mr. Haig, we will contact you when we get them out. Please be assured that we will succeed. Before we decide on the specifics of the operation, General. Are there any questions from the group for NATO or CBN?"

There were none. Sid Collins thought, *Fly by the seat of our pants time, kids. Literally.*

McGrath said, "You got all we have, Major. No need to keep me informed of the details. The less I know, the better. Your reputation and pledge for successful mission completion on this are all I need. Your folks are specialists in saving lives in that part of the world."

"Thank you, General. Mr. Haig. I will be in contact."

***

After the tactical side of the meeting was completed, Lieutenant Sid Collins and Major Brian Porfilio stepped out on the balcony for a smoke. In the bright African sun, Camp Montgomery's buildings and armaments were laid out before them.

"Do not, I repeat, do not, fuck this one up, Sid."

"Bri, did you mean it when you did the brag on my team?"

He did not flinch at the familiarity of the lieutenant's address. In all the world, Sid Collins was the only one he let call him "Bri."

"Yes, I know quality, strength, and bravery when I see it."

"Hey, thanks."

They blew smoke into the hot air. Funny how having a smoke could bring together some old comrades in arms.

Collins said, "I got one for you, Major. You know I am a big dyke, right?"

"Don't care."

"Cool, 'cause in that room of tried and true heroes-- my kick-ass team from the US Armed Forces here at Montgomery-- is an assortment of dykes, 'mos, straights, and trans soldiers, all ready to sacrifice everything, including their lives, for their country."

She tapped the chest of her commander.

"Something for you and the Pentagon folks to think about – just sayin', Boss."

Chapter Forty-Four: The Scourge of God

TA'IZZ, YEMEN

The three bearded men approached the stronghold in the dead of night. They were peasants, all but one. The smallest of the three was dressed in priestly robes that bore the marks and style of the Coptic Orthodox Community. The cleric moved with halting steps assisted by his ornate walking staff. Somewhat feeble, he raised his head with authority as he walked up to the fortress checkpoint. The man of God clutched a large cross almost beneath the open folds of his black robes. His two bodyguards carried heavy duffle bags but were unarmed.

The tallest addressed the guard. "We have come to see the Sharif, *effendi*. I am honored to present His Excellency Bishop Cosmas Nassif Mus'ad, Holy Suffragan Bishop of the Throne, Metropolitan, and Ethnarch of the Coptic Christian Community in Yemen and Saudi Arabia. We are his sons and have brought gifts for the Lord of Ta'izz."

The escort indicated the large, heavy canvas bags.

Soldiers of The Scourge of God began to frisk the three visitors for weapons, but the old bishop stopped them, speaking in a firm voice. "Please, for your purity and ours, accept my word as a man of God. We come in peace, my children and I." He stooped and opened one of the rucksacks and indicated food, which the soldiers eyed hungrily. Sounds of fighting filled the streets not far from the foot of the road up to the headquarters of Ali Ibn Zalid.

A tall officer stepped from a newly arrived Jeep at the entrance bunker. General Yasser Abdulkhalek looked suspiciously at the intruders. "What is your business with the Chieftain?"

The taller of the Bishop's guards answered. "We have come to broker a transaction. We serve as agents of an interested party to arrange for the transfer of your prisoners at a considerable ransom."

"You are not our contacts. If you are, produce the proof of our agreement."

The bishop answered, "We come with a very lucrative offer, my Lord. Possibly a better one, but let us not do our business in the streets."

The General motioned the three to precede him up the steep road to the darkened castle. The old bishop leaned on his sons to make the climb. Abdulkhalek made no offer to share his transport.

Inside the walls, the depths of the buildings were illuminated by lanterns, candles, and oil lamps. Bonfires blazed in the courtyards. Electricity was nowhere to be found except for a sputtering generator that powered three computers near the inner sanctum of the headquarters.

The Chieftan was in the middle of a conversation when the strangers entered his chambers. He barked orders to a handful of soldiers concerning the night battle that raged at the base of the mount.

"Peace be to this house."

The Chieftan looked suspiciously at his visitors and did not exchange the greeting.

The Bishop continued. "I will be direct, my Lord, as you have urgent matters of life and death over which to preside this night."

"How is it possible that you have entered this battleground of a city?"

"The Copts have been in this part of Yemen for centuries, Sharif Ali. We are respected by other 'People of the Book.' The Holy Scriptures are common to the three faiths and underly our spiritual integrity. We have survived many conflicts throughout history. The little people hiding from your war have helped us get to you on this night."

"I have no time for religious emissaries and theological discussions. Do not waste time. Tell me of your reason for invading my compound."

"We want to buy your hostages in the name of God."

The Chieftan laughed and said, "The gossip of 'the little people,' as you call them, travels far. You and your scum are enemies of Islam. As a member of the local clergy, have you learned nothing from our war in this country?"

The Ethnarch said, "Although my community is few in number in this land and you have continued to target our churches, we come offering forgiveness. To that end, the people I serve have undertaken a divine mission to save the unfortunate victims of the war."

It was General Yasser Abdulkhalek who responded. "Christian devils. Do not disguise your hate and revenge. As recently as last year, Houthi militias stormed the St. Anthony Church in al-Tawahi, Aden, in Yemen."

He continued by addressing the Sharif, "There is no sincerity here, *Qayid Baladiin*. This Christian dog's words mock the Scourge of God."

The taller of the bishop's guards broke in, "It was His Excellency who called for the reconciliation and community discourse after the Islamists took responsibility for the kidnapping and beheading of our brothers and sisters in Libya in 2015. We come in that same spirit of concord."

"Your accent betrays you, mixed-racial dog. Enough of these political lies." Abdulkhalek spat and moved forward to strike the Bishop's bodyguard. The Chieftan called the name of his Number One and ordered him to stand down.

The old Ethnarch extended a shaking hand to stop the boisterous soldier who was zealous for his cause. The General stopped his assault and caught the eyes of the Bishop. The cleric closed his hand but pointed up to the heavens. Mus'ad quoted the Holy Quran.

"Allah spreads out his hand at night to accept the repentance of those who did wrong during the day, and he spreads out his hand during the day to accept the repentance of those who did wrong during the night. This will continue until the sun rises from the west."

"Blasphemer."

The Bishop lowered his hand and pointed to the General as he continued, "You and your band are human traffickers, my son, selling the children of God to the highest bidder. At one time, you were looked up to by children the world over, a hero of the stadium. Your name is famous in the world of sports. How did you come to forsake all of that? Surely not in the name of God.

"The Holy Scriptures forbid this atrocity. You believe you are righteous in this, but you deal in evil. And so your God has abandoned you, and you are losing battle after battle. In that respect, we want you to consider a higher offer and be free of the sin you intend. Regain the blessings of God."

He spoke with divine authority and great conviction. The Bishop had the attention of all in the room. A strange member of the rebel group, not a soldier, dressed in dark robes, lingered in the shadows, listening intently to the conversation.

Bishop Mus'ad said to the Chieftan, "Give us the hostages, *effendi*. We bring forgiveness, and we bring gold. God will forgive you, but only if you show mercy. At least consider our offer. You will not be disappointed."

The smaller member of the bishop's retinue stepped to a computer console. The young rebel technology soldier looked up at the Chieftain and received a nod.

"Do as this Christian has asked, Captain Mustafa."

The boy soldier allowed the stranger access to the keyboard.

The Copt typed and motioned for the young rebel captain to enter information on the screen. He turned away to ensure that the boy's entry was confidential. Taking back the console for a final set of data entries, the attendant hit Enter, stood, and returned to the bishop's side.

Mustafa's eyes grew large. "God be praised. Look, my Sharif, a fortune in gold, a vast treasure. And it is ours."

Members of the Scourge of God brigade gathered before the computer monitor. The amount about to be deposited in their bank account blinked in the report on the screen along with, "Please Confirm Transfer."

It was indeed a king's ransom. The rebels exchanged a rush of expressions of astonishment.

The tall cleric spoke, "The payment is pending, as you can see. His Excellency must give the codes for final approval."

The General shouted, "Another lie, my Sharif. This is a computer trick. These Christians are notoriously poor. They could not have access to this amount. We must imprison these enemies of God and execute them."

The Bishop said, "We have the assets of the treasury of the Throne of our Pope, Theotokos II, at our disposal and his approval to intercede for the hostages. The offer is conditional, and you must decide quickly. On behalf of His Holiness, I insist on seeing your prisoners as a guarantee of their safety before I authorize payment in his name."

The Bishop's voice was failing. His fatigue became apparent as he fingered his pectoral cross and stroked his beard. The Chieftan waved at his soldiers.

"Take them."

***

They were indeed starving and in need of medical attention. The small entourage from the Coptic Church passed among the children and their teachers. The old Bishop was dumbfounded. They distributed high protein rations from the folds of their robes, bars of nuts, and chocolate. The youngest of the priests called for water.

The Bishop cradled more than one of the youngsters in his arms, moving among the children. The excitement among the group was elevated as the prisoners recognized the chance of rescue despite the presence of the small group of rebel soldiers.

The Bishop whispered, "In the name of God, Lord Ali, give them to me."

A newly arrived soldier interrupted Ibn Zalid.

My Sharif, the transports for the women and children have arrived at the checkpoint. They demand that you honor the agreement made over a month ago.

The Sharif was silent, considering the two options. Finally, he spoke to the soldier. "Go to the fortress gates and tell them the hostages are dead."

"Lord, there will be repercussions."

"Do not question me. Follow my orders." The commander snarled.

Next, he addressed the Bishop, "Take them, priest. Complete the transaction-- the electronic bank transfer. Your offer is far better. You may have them all. All but this one. The reporter will stay. The American is a powerful bargaining chip with the international community. His execution will bring the cause of The Scourge of God to the world. I believe it is called 'publicity' in the West."

The man who lay face down in the filthy cage had recently been beaten. He was barely conscious. The Bishop's younger attendant gasped at the sight of the prisoner. Mus'ad motioned for his staffer to retreat and directed one word to General.

"Open."

His Excellency, Bishop Cosmas Nassif Mus'ad, Holy Suffragan Bishop of the Throne, Metropolitan, and Ethnarch of the Coptic Christian Community in Yemen and Saudi Arabia, knelt in the dirt and raised Mark's head to his lap.

A plaintive voice came from the battered man, eyes closed, face bruised and battered, one leg twisted unnaturally.

"Mae hen wlad fy nhadau yn annwyl i mi,

Gwlad beirdd a chantorion, enwogion o fri;

Ei gwrol ryfelwyr, gwladgarwyr tra mad,

Dros ryddid gollasant eu gwaed."

The sound was no more than a whisper, filled with a struggle for breath and wracked with pain.

One of the soldiers said with disgust, "See, he calls upon the devil."

The Bishop turned from his ministering to look into the eyes of the soldier and quoted with profound sadness:

"O Land of my fathers, O land of my love,

Dear mother of minstrels who kindle and move,

And hero on hero, who at honor's proud call,

For freedom, their lifeblood let fall.

"The man you are slowly murdering, my son, is trying to sing the Welsh National Anthem."

"Get the fuck out of my way."

A woman from among the prisoners pushed her way past the soldiers and into the cell. She addressed the Bishop, "I am a doctor, Your Excellency. They have left him to die. He needs medical attention. He will not last much longer."

She shouted to the captors, "Bring water, you inhuman bastards."

Approval was given with a raised hand by the Chieftan.

The medic tore at her clothing to create bandages. The Bishop's taller bodyguard moved in to take a position next to the journalist. He removed a small leather pouch from his robes and handed it to Dr. Susan Russell. She loaded a syringe with antibiotics and injected the American.

Bishop Mus'ad reached up and raised the chain of the large cross above his black headdress and placed the holy metal on the chest of the dying journalist. He made the sign of the cross in the Eastern manner and rocked in silent prayer. A soft light seemed to emanate from the cell.

***

Behind the observers, a hand reached out to pull the younger, weeping Copt into the shadows.

"Quickly, Ms. Quinto, give me the coordinates of the rescue forces. We do not have much time."

"No. Take me back up. I... how?"

"Your hands... even without the manicure... dead giveaway, beard or no beard."

Youssef Kamil hurried Rebecca up the stairs to the Sharif's operations room without being observed. The old PCs were rebooting as the generator in the adjacent courtyard began to sputter again. The only light in the room came from the monitors. Kamil dashed into the yard to refill the machine's gas tank and returned as Rebecca pulled a slip of paper from her clothing. The spy's hands flew over the keyboard.

"Stand away from the table and keep your hands up, both of you."

"Lord Abdulkhalek, I am assisting the Copt in completing the transaction before the power dies. The deal is set to timeout very soon, and the power to our computers is sporadic. We are attempting to please the noble *Sharif*."

The rebel general wasn't buying it. He spoke in English to the Christian. "You are a fake. You have remained silent all this time because you speak no Arabic."

He pointed and continued, "You are that woman…."

Rebecca faced her captor. She peeled off her beard and dropped her disguise. "You're damn right. I am <u>that</u> woman. Look, asshole, you want the money or not?" She turned back, attempting to send the coordinates.

Abdulkhalek took her by one shoulder and bitch-slapped her to the floor. Kamil raised his hands and stepped to the side with his back to the console as the rebel leader stood over his captive. As a dazed Rebecca came up, Kamil shouted, "The power is going. We are losing the bank connection."

The General's first mistake was that he did a half turn to the hysterical spy as the monitor flashed. His second was underestimating the woman who was rising from the floor.

As she stood, Rebecca grabbed the General's shoulders and racked him with all her might. The smash to his testicles was audible as the breath rushed out of him, and he doubled over.

"How are those squashed plums, fuckwad?"

She pulled the rifle from him and did a spin kick against his right leg, sending him crashing into Youssef and the computers.

As the table collapsed and the parts of the PCs began to scatter around the fallen, agonizing soldier, the repentant Judas fought to regain his balance, grabbed the keyboard, and pressed Enter.

Chapter Forty-Five: *Deus Ex Machina*

TA'IZZ, YEMEN

"We bring this bird down, and they are not there, and we are so fucked, bud. We are talking heavy US machinery coming from the sky. Huge targets for the anti-aircraft guns that surround the city. *Capice?*"

"Roger that, Sid. We need confirmation from the ground. Our intercept needs to be pinpointed. They could be anywhere in these mountains. We engage the wrong troops in the wrong place, and bingo, international fuck-up. Half the problem down there is knowing who's who. Stay high."

Sid Collins spoke into her headset while flying the Sikorsky CH-53E Super Stallion. Her team had piled into a heavy-lift helicopter about an hour ago. Technically, it was a troop carrier capable of carrying 55. Still, tonight, it bore the Red Cross/Red Cresent insignia.

"This is Red Leader. Mama's trying to look busy, kids, and stay high, awaiting the confirmed location for our drop-in. Mama saying stay cool."

She flipped a switch and turned a fraction of her attention to her co-pilot, Jack Tersegno.

"Been so hot to fly one of these. I am in grunt heaven, boy. They were going to mothball this beauty, re-tool her for recon, or make her a Hanger Queen, you know, spare parts. The new ones are way slick, more room, more power, quiet and fast. Talking twin transverse rotors and the lifting power of forty-four tons. Beats the Ruskie version all to shit. But I am happy to be flying this doll, baby. "

Jack said, "Old and outclassed, she still comes with a twenty-four million dollar price tag. Not to mention the expensive payload. No pressure, Boss."

Sergeant Karen Olsen stepped into the cockpit. "Speaking of pressure, Lieutenant, the window is closing. We either know exactly where we are going soon, or we head back to Montgomery and get tucked into our beds for the night. Porfilio can find excuses for McGrath."

"You take care of your Jawas, Sargeant. Make sure they are locked and loaded, and leave me to fly this bird. No way of knowing how many of the enemy we are facing. The Scourge is a super unknown."

Sid continued, "Damn shame. This was supposed to be a surgical operation. Quick in and quick out. Now we got nothing. C'mon... where the fuck are you? Those guys get snuffed, and it will be an international shitstorm." She began to bank the transport back to the west and The Horn.

***

"My Sharif, we must hurry this along. Imprison these Christian devils and raise the ransom. They are toying with you. Are you in charge of this brigade or not? We are losing ground by the minute. Soon, we will all be prisoners of the enemy."

The soldier who spoke gave voice to the growing unrest of the troops.

The General stumbled into the room, landing on the floor next to the soldier who had been speaking. Behind them, Victoria was returning the bishop's ceremonial cross to her robes. She spoke softly to the women ministering to Mark.

Dr. Susan Russel said, "His pulse is stronger, but he is not out of danger, Sir."

As he stood, Rebecca and Youssef came up behind the fallen General with Abdulkhalek's assault weapon trained on the band of insurgents.

The armed woman said, "Back off, fellas. This ain't my first time at the rodeo." Youssef translated, and the soldiers of the Scourge lowered their weapons.

Loic snagged a rifle and moved the soldiers against a nearby wall, ordering them to leave their weapons a safe distance away and keep their hands raised. Dr. Russel directed a few of the bigger schoolboys to find a sturdy blanket to act as a stretcher for moving Mark out of the dungeon. Amat Al Kindi roused the children and the other educators to prepare to depart the prison enclosure.

Youssouf threw back his hood and took up a weapon. He motioned for some of the stragglers to join Loic's band of captives as they were herded into the cell, "Make haste, dogs." He raised his rifle. "Who wants to be the first to enter Paradise?"

The humiliated Sharif said, "It is my wish that we make the first to die you. You have bungled this operation for months. You have failed me and have cost us the divine mandate. Now we have nothing."

He reached inside his tunic for a handgun and fired six shots into the head of his target. General Abdulkhalek spasmed on the dungeon floor, his eyes an expression of surprise and then of the blankness that comes with death.

Lying inches from the Chieftan and behind him, Victoria pulled a metal object from its holster strapped to her forearm beneath her voluminous sleeve. She stabbed and yanked twice through deteriorated leather, ripping the tendon and muscle of Ibn Zalid's Achilles tendons with six inches of razor-sharp Toledo steel.

The force of the attack turned the commander, who screamed in pain, fell against the Diva, and dropped his gun. Victoria pulled him close as he fell. She stabbed up and deep into his ribcage. Sharif Ali Ibn Zalid, anointed commander of The Scourge of God, slid down her body to the floor.

La Gloriosa sang softly in Italian. It was a lyric from a role she performed many times the world over.

"This is the kiss of Tosca. Die accursed! Die! Die! Die!"

In the following seconds, the ruined prison was filled with blinding lights and roaring winds from the heavens above.

Chapter Forty-Six: Pegasus

TA'IZZ, YEMEN

The dust and the roaring winds were as if heaven itself had opened above the ruins of the Fortress of Ta'izz. The building itself shook as if an apocalyptic cataclysm.

Loic took the point, an assault rifle at the ready, and one more slung across his shoulders. Youssef Kamil had his back at the rear of the escaping band. The adults helped the terrified children ascend the stairs, following the blanket stretcher holding Mark Gadarn. Victoria held the hands of two small children. Rebecca came up behind the group after locking the defeated band in the cell below. She detoured into the computer room and sprayed the machines with gunfire. Then, she brought up the rear of the escaping group.

Above the east side of the stronghold, the Super Stallion helicopter hovered over the partially destroyed buildings. Sid had the helicopter's night vision system in operation. She brought the aircraft in low. Below, a corridor seemed to open up, and a soldier led a ragtag band of fugitives away from the most fortified sections of the fort. But to where?

She muttered, "They need a fuckin' miracle."

Youssef yelled over the din to Loic, who struggled to find the way out to safety. Access gates to the stronghold would be heavily guarded. The young spy yelled, "Into the garden, quickly. This way."

Crossing to the garden archway, the group encountered shouts and shooting. As the helicopter hovered low, gunfire erupted from its open bay. Two 0.50-caliber machine guns mounted in the ports on the sides of the aircraft cut into the approaching rebel guards scrambling up the access road. Sid's crew did their best to hold off pursuing hostiles approaching the escapees in many directions.

In the cockpit, Karen Olsen yelled to her pilot, "They're headed to that walled space with the truck."

Sid said, "Tighter than a gay boy's butthole. I can't land this thing anywhere near there. Tersegno, strap on your wings, ya big fairy. Go dope on a rope and get those people, for fuck sake."

As the refugees with the makeshift stretcher reached the walled plot beneath the heavy-lift helicopter, an airborne soldier rode a line to the ground. As he landed, Jack Tersegno yelled to Loic above the roar, "Into the truck, big guy."

He helped the Frenchman open the empty Saudi intermodal shipping container and get the evacuees inside. Two rebels ran at the group. Tersegno turned, raised his rifle, and took them out.

A surface-to-air rocket screamed above but missed the helicopter. A returning missile took out the bazooka nest on the roof of a tower above the garden area. Rebels flew into the air from the impact, and bodies dropped to the ground. The soldiers of the Scourage closed in, leaping on walls and rooftops and spraying gunfire.

The Helicopter released a sling assemblage above the container as the last of the hostages dodged bullets and boarded the huge supply locker. As Tersegno sprayed cover fire, Loic climbed to the roof to guide the cables over the vessel's side between firing into groups of insurgents. A bullet ripped the tail of his t-shirt at the level of his belt, grazing his taut midsection. On the ground, Rebecca and Jack secured the lines to the two long sides of the container. Youssef kept them covered.

Above them, Sid Collins chomped her cigar and commented, "Move your asses, people. We are leaving."

Loic dropped to the ground as the helicopter started to lift but settled its load back down. The container shifted and seemed to be off-balance during ascent. Loic shouted to Rebecca and Jack to get in and move the occupants to the center and against the unit's walls.

"It's the cable, Sir."

Not waiting, Youssef scrambled up the side as Loic closed the doors and slid the heavy bolts home. He followed the young man up the outside ladder of the enclosure just in time to see him sitting and using his booted feet to slam the loose clip securing one of the cables to the payload. As the craft went airborne, slung below the helicopter, Youssef stood and made for the small hatch on the roof.

It was there that he caught the bullet to his upper chest. Loic tackled the man and used his body to cover the wounded spy and secure them both to the container's roof. He reached with his hands and feet to find any and every holdfast.

Their faces met as Loic pressed into the body of the wounded man. He said, "Stay with me, *mon ami*. It's a short trip, and you and I, we're making it the hard way."

In the 'copter, Karen Olsen gave the order, "Unleash Porfilio's dogs."

Twenty-five drones swarmed from the belly of the flying beast, firing round after round to keep the ground troops contained. A drone's missile slammed into the entrance arch of the garden and exploded, taking out several gunmen. Two more smashed into the headquarters ruins from the swarm of robot warriors.

The winged Stallion continued to take flight lifting its cargo high into the night sky above Ta'izz, protected by the deadly, flying horde. The drones circled, dove in for another raid, and then hurried after the mother ship as the flying convoy disappeared in the skies above.

Chapter Forty-Seven: *Denouement*

IN THE AIR ABOVE THE BAB AL-MANDAB STRAIT, THE RED SEA

From the inside, it was apparent that Loic and the young turncoat had not made it. Victoria tried to comfort the children clinging to her in the dark, windowless, relatively airless, flying enclosure. The thrown-back cover of the ceiling hatch gave the only relief. The roar of the seven-bladed main rotor in the sky above them was constant.

Rebecca held Mark, encouraging him with loving words and gentle caresses. Susan Russel tended to the fallen journalist as best she could in the rocking transport. As their eyes met, the doctor said to Victoria. "That has to be Lieutenant Sid Collins up there. She's got us."

Sitting on the steel floor, the Diva clutched for her cross and closed her eyes in fatigue. It was then that the memories came.

Chapter Forty-Eight: The Architect in Chains

SPANDAU PRISON, BERLIN, 1946

"Your papers are in order. I will escort you, Madam."

Prisoner Number Five was writing as she approached the cell. Behind him, on a wall map, he had plotted an imaginary trip around the globe. Books were stacked around the cell.

He looked for a long time at the visitor before requesting his walk in the prison gardens from the guard. As they walked outside into the sunshine, his first words to her were, "You have not aged. Project Peter Pan, named for the boy who would not grow up, seems to have worked."

"Yes, Albert."

"And you brought us all down-- a woman."

"One among thousands, my dear-- men, women, and even children, countless heroes. It was ever ordained. Evil regimes always underestimate the little people. And it is small bands of passionate believers in goodness and justice that topple the tyrants. Happens every time. You ignored the lessons of history."

He walked slightly ahead of her into the gardens of the prison. He considered her remarks but did not respond. He pointed to the gardens. "We are each given a plot of land to plant. As prisoners die, lose interest, or are... well, I asked the supervisors to give their plots to me."

He gestured to the neatly trimmed lawns, flowerbeds, and fruit trees.

"I seem to still be an architect, even if it is landscaping. It passes the time."

"My sources tell me you are still a man of controversy, Albert. Many are advocating for your release."

"Not the Soviets, my dear. They wanted the death penalty."

“I also hear of your forbidden correspondence with the outside and the money being raised for your family.”

“Do not interfere, my dear, for the sake of what we once had or thought we had, stay out of all that. We ended our story quite a while ago, it would seem.”

They were silent for a long time. Settling on a bench in the morning sun, Victoria asked, “Your regrets must be overpowering, Albert?”

He took a while to answer.

“Some and none. I will sort through it all. Twenty years is time enough to consider the tragedy of the life I have lived... the selling of Speer’s soul for fame and fortune. Part of what we shared I can never regret.”

She felt uneasy.

“I must go.”

“The holy relic-- I know you have it. You must use it only for good, Victoria. For truth.”

La Gloriosa turned to look at Albert Speer. She took a deep breath and spoke what would be her final words to him. It was a quote.

“And Pilate said, ‘Truth? What is that?’”

Chapter Forty-Nine: The Interview

FORT LAUDERDALE, FLORIDA

QUE: Fly-over of the Fritcher Museum and street shots of the Tribal Blood banners and crowds.

Voice over: Rebecca Quinto is the CEO and Head Curator for the Fritcher Museum of Art in Fort Lauderdale, Florida. On March 20, the first day of Spring, the Board of Directors of the Museum, led by Board Chair T. Jackson Harkness, opened an extraordinary exhibit, *Tribal Blood: 3,000 years of the Indigenous People of America*. CBN attended the opening and the after-party with Ms. Quinto and Mr. Harkness.

QUE: The courtyard of the Fritcher Museum. Rebecca Quinto and Jack Harkness are in director's chairs across from the CBN reporter, Martin Walker. Graphics of their titles concerning their relationship to the Fritcher Museum.

CBN: Martin Walker of CBN here with an exclusive on the opening of *Tribal Blood* at the Fritcher Museum in F. Lauderdale. I am here with Rebecca Quinto and Jack Harkness after an extraordinary first look at the much-anticipated exhibit at the always cutting-edge Fritcher. I understand this has been almost two years in the making.

RQ: Yes, Martin, we began with Board approval, followed by research and a trip to Colorado to meet with our Native American partners in this project. Yes, I would say it came together quickly after last year. (Looks to Harkness, who nods.)

CBN: Can you tell me what is happening around us?

RQ: We have invited members of many indigenous communities across the country to celebrate the Spring Equinox, the rebirth of the sun after the regression of the winter months.

(Points)

The stylized, blazing serpent of light that you see descending from the roof of the Museum to the plaza is one of the traditional representations of the Native American celebration of reawakening, migration, and sacrifice associated with the return of the sun. The piece was designed to align with the dawn over downtown Fort Lauderdale. There are sun daggers throughout the concourse, marking this stunning event in the cultures of our indigenous peoples.

CBN: So, you have not set up a market of exotic cultures to promo your exhibit.

RQ: Hardly, Darling. We don't do street fairs at the Fritcher. That would be another exploitation of the first peoples of the Americas – we are making a political and cultural statement.

CBN: And that is?

RQ: Enough discrimination, repression, and extermination. The history of the European colonists in America and the subsequent stealing of Native American Lands is unconscionable. We want the world to learn and make progress.

CUE: Split screen: The interview, side by side with religious rites going on in the courtyard, alternating with pieces from the exhibit...

CBN: (Switches the microphone to Harkness) Mr. Harkness, as Chair of the Museum Board, do you feel that art can afford to make political statements?

(The Board chair exchanged a look with the CEO.)

JH: We have no choice. Our mission is clear. The Fritcher Museum has a responsibility to educate the public. (He stumbled slightly.) We... we... cannot just house beautiful objects. We have to send a message....

This was the legacy of our Board Chair for Education, Arva St. Genevieve. She was passionate about our mission of education.

RQ: What Mr. Harkness emphasizes here is the need for our American Institutions to raise the public consciousness on the fundamentals of our democracy – inclusion, acceptance, the value of diversity in all its forms, as well as defiance in the face of tyranny and oppression. We remind the public of the fundamental rights of freedom and self-determination embraced by the human family from the onset of history. Nothing is more evocative of that spirit than art.

CBN: Quite elegantly presented, Ms. Quinto. And speaking of elegance, the red carpet crowd was an impressive collection of international glitterati.

RQ: We did a special opening for school children and are holding Tuesday mornings during the Spring for students and educators. For them, admission is free to the exhibition, the lectures, and the interactive workshops. Thank you, National Endowment for the Arts.

CUE: Single screenshot of the artifacts in the exhibit. Quinto's voiceover explains the objects on the screen. Close with a full shot of Quinto and Harkness.

CBN: Thank you for the tour. Before we go, I want to compliment you on your gown.

RQ: Thank you. The famous Navajo designer Orlando Dugi did the dress. The incredible Stéphane Rousteing did the boots from a design by Jamie Okuma, another renowned Native American Artist. They have been given to the Fritcher by our extraordinary *Tribal Blood* partners, the Phelan Museum of Fine Arts and the Silverman Museum of Native American Arts.

CBN: Thank you, Ms. Quinto and Mr. Harkness, for this extraordinary adventure. For those coming to the exhibit, there are many more beautiful pieces of Native American history at the Fort Lauderdale Fritcher Museum's show, *Tribal Blood*, going on now through July 31.

Chapter Fifty: Judas

FRITCHER MUSEUM EXECUTIVE OFFICES, FORT LAUDERDALE

"Thanks for the coverage, Martin. Let my office know if CBN needs anything additional."

The crew began to disassemble.

The Honorable T. Jackson Harkness congratulated Rebecca again on the opening. "My only regret is that Ms. Arva was not here to see this."

"Will you excuse me, Jack? I am getting the look from my assistant."

Micah approached in his tux. Hud was talking with the folks from New Orleans near the rear of the plaza.

"Rebecca, the representative of the Patriarch is in your office for the transfer."

"Micha, I am on my way. I just want to make sure that the Board Chair has no notion about what I am about to do. All of this is off the record."

"Got it."

"Come up when you can."

The CEO stepped off the elevator on the sixth floor and greeted Archbishop Péter Sidrak, Special Emissary for the Ecumenical Patriarch of Constantinople.

She bowed and kissed his ring.

More clerics. This one's the real thing.

"Your Excellency, How nice to see you again."

The tall, distinguished prelate was dressed in a black Western-style suit. The only evidence of his office was a chain and the *Engolpion*, the medallion depicting the Blessed Virgin and the Christ Child, the insignia of his office. An Orthodox priest, Father Bartholomew, served as his staff.

"The last time we were together, Ms. Quinto, was for your museum's exhibit on the martyrs of the early church. So beautiful and reverently done."

Micah and Michele stepped off the elevator and were introduced.

"Micah, please bring the case from the safe."

The Administrative assistant placed the leather valise on the conference table. Rebecca set a manila envelope next to it.

"I apologize for the secrecy surrounding this, but, as I mentioned when we first spoke, the donor insists on being anonymous. Also, I can share no information on how the Museum came into possession of this object. Suffice it to say that someone who has cared for it for a long time is now entrusting it to your care."

Rebecca continued, "I suspect that, if this is what many believe it to be, the political issues that will come into play are best handled by the Church as the rightful custodians of the relic."

She opened the case, and the holy fathers moved forward to view the contents. No one spoke for a long time.

Rebecca said, "The folder contains the provenance of the cross as far as the tests reveal and is, therefore, a comprehensive report on the authenticity of the relic. Non-destructive analysis of the piece was conducted independently by the Centre for Archaeological and Forensic Analysis at Cranfield University, United Kingdom, and by the Centre for Archaeological Science, Katholieke Universiteit Leuven, Belgium. It pays to have friends."

Without touching the case's contents, she indicated parts of the object with a short, wooden pointer as she spoke. A jeweler's loop sat next to the box with a pair of preparator's nitrile-coated gloves.

"The transverse pieces are burnished Toledo steel and have recently been added. You can see that they are temporary and may be easily removed without damaging the older materials. The longitudinal piece is bronze. It has been embellished with a partial gold sleeve here at the center. The gold there and on the chain, together with the jewels, are from the 9th century, believed to be from the Holy Roman Empire territory that is present-day Bavaria."

She stopped and looked at the Archbishop as she said, "The bronze shaft of the cross is 34 cm by 10 cm, tapered at one end and blunted here at the other. The approximate size and shape are that of a Roman spearhead. Grooves on the blunt end would have supported leather strips that secured the metal set in the groove of a wooden shaft, estimated to be 7 to 8 cm in diameter. The markings on the bronze and high-quality X-ray diffraction of the metal's crystalline structure indicate it is from the First Century of the Common Era. It is, in fact, Roman and from the eastern Mediterranean-- the Roman province of Syria. This object is from Palestine."

The Archbishop was transfixed as he heard the words of the Head Curator. He stepped forward, donned the gloves, and examined the artifact with the loop. The Archbishop carefully lifted the cross from its case. Holding it flat in both hands, he kissed the relic and offered it to Father Bartholomew, who knelt and did the same.

Rebecca and her staff were so moved by the piety of the clerics that they were unaware of what was about to happen. Behind them, two men and a woman came off the elevator and approached the glass wall of the CEO's office, pushing open the door as they entered.

***

"Good evening, my friends. I am delighted to meet the hero of Ta'izz. Ms. Quinto, your adventures have delighted both my husband and me."

Micah said, "Boss, I locked the elevator."

Rebecca remained calm as she said, "Madam Lu. I knew the viper would slither out from under its rock sooner or later. Gentlemen, enter the snake of the Garden of Eden, or, more accurately, of the Ghost Hand."

The woman ignored the priests and touched Rebecca's hair and gown with her long red nails. She seemed to hiss as she spoke, "Rebecca, if I may. So classy, yes. We so enjoyed the museum's little show. Please allow me to introduce my husband, Dao Luang Kham."

The Red Spectre of the Ghost Hand skipped the formalities and came right to the point.

"Your interference in Ta'izz will not be tolerated. You and your confederates absconded with my property. No mere woman brings down my enterprise. I am here for the spear." He pointed to Rebecca. "And you will hand it to me."

Archbishop Péter held the relic closer and stepped back, saying, "No."

The third intruder, a tiny person with unrecognizable ethnic features, drew a gun and pointed it at the cleric as he stepped forward. The three criminals began to move forward to force the handover of the treasure of the Holy Church.

As the drama reached a climax, Rebecca was distracted, as was Micah, by the subsequent intrusion. Coming to a quick realization, Rebecca spoke with mock politeness in her voice.

"Please allow me to introduce Special Agent Mary Chaffee of the FBI and Detective Michael McCullough of the New Orleans Police."

A man and a woman stepped through the door between Rebecca's and Micah's office, guns drawn.

"Drop the gun, little crud. And get on the ground."

FBI agent Chaffee addressed the Daos, "We are holding you both as well as your associate for an assortment of capital crimes beginning with the murder of Arva St. Genevieve."

The Archbishop moved to the conference table, replaced the cross in the case, and closed it.

Mary said, "Fathers, you are free to go. We have escorts waiting for you in the Museum lobby. My office will be in touch."

Father Bartholomew handed her his card as the Archbishop took the case and followed his colleague to the elevator.

Rebecca said, "Looks like you got women all over your ass, Red. Fancy that. Hey, Snake Lady, I'm here to tell you manicures suck in the penitentiary, and honey, in orange, you're gonna look like a leper. How's that for class?"

The Specter and the Cobra looked dumbfounded.

Mike said, "Spotted them at the gala, hiding in plain sight." He addressed the suspects, " How'd ya get the security uniforms? This little guy here was a dead giveaway. You just didn't look like a fourth-grader, Mac. Five o'clock shadow... really? So freakin' obvious. They're gonna love you in Angola. Beg for solitary, Ace."

The miniature assassin growled at the police officer.

"Hey Mike, Get these Bozos the fuck outta my office."

Mary smiled at her friend's brashness as Rebecca sank into a chair. Before they turned to leave with the three suspects, Mary spoke softly to Rebecca, "Be careful. These folks have a way of getting loose or running a vendetta, even from prison. Call me, girl."

Rebecca put a hand on the Special Agent's arm.

"One second, please." She turned and said, "Michele, you are sweating like a Republican at a gay bath house. The dysautonomia?"

"Yes."

"Hey, may I have your office keys? Mine are downstairs."

Michele looked up at her boss. She was pale and astonished.

Mike reached into the pocket of the small thug and tossed a set of keys onto the conference table.

Rebecca said one word, "Why?"

Michele raised her head. She started slowly, but her anger increased the passion in her voice as she continued.

"Why? Huh... know what it's like to run from a step-monster when you are twelve years old? Once I got out of the hospital, I left that fucker. Better on the streets, on my own. Too late for my younger sister. He killed her. Been running ever since, really. The scars never heal.

"Why? Why. Because I got nothing in this life but a crap-assed disease, and they offered a shit load of money. Why the fuck not? No one has ever given a rat's ass about me. It was my time."

Rebecca touched the keys of the Executive Assistant of the Fritcher Museum of Art, Fort Lauderdale, Florida.

She looked at the woman and spoke one final remark.

"No one?"

Chapter Fifty-One: Mark

LA SERENA, RIVERWALK, FORT LAUDERDALE, FLORIDA

"Sorry I missed the grand opening, Beautiful. I still think I could have made it. "

"Mark, you arrived from Brussels yesterday after three weeks in the hospital. They wanted more time, but you promised you would meet with your doctors here and do complete bed rest until they say differently."

Rebecca walked into her condo, dropped her bags on a chair, and moved his crutches off the arm of the lounge chair so that she could sit with her back to him. She gestured with one hand over her shoulder. With the other, she raised the mane of her black hair. He reached up and unfastened the back of her gown. His caress lingered as he slid his hand beneath the back of her dress.

He was in the white silk pajamas she bought him for his birthday. When he unwrapped them, he said, "Hey, these will be great in the bunkers over in Syria. Can't wait." His leg cast looked huge, and the coat of his pajamas hung open.

Sexy invalid.

"How was the event?"

"Fuckin' fantastic."

Still balancing on the chair's arm, Rebecca bent and unzipped her boots, sighing as her feet came free. She looked at the impossibly sharp, tall heels. She mused, "One of the concessions this woman will give to the subjugating male hegemony-- stilettos. They make such a fashion statement."

He rubbed her back and said, "Right, makes your legs look even more spectacular."

She stood and left the room, returning a few moments later in her white monogrammed robe. Rebecca was in the process of pining up her hair when, without looking at Mark, she took the remote and turned the TV off.

Mark wined, "Rebecca, Cardiff was about to score on Manchester United. Have a heart." He pointed to the darkened screen.

She glared, made an "as if" face, and moved to fix herself a cocktail, bringing his cell phone from the side table and placing it on the bar.

Mark thought, *All signs point to a "we-need-to-talk" session. Shit.*

"Pills?"

"Took' em."

"What time did the nurse leave?"

"Just before nine."

"Pain?"

"Physical or mental?"

She did a pursed lips frown.

Then she said, "Do not even give me the 'I can't take being in this cast and confined to this condo; I am a man of action' speech. So help me, I will heave those crutches right over that balcony."

"Ouch. Gonna tell me what's going on, or do I have to wait for the entire explosion of my fiery Latina. Because the initial rumblings indicate that the volcano is close to eruption."

Rebecca stuck her tongue out at him. She sat opposite him on the couch, feet on the ottoman, her robe held loosely around her naked body. His libido stirred-- the first time in quite a while. Thankfully, some things still worked.

She tried to calm down a bit, her eyes avoiding his.

"I am so damn angry at you, Mark. Reasons? Let's run 'em off."

She finger counted.

He thought, *Folks, we have the 'I told you so' moment.*

"Rage… that is a big one… fear… yeah, that you were dead or worse… terror… suspicion… helplessness… did I mention rage and fear?

"Oh, and Markie – yes, Markie, that little arrangement you have with your hot hacker to refer to me as 'Becky'-- change it ASAP, boy."

"OK. I'm thinking 'Rebecca of Sunnybrook Farm.' Shirley Temple ringlets, the whole nine yards…."

He froze. The expression on Rebecca's face was deadly, a nut-sack-shriveler. He deadpanned.

If you value any continuance of your connubial pleasures, do not make fun, Mark boy.

She breathed heavily, "I am so God-damned mad… and… and tired of being scared."

He said tenderly, "Rebecca, you can feel whatever you feel, Beautiful, but you will never actually be helpless. I believe you may even be invincible."

He reached for her hand as he continued. "I am so in love with you, Beautiful, but this is what I do. I am stubborn, headstrong, and behave like a tightrope walker caught in a twenty-four-seven crosswind. I apologize that my shit-headedness puts others in danger. But what I do… and what you do… hopefully, is so that justice has a voice. This is bigger than just us."

She listened and stared at her man as if trying to see into his mind and soul.

"This world is a fucked up place. It desperately needs heroes. We have no choice. Somebody's gotta call BS. Jesus, the heroes of old are not dead. We are here, you and me and those soldiers, Loic, Davia, Sid, Youssef, Ms. Arva, and all the little folks who each day overcome adversity and the crimes of the tyrants. We gotta resist, as painful as it is sometimes."

He finished with a soft, solemn tone.

"Because so many cannot."

She continued to stare at him, gradually seeing how magnificent this man whom the Fates had brought into her life.

After a sip of her cocktail, Rebecca said, "You mean, I don't even get a 'this is the thanks I get' speech?"

"Nope. But speaking of thanks, I have a suggestion for showing you some of my profoundly, deep... and I am talkin' deep-felt gratitude. That is if you are not too tired."

She ignored his friskiness and the lust devil in his Welsh eyes. She sat back and said, "We got 'em tonight – the Red Specter and the Cobra Woman. They showed at the Museum."

"Fuck me. That is great, Rebecca. Detail, details – I'm a reporter, remember."

She recounted the events of the capture of the Daos and their petite bandit by Mike McCullough and Mary Chaffee. She left out specific details of the transfer of the Spear of Destiny to the Greek Orthodox Church officials. She just indicated that a valuable relic was involved. Rebecca ended with the arrest of Michele Larson.

She said, "I guess no good deed goes unpunished."

"Disloyalty is a bit hard to take when you have tried to help someone, Beautiful. Love hurts, as the song goes."

She took a deep breath and fought back a few tears as she changed the subject.

"Anyway, the interview was pretty good. Harkness did a one-eighty on Museum policy. I hate it when I'm right. So, I guess I nailed my performance review for this year." Rebecca took a deep draw on her vodka rocks, softly clinking the ice cubes.

Mark said, "Got a check-in call from Haig a bit ago. My story on Yemen is airing next week. They got some video patched in. They are all over the personal stuff, the daring-do of their fearless reporter. I really do not like that angle. I went there so that folks could become informed on the plight of those poor people. I am insisting on a rewrite. We'll see if it is any good."

"Darling, it will turn out to be a significant piece of journalism. CBN or any other media company has no one to compare with you."

She stood and crossed the room to refresh her drink. As she passed, Mark retook her hand.

"And I have the incomparable Rebecca Quinto."

She gently pulled her hand from his, did a rough mussing of his hair, and teased, "We'll see about that."

"Say what?"

She felt his eyes on her as she continued to walk to the bar. She made her drink and opened the sliding door to the balcony. She said, "I guess you haven't been paying attention, Mr. Gadarn. This woman's been hanging with the studlies."

She purred, "Oh my, those inexhaustible men."

As she did a roll call of her hot male friends, she did a striptease at the open door, doing her best Gypsy Rose Lee at Minsky's Burlesque.

"There's Remy ...

She dropped a shoulder of her robe.

"... such Cajan savagery... and Mike the Cop.... honestly, you white boys... so energetic."

Another shoulder-- holding the upper part of the robe against her breasts.

" ... always did like my ginger extra spicy ... and ooh la la ... the muscles on that French soldier's arms, back, and legs... mmm... Loic, my guiding star... know that thing where you hold me up off the ground? NATO boy, well, he just...."

She turned her back to him and dropped the robe completely. Using the door frame like a pole-dancer, she looked over her shoulder for his reaction.

Mark grinned, palmed his erection, and said, "Now you're talking, sexy woman. Promised that muscled-up sex bomb, I'd make him my bitch as soon as… wanna watch?" He stuck out his tongue in imitation of a savage rut.

She bristled and heaved a throw pillow, which hit him squarely in the head.

"Heyyy, easy. Injured here, remember?"

"You are a piece of work, Gadarn, a monumental tease, and you know me too well."

"Look who's talking, naked lady."

She walked onto the balcony and mounted the steps to the infinity pool. Mark lifted up from the lounger and pulled into his crutches. He slowly followed her into the spring night with its full moon shining on the Atlantic.

The ambient lighting played across her naked body as she luxuriated in the warm water. She quaffed the Belvidere on the rocks. He eased onto one of the steps of the pool and dangled a hand in aquamarine and black water near her.

He offered, "Haig also said that thanks to McGrath, our boy, Youssef, is in one of those Dutch programs to deprogram the radicalized. Hope he makes it. Still can't believe that Loic held on to him all the way across to Montgomery base."

"Told you the lad is fit. Ohhh, my yes."

"What's the deal with the Diva?"

"Back in Spain, teaching the children. She revels in the solitude. Says it helps her to forget."

She drank from her cocktail and asked, "What are you thinking about?"

"Really want to know?"

"Of course."

She came up close to him on the waterside of the pool and took his hand.

"I think it's the drugs, but my imagination has been freaking me out lately, Rebecca."

"Go on."

"So, you know how those adventure movies have like ambiguous endings 'cause the bad guys never really die? Well, I was imagining that one of those blood-thirsty pigmy dudes climbs up the side of this building and onto your balcony with a terrifying knife in his... OH, MY GOD!"

Mark pulled himself up, grabbed one of his crutches, and swung it at the dark phantom climbing onto the pool's edge.

Rebecca screamed.

Mark dissolved in laughter and sat back down.

"You son of a bitch."

Rebecca cursed in English and Spanish. She splashed him, giving him a good soak, and he roared.

They both were panting.

"You know... I thought that cast would not be much of a hindrance for some, ah... but after that little bullshit, Gadarn, I am here to tell you that this shop is closed until further notice. Good luck with your hand."

She swam to the outer side of the pool, palming a final splash in his direction.

Mark raised up again and removed the dripping coat of his silk pajamas. The light took a turn at playing with his wet skin and hard muscles.

Rebecca regarded the semi-naked, wet beauty and thought, *Well, my, my, my – I guess I spoke in haste. Temperance was never my strong suit.*

As he sat back down, she glided over and kissed him for the first time since she arrived home, hands moving over his broad shoulders and strong neck.

Mark caressed her and spoke softly in her ear, "Thank you for saving me, Rebecca. I promise to be more careful."

She replied huskily, "No, you won't, but I do love you so, Mark."

They kissed a bit more. Mark tasted the vodka on her lips and tongue. His hands continued to caress her neck and face.

Mark came up for air and said, "But what is more important is that I love you."

"Such a doofuss."

Her hand moved down the planes of his chest to his abs. She leaned back a bit as the light again caught his torso.

"Still there?"

He looked down. "Yeah, the doctors don't know what it is. X-rays and MRIs show no abnormalities beneath. At first, they thought it was a burn, but there is no tissue damage. Some kinda intense light imaging."

He traced the mark-- about 34 cm by 10 cm, sternum to upper abdominals.

"Anyway, it seems to be fading."

Epilogue: Limelight

THE BROWARD CENTER FOR THE PERFORMING ARTS, FORT LAUDERDALE, FLORIDA

The soprano stepped forward as the conductor raised his baton. The orchestra began the soaring strains of Mozart's "Der Hölle Rache," the Queen of the Night's aria from *The Magic Flute*. As the young woman from Ghana performed the utterly stunning vocal acrobatics, behind her, a series of screens and drops flashed with memorable scenes from the honoree's illustrious career.

Four fashion models, each, in turn, descended a staircase at the rear of the stage in vintage costumes from the opera. With stylized moves, they walked behind the performer and onto the thrust stage, turned, and returned upstage.

The audience was in awe.

Performances of many of the world's greatest operas for soprano and mezzo-soprano by guest artists from all over the world filled the bill. The program included a scene from a new work, *La Gloriosa*, an opera in progress with music and libretto, by two students from *Conservatorio de Música de Granada*. Written in Italian, the first glimpse included a scene in which the heroine and a handsome Nazi officer sang of love, fidelity, and hidden treachery. Two other women joined the principals in the performance, the star's dresser and companion and the officer's wife. The music and drama were electrifying.

The Members of the Board of Trustees of *La Gloriosa* Foundation were introduced, and each took their place on the stage. When the final director, Rebecca Quinto, was announced, the upstage set opened. A woman dressed in a brown, black, and white nun's habit walked downstage. A microphone rose from the floor to meet her.

Rebecca addressed the assembly, "My mother would have been so proud."

The audience laughed.

"I wanted Carmen as it would have better suited my personality, but…."

She shrugged and twirled her rosary beads from the hip.

The laughter continued, followed by a smattering of applause.

"Good evening. I am dressed as Sister Blanche de la Force from Poulenc's *Dialogues of the Carmelites*, a masterpiece of personal conviction, resistance, and the fearless sacrifice of self-interest. One of the remarkable women portrayed by our guest of honor.

"The life of Victoria Ricci is reflected in the legendary roles she brought to life to the delight of international audiences for more than three generations. Like them, she is a woman of strength, beauty, and unmatched artistry with the determination of Floria Tosca, the faithfulness of Madama Butterfly, the devotion of Violetta, the courage of Aida, the beauty of Cleopatra, the seduction of Delilah, and the justice-demanding determination of the Queen of the Night. It is in her triumphs that the world best knows *La Gloriosa.*

The stage held one large portrait of the famous soprano. It was a headshot of Victoria looking into a dressing room mirror, preparing for a performance. The eyes were full of mystery and inner secrets, the countenance beautiful and wondrous, framed by hair the color of burnished gold.

"Following the defeat of the Axis in World War II, Dame Ricci was honored by the Allies for her intelligence work that contributed to the defeat of the Fascists in Europe. This incredible beauty and talented artist, caught in a web of politics, corruption, lies, and lust – she wouldn't mind me saying that-- made many courageous choices."

Now, the screens dropped a series of photographs of architectural drawings, espionage communications, and aerial shots of strategic locations from the war.

"All of her victories were not just on stage. Victoria Ricci provided secret information to the English and the French Resistance, with photos of detailed plans of munitions factories and armed installations as well as the location of concentration camps in France, Germany, and

Poland. All this from within the highest levels of the German Reich and at the risk of her life."

The stage visuals now showed vintage pictures and videos of the War in Europe-- Nazis in the European capitals.

Rebecca continued, "On October 1, 1943, The German Chancellor, Adolf Hitler, ordered Danish Jews to be arrested and deported to the camps. Five days prior, despite enormous personal risk, Victoria Ricci hid 203 of the Jews of Copenhagen in the railroad transport used to move the colossal Fall production of Wagner's *The Ring of the Nibelung* from the Danish capital to Stockholm. It was she who obtained the round-up date for the Danish Underground. Knowing of the coming arrests, the valiant Danish citizens evacuated 7,220 of Denmark's 7,800 Jews, plus 686 non-Jewish spouses, by sea to nearby neutral Sweden before the Nazis could interfere.

The backdrops faded and brought up images of Victoria in Jerusalem.

Rebecca continued, "In 1953, Israel's Holocaust Martyrs and Heroes Remembrance Authority, *Yad Vashem*, recognized Victoria Ricci as one of the Righteous Among the Nations for her efforts to aid in the liberation of the camps.

"In 1975, after a remarkable career, the Diva of Divas retired from public view. She continues to be a dedicated educator in some of the most remote areas of Europe with an extraordinary passion for the empowerment of girls and women."

The logo of the Diva's foundation appeared across the stage behind the speaker.

"The mission of the *La Gloriosa* Foundation is to provide women and girls with greater opportunities through education, financial investment, and skills training in the arts, technology, engineering, science, and the media.

Rebecca paused and looked up and out to the highest reaches of the opera house.

"My friends, please welcome my friend, Dame Victoria Ricci."

The stage went dark, and then, from a vintage 1961 recital in Rome, *La Gloriosa* appeared performing her signature aria "Vissi d'arte" from *Tosca*. Titles scrolled below the film of the soprano, translating the Italian as the music swelled.

> I lived for my art, I lived for love,
>
> I never did harm to a living soul!
>
> With a secret hand
>
> I relieved as many misfortunes as I knew of.
>
> Always with true faith....
>
> I gave my song to the stars, to heaven.

As the aria continued, the lights came up, and a solitary figure walked through the image toward her adoring audience, which had risen with a thunderous ovation.

La Gloriosa clasped her hands to her heart and bowed.

The End

Acknowledgments

I am grateful to my husband, Anton S. Wallner, for his expert advice in creating The Frozen Diva. Your insight into the human experience and scientific knowledge are invaluable. I am forever mindful of your loving presence in my life, and much of what I write about travel, romance, and love comes from the path we have walked together for all these years. "Po-tay-to/po-tah-to" – also, thanks, Tony, for the skillful copy editing.

My gym buddy, the former USMC, Antonio Guerrero, gave me excellent advice about the martial arts action in the story and inspired the military aspects of the plot. Thank you for your expertise and your service to our country. You have helped to make my story more exciting and authentic.

I am deeply appreciative of the friendship of courageous women. My sister-in-law, Liza, is such a woman... with admiration, love, and profound appreciation for your encouragement.

When Rebecca speaks to me from my imagination, my good friend, Joanne Mena, always comes to mind. I am grateful for her example of strong women who lead, and I find it genuinely inspiring.

Finally, to all those who are willing to risk everything, setting self-gratification aside for the sake of those most in need, I am most thankful.

Afterword

Thank you for reading The Frozen Diva, Book One of The Amazing Adventures of Rebecca Quinto. I hope you found it enjoyable.

Rebecca returns in her next adventure, The Lost Museum. The intrigue and suspense continue. Be on the lookout at tomseverino.com and on Amazon.

The Lost Museum

The Amazing Adventures of Rebecca Quinto

Thomas Paul Severino

Prologue: The God of the Ptolemies

Alexandria, Egypt, 282 BCE

The Pharoah coughed. The spasm wracked his body, and the cloth the servant brought to his mouth reddened with more blood. The Queen rose from his desk and started towards him, but he motioned her back into her place.

He turned on the royal bed and spoke to his son and co-ruler of Egypt,

"Hear the wish of a dying man and your father, my son."

The young prince took the hand of the old king. "What is it, my Lord?"

Despite his near-death condition, the Divine Ptolemy I Soter roared, "Make those damned priests out there stop that infernal chanting. Send them away."

The prince of Egypt gave a hand signal, and the servant went into the corridor. The dirge stopped instantly.

The King coughed again. "That damn incense will kill me before whatever it is that is killing me kills me."

The returning servant spoke softly to the Queen, who said, "My lords, the King's doctors are insisting...."

Again, the Pharoah rasped with aggravation. "No doctors. That time is past. Bernice, I want to be here with the three of you– just you, Philadelphus, and my friend Euclid. The entire Kingdom knows that the Pharaoh will soon travel to meet the sun god, Ra. It is ordained. The royal mortuary boat has been prepared to bring me to the Hall of Maat for the judgment of my soul."

He looked at each of them in turn and then continued, "I am aware that this journey is about to begin, and so are the three of you. It is the will of the gods. But I am not ready. My conscience weighs heavy. I will be barred from the Kingdom of Osiris unless I can purge myself of the guilt I bear."

Ptolemy II Philadelphus applied a cool compress to his father's fevered brow. The King spoke again to his wife.

"Bernice, continue reading from the Chronicles. Go back to the beginning– the invocation of the goddess and the attribution of authorship."

The Queen bent over the large scroll on the desk in the royal bedroom. She read the words written so many years before by the young Macedonian, now Pharoah of Upper and Lower Egypt.

> Hear me, Divine Clio, daughter of Immortal Zeus, Proclaimer Goddess, clear-eyed Muse of History, and bestower of Fame. I, Ptolemy, brother of Alexander, sing of his glorious campaign to conquer the world. I sing of his great deeds and accomplishments.

The mathematician and friend of the King interrupted, "Great Ptolemy, you were the friend of the God Alexander, a member of the Royal Companions and served as a General throughout his conquests. Your history is a straightforward and honest account. There is no guilt for which you need to atone on your deathbed."

The King gazed into the space above him as if searching for a divine presence in these his last moments. He spoke to invisible phantoms gathering near the royal bed.

"Yes, yes, my account is accurate. Your accusations are false. May Alexander himself attest to the sincerity in my heart."

He grew even more feverish in his rant. "I could not part from you, my Lord and my God. You wanted to be buried at Siwa, where the oracle confirmed you as the son of Zeus. Those idiots, Perdiccas and the rest, wanted to bury you in Macedonia, in Aegae, next to your father."

The dying King suddenly became lucid. He turned to those attending him. "That idea was an abomination to Alexander, for he truly hated Philip."

The Queen skipped ahead in the Chronicles.

> The idea came to me a few days after the death of the King. The embalmers had arrived from Egypt, and the

> Generals were formulating their plan for the cortege to march to Macedonia. That is when I knew that I would steal the body of the god and bring him to Sacred Egypt. Thus began the War of the Generals, the *Diadochi*.

"Alexander lies below us in the Sema, my Lord. You were wise to bring him here. The one who possesses the Divine Alexander can never be judged anything but the rightful ruler of his legacy."

The king looked at the speaker, struggling to remember who he was. His mind wandered along the interface between life and death. Finally, he recognized the great teacher and author of the *Elements.*

"Master Euclid, have you and my son completed the plans for the Library?"

The Master of Geometry raised up and walked to the wall where the plans for the campus of the Great Library of Alexandria were hung.

"Yes, my Lord, Ptolemy. You approved them over a year ago, and construction is underway to create a campus of great knowledge with no rivals throughout the world. See here, the Library itself and the housing for the scholars, the spaces for instruction, The Great Hall of the Treasures, the gymnasium, the ambulatories, as suggested by Master Aristotle, the Walking Philosopher – the Gods forbid he should sit still while teaching-- the proximity to the harbor for receiving the books and artifacts...."

"And the centerpiece, Father– the Sema, the Tomb of the Great Alexander."

The Pharoah reached for the hands of his heir. "Never, my son. Never. Alexander can never leave Egypt and this dynasty. "

Philadelphus tried to calm his father, who was slipping again into delirium.

"My Lord, ease your mind. You brought the god to Egypt to safeguard the eternal rule of this family. The Ptolemies will rule this Land of the Gods forever. There is no shame in that. You die having a united and stable country that enjoys divine favor because of the presence of the Glorious Alexander. You, Father, are 'Soter,' the Savior of the Land of Egypt."

Barely able to speak now, Ptolemy persisted as he gestured to the plans behind the master of mathematics. "The safety features... for the books... the treasures... the sarcophagus itself...."

Bernice came to the bedside of her spouse and settled him back on the pillows. As her son nodded, she assured the dying king, "Great Ptolemy, my dear husband, give ease to your soul and mind. Master Euclid, the Royal Architects, our son, who is your namesake – they have done it all according to your will. The Great Library rises and will be safeguarded against all destruction. It is your eternal legacy."

"Yes, Father. Your great thievery will forever bestow upon us the blessings of the Gods. There is no shame there. Alexander would agree. No power on earth will take him from Egypt."

Lord Ptolemy, Son of Horus and Master of the Two Lands, could speak no more. He looked into the eyes of his wife and mother of the next Pharoah.

Bernice understood. She gave the command.

Beneath the gaze of his enormous, granite effigy as the founder of the dynasty, the servants carefully bore Ptolemy's litter down through the royal enclosure to the crypt of the Soma. The beautiful goddesses that lined the walls seemed to fan the feverous monarch with their outstretched wings. The hieroglyphs before the steps down to the crypt announced, "Nothing is lost that is under the protection of the Gods."

The litter bearers set the throne of the King on top of the giant stone scarab before the gold and glass tomb. The family of the Pharoah drew close to the sarcophagus.

Ptolemy I Soter would come to the end of his life gazing on the body of the Divine Alexander...

... which was destined to rest in this place forever.

www.ingramcontent.com/pod-product-compliance
Lightning Source LLC
Chambersburg PA
CBHW061937170626
46813CB00006B/2442

* 9 7 8 1 7 3 2 2 2 7 8 9 7 *